Did I Mention I Won the Lottery?

By Julie Butterfield

For my bemused husband
and my amused children

Chapter 1

Rebecca looked down at the ticket in her hand. She knew the numbers by heart but she read them to herself again before pushing the ticket back into her pocket and walking over to the kiosk.

'Sorry - could you tell me - are those the winning numbers from this week?'

The large woman behind the counter nodded, pointing to the notice board behind the counter.

'They certainly are my darling why, do you think you've won? Here, give me your ticket and I'll put it through the machine. That'll soon tell us!'

She laughed as she spoke, holding her hand out for Rebecca's ticket.

'Oh no, I can't… I mean, I haven't got it with me. I just wondered if those were the numbers. This week's numbers I mean, then I could check them when I get home.'

Her fingers tightened around the ticket still in her pocket, her cheeks flushing a little.

'Well those are the numbers. Look, why don't I write them down for you. Who knows, you might have won the jackpot,' and she laughed again, a deep belly laugh that shook her ample frame as she reached for a pen.

'Right. Thanks. Thank you,' and Rebecca took the scrap of paper, smiled politely and turned towards the door.

She walked across the car park, hunching slightly against the bitter wind that blew in her face and swirled around her legs until she reached her car and sat, slightly breathless with her hands against the steering wheel.

She would check when she got home. She didn't need to check now because it wasn't really true. She hadn't actually won the lottery. She had looked at the wrong week when she checked online yesterday. She had gotten confused when she read the numbers in the local paper the day before. She hadn't won. Of course she hadn't won because that was something that happened to other people, not to her. She put her hand into her pocket again and felt for the ticket. It had been joined by the scrap of paper containing the winning numbers and she could feel them sitting side by side, touching. Of course she hadn't won, it was silly to even imagine that she had. She took her hand out of her pocket and turned the key, listening for a moment to the engine.

Maybe she should just check them quickly, then she would know that she hadn't won and she could stop thinking about it. Stop imagining what it would mean if the winning numbers were actually her numbers.

She pulled the ticket from her pocket and smoothed it out. It was creased and stained. She had barely let go of it since Sunday morning when with a coffee in her hand and a smile on her face, she had switched on the computer to see if she had won £10.00 on the Saturday night lottery. She stared at the ticket, slowly reading the numbers out loud. Once she checked and admitted that she hadn't won, the daydream was over. She would have to stop imagining what it would mean to her life. Stop those delicious little fantasies where she woke up each morning able to do whatever she chose, able to go where ever she wanted. The warm feeling that was surrounding her, that wonderful warm feeling of relief would go and she wouldn't be able to sit with her feet curled under her, not listening to the TV as she planned her first trip away, what she would do, where she would live.

She stared at the ticket for a moment longer then carefully folded it into a small square and pushed it back into her pocket. She would check later.

'Bec! Where are you?'

Rebecca didn't bother answering. She was where she always was at this time of the day. In the kitchen getting the evening meal started.

'God what a bloody day.'

Daniel walked past her on his way to the fridge. The hiss of a beer being opened was followed by silence as he took a long drink.

'You have no idea what a complete waste today has been. That bloody git Peter tried to get us to do team building! Team building -how's that supposed to help for crying out loud? We're a sales team, we don't need to build anything apart from bloody sales!'

He snorted and took another deep drink of his beer. 'What's for tea?'

'Shepherd's Pie,' Rebecca answered, ignoring his screwed up nose as she spread grated cheese over mashed potato and opened the oven door.

'Right - I'll go get changed then,' and he finished his beer, dropping the can on the surface as he left the kitchen.

Rebecca took off her oven glove and stared at the beer can for a moment then picked it up and put it in the recycling bin. She could leave it on the surface for Daniel to get rid of but he would ignore it and if she asked him to move it, he would throw it in with the kitchen rubbish. Then he would lecture her on what a waste of time it was trying to recycle because when the rubbish was collected it would all be piled up in the same place anyway regardless of what colour box she'd put it in.

That was one of his favourite theories of the moment. Given any opportunity he would describe how the population of Britain were all being taken advantage off, how the landfills were full of all the rubbish that people threw away, regardless of how carefully it had been sorted out before being collected by the weekly refuse men.

She had detected the glaze of boredom in their neighbours' eyes on Saturday night. Rebecca had laughed at Daniel's story and tried to take the edge away by poking fun at herself for all the hours she spent sorting her tins and her plastics, her paper and her kitchen refuse.

'Is it ready?'

Rebecca jumped as Daniel reappeared in the kitchen doorway and smiled at him, feeling guilty.

'Should be, let's serve up.'

They ate the meal on their knees while Daniel watched yet another episode about yet another car being rescued from the scrap yard. Rebecca loaded up the dishwasher because Daniel suddenly remembered he needed to check his emails. Then she made the cup of tea that he said he would make but first he needed to check something online. Finally, she ended up in her favourite corner of the settee, not listening to the TV as she slipped back into the warm welcoming daydream that had begun on Sunday morning when she had turned on her computer to see if she had won anything on the lottery.

The next two days were frantically busy. Susie had called in sick at work and Rebecca had been covering both their shifts. Daniel had invited two prospective clients around for dinner in an effort to win their business, leaving Rebecca a note with a suggestion of what she could make as an evening meal. She had spent the evening smiling until she felt that her face would split in two, laughing obediently as Daniel launched into his theory about recycling, nodding appropriately as Daniel discussed the packaging industry then clearing away in a blur of exhaustion when finally, full on wine, brandy and cigars the guests said a protracted goodbye and Rebecca started filling the dishwasher.

Daniel had lounged in the kitchen doorway looking smug as he watched Rebecca clear away.

'They seemed very interested,' he said, rubbing his hands together. 'I wouldn't be surprised if they phone back tomorrow and say they want to put their business with White's.'

Rebecca stared at him. She would be amazed if Daniel ever heard from them again. They seemed perfectly happy with the idea of drinking as much wine as they possible could and eating a free meal. She had seen the lack of interest in their faces as Daniel pontificated about White's packaging business and his own personal success. Only several more brandies had kept them in their seats.

Tonight he was wining and dining another business client at a local restaurant and finally Rebecca was home alone. And instead of more cars being dragged out of garages to be given the once over she had turned the TV off and taken from her coat pocket the ticket and the piece of paper she'd collected from the kiosk. She laid both on the coffee table in front of her, smoothing out the wrinkles in the paper.

It was time to check the numbers. The daydream still kept her warm at night. It still filled her thoughts during the day but it had started to become limited. It was all very well spending a few days thinking what you would do it you won the lottery. But that only took you so far. The dreams soon started to fade and eventually you had to let it go - unless it turned into reality.

She took the piece of paper from the kiosk first and following the numbers with her finger she read them out loud, saying each number clearly and letting it hang in the air for a moment before she read the next. She paused and then read them again, trailing her finger along each number as she read.

Then she picked up the lottery ticket and smoothed it out. She didn't really need to check the numbers on her ticket. She knew those numbers like old friends. They ordered themselves in her mind as she drifted off to sleep. They welcomed her as she opened her eyes in the morning. She knew each and every one of them.

In truth, Rebecca didn't really need to check the lottery ticket at all. She hadn't needed to check it for the last two days. She had watched the kiosk lady write down each number and she knew. She knew that every number on the scrap of paper matched a number on her ticket. She had known immediately that they were the same. But this was making it real. This meant that it was actually happening.

She placed the ticket next to the scrap paper and this time as she read the numbers from the paper she followed the ticket with her finger. Every number matched.

She got a pen from the kitchen drawer and returned to the coffee table. She didn't want to mark her ticket so this time she read each number on the ticket and then ticked the matching number on the scrap paper. Every number matched.

She wrote down the numbers from her ticket. She wrote down the numbers from the scrap paper. Every number matched.

She stared at the pieces of paper sitting side by side on the coffee table and then closed her eyes. She said out loud each number that was on her ticket. She opened her eyes and read each number that was on the scrap paper. Every number matched.

Rebecca picked up her ticket and stared at it. The dream was over. Reality had arrived. Rebecca Miles had won the lottery.

Chapter 2

It was Sunday morning and Rebecca had slipped downstairs to make a cup of tea and have 5 minutes peace before Daniel woke. She went into the conservatory where the laptop rested on a small computer desk in the corner and sat with a mug of coffee in her hand as she flicked from screen to screen. This week she didn't have any new numbers to check. She hadn't bought a lottery ticket on her way home on Friday as she usually did. On Saturday as they watched TV together, Daniel had flicked through the channels, resting briefly on the big ball draw of the lottery.

'Do you need to check your numbers?' he had sneered. 'Are we millions better off?'

Rebecca hadn't answered. She had taken another sip of her wine and made no reply as he sniggered and carried on channel hopping.

It had been Friday night when Rebecca had checked her numbers against the scrap of paper she had brought home. She hadn't looked at the numbers since. She hadn't checked to see how much she had won. And she hadn't mentioned the winning ticket to Daniel.

There hadn't seemed much point when she didn't know what to tell him. All she knew was that she had a winning ticket. She had no idea what her prize was but the daydreams had returned full force. Now they were real and strong. Now it wasn't an if but a when. Rebecca didn't know how much she had won but surely it was enough to change her life. It wouldn't take much after all.

Clutching the coffee mug with one hand, Rebecca soon found the lottery web page that gave all the detail she needed. Every draw, every week, every winning ticket and how much each ticket had won. She scrolled to her week. There had been only one winner that week. Was it Rebecca? She supposed so, she had matched every number. Didn't that mean she got the jackpot? She scrolled down a little more - and how much had she won?

The cup fell out of her hand as though in slow motion. Rebecca watched as it flew gracefully towards the floor, landed and then bounced upwards throwing its contents across the tiles and her feet before landing again to smash into one large piece and a dozen smaller pieces. She watched for a moment as the pale brown pool of coffee trickled between her toes and round the chair leg then hearing Daniel's feet thumping down the stairs she reached forward and snapped closed the computer.

'What have you done? Don't just sit and look at it, it's spreading everywhere!' and with a grunt Daniel grabbed the paper towel from the kitchen and threw it in Rebecca's direction.

Catching it on reflex, Rebecca tore off a sheet and looked downwards at the spreading pool.

15.7 million pounds. The numbers jumped around in front of her eyes as she stared at the coffee. 15.7 million pounds. Rebecca had won 15.7 million pounds.

'For God's sake Bec, what's the matter with you? Give it here,' and snatching the paper towel from her hand Daniel bent down to start mopping at the floor.

15.7 million pounds. For a moment Rebecca wondered if she had said it out loud but Daniel didn't react. Mopping roughly at the floor and grunting, he grabbed more handfuls of towel until the lake of coffee was gone.

'I'll get a brush,' he muttered and walked back towards the kitchen.

15.7 million pounds. Rebecca could still see the amount printed on the screen, the numbers neat and organised. 15.7 million pounds written next to her lottery numbers.

Her hands started to shake and she pushed them into her dressing gown pocket as Daniel came back with the brush. She suddenly realised that he was fully dressed.

'I told you I was playing golf today,' he started defensively as he saw Rebecca take in his outfit. 'It's an important day. I'm taking old Murgatroyd and his son for golf and then a meal. They used to be one of our best customers and I haven't had a sniff of business from them in ages. I need to get him back on side!'

Rebecca nodded.

'I did tell you Bec, I told you last week I would be out all day. I said that …'

'I remember,' interrupted Rebecca who had absolutely no recall of the conversation. 'It's not a problem. Give me the brush, I'll do this. Go on, get off, you don't want to be late.'

Daniel's eyebrows shot up as Rebecca grabbed the brush from him and all but pushed him towards the door.

'Right… well,' he started 'as long as you realise how important this is…'

'It is, I agree, I remember.'

Rebecca took a deep breath and tried to control her breathing. 'Of course it is Daniel, go on, I'll clean this up. Have a good time.'

It took another few minutes to get Daniel to the door and then Rebecca stood in the front room, slightly to the side of the window and watched as Daniel's car pulled out of the drive and set off down the road.

15.7 million pounds. She had won 15.7 million pounds.

Two hours later Rebecca had cleaned the house, put in the washing and was sitting in front of her computer again with her heart hammering. She turned on the screen and scrolled to the lottery results page. There it was, one winner only, one winning ticket, a 15.7 million pound ticket. She had checked the screen every 15 minutes as she cleaned, convinced that she would suddenly realise it didn't say anything about millions. In a daze she had wiped the kitchen surface and mopped the floor where she had spilled her coffee. No of course it hadn't said 15.7 million. She would finish the cleaning and check again. But after the cleaning was done and Rebecca checked for one last time, there it was, 15.7 million pounds.

Taking a deep breath, Rebecca pulled the lottery ticket from her pocket and spread it out next to the screen. Her hand shaking, she reached for the phone and dialled.

'Hello. Er… I'm Rebecca. Rebecca Miles. I've got…I have…. I think I've won the lottery.'

30 minutes later Rebecca was sitting in her favourite chair in the conservatory, a brandy in her hand as she watched a robin hopping around the garden. Her toes were almost blue with cold and her hand still shook slightly as she lifted the glass to her lips. She really ought to find her slippers, she thought but didn't move from her chair.

A very nice lady called Leslie from the Lottery Help line had spoken to her. She had validated Rebecca's ticket and confirmed that she had indeed won 15.7 million pounds. She had waited calmly as Rebecca lost the power of speech, sympathised as she burst into tears and had tried to give her a little practical advice which was all falling on deaf ears. In the end they had agreed that she would speak to Rebecca tomorrow after the shock had worn off a little. They would talk about the team of people who would be on hand to guide Rebecca through the legalities of winning so much money, offer her investment advice and generally look after her.

The only decision Rebecca had already made was about publicity. When Leslie told her that a team would deal with it all in her behalf, she was quite, quite clear that this would remain private. No publicity at all,

'That's not a problem at all Rebecca. If you don't want to go public that's okay. But these things have a habit of coming out anyway. You tell your neighbour and she tells her friend and they tell someone at the pub and pretty soon everyone knows. If you want to go public we'll help, we'll protect you as much as possible and help you deal with it. But if you turn down the publicity team you'll be on your own when everyone in the street is knocking on your door wanting a share. It's surprising how many people suddenly remember you as their long lost friend and feel that you should be sharing the wealth - and I have to say families are often the worst ones!'

But Rebecca had been firm - no publicity. She didn't tell Leslie that there was no chance of anyone in the street finding out because she hadn't told a soul, not even her husband. But she assured Leslie that since checking the numbers she had been very discreet and she didn't feel publicity would be a problem and she promised that she would follow Leslie's advice and tell only her nearest and dearest until she had met with the Lottery team.

She needed to meet someone as soon as possible and in the meantime she had followed Leslie's advice and written her name and address on the back of the ticket. She hadn't put it in a safe place, it was still clutched in her hand.

As the conversation drew to a close Rebecca had a final question.

'There couldn't be a mistake could there? I mean, I have definitely won?'

Leslie chuckled, it was clear that this wasn't the first time she had been asked this question as she assured Rebecca that there was absolutely no mistake. She had won 15.7 million pounds. Her life had changed forever.

So now Rebecca was sitting in the chair, gazing out onto the garden knowing that in a few days there would be millions of pounds in her bank account. Leslie had mentioned it might be an idea to have a word with her bank manager and mention that a large amount of money would be arriving shortly. She should also get herself a lawyer - it was a lot of money to suddenly be responsible for. When Leslie had asked for bank account details, Rebecca had paused for the briefest of seconds before she gave the number. It was an account Rebecca had held for years. She would squirrel away money during the year and then use it to buy the children's Christmas and birthday presents. As they got older she started putting away whatever she could whenever she could and now she used it to help them out when they were down to their last tin of beans, had to spend another £100 on books or whenever life at university became that little bit too expensive for them.

Daniel didn't think they should help the children now they had left home. They were independent he said, it was time they learned the value of money, learned how to budget and also learned how to do without. He hadn't been like that when they were little. Daniel had been a wonderful father when they had two small children running around the house. But as he had gotten older and more disenchanted with his own lot in life, he had become a mean person. And not just regarding money. He was mean with his time, his praise, his love. He had recently spent a fortune renewing his golf membership, which they could little afford in light of his plummeting salary, but he had told Sarah quite firmly only last month that he wasn't prepared to lend her any money and if she couldn't afford life at university then maybe she should pack it in and get a job.

Rebecca hadn't argued with him. She had stopped arguing with him a long time ago. She had simply emptied what was left in her account and shared it between Sarah and Toby until the next instalment of their student loans came through. The account had been empty ever since.

Rebecca wondered if she should have put the money in the main bank account. After all that was the account that paid the mortgage, the bills etc. That was the account that was severely in need of a little help as Daniel's sales commissions had dropped lower and lower over the last few years. But, she reasoned, it was probably for the best. Just until it was all sorted and definite. Once the money was in the bank and she knew there was no mistake, then she could transfer it into whichever account she wanted. But for now, it was best to put it into her account. Just until everything was sorted.

Suddenly Rebecca gave an almighty whoop, so loud that the little robin looked up in surprise and flew onto the garden fence.

She had won the lottery. She had won 15.7 million pounds!

For the first time Rebecca actually let herself believe that it was true and slamming the glass down she leapt to her feet and threw her arms out.

'Oh my God I've won!' and to the amazement of the robin who was watching Rebecca and next door's cat who was watching the robin, she began to dance and spin and whirl around the conservatory laughing and whooping and flinging her arms around as the tears poured down her cheeks.

Breathless, tear stained, Rebecca stopped. The brandy had warmed her stomach but her feet were still icy cold. She stared down at them. She really couldn't remember where her slippers were but it didn't matter - she could always buy some more.

She sank back into her seat. It was Sunday lunch time. The weather was cold and blustery. Her husband was playing golf and she had just won 15.7 million pounds. What should she do next?

Tesco would be open, but it was hardly the place to splash millions. Besides, she didn't actually have it in her bank yet. She could plan but not actually spend. Rebecca jumped up and started pacing the floor. How frustrating. To have all that money but not actually have it in her hand! She wondered what other people did when they won the lottery. She ignored the little voice inside her that said they told their family and went back to the computer. A few minutes later she knew that the first purchase of most lottery winners was a car. Closely followed by a house and a holiday.

That didn't really help - she couldn't buy any of those things at Tesco on a Sunday afternoon. And besides she knew nothing about cars. Or holidays come to that. Other than the odd week away in Greece or Spain, she and Daniel didn't really go on holiday much. They had when the children were small; lovely family breaks where they would play on the beach, drink Sangria and laze around. But as time moved on Daniel had declared them a waste of time and money. At least he had declared family holidays a waste of time and money - he often went away for long weekends of golf, even a week to the Algarve once. Rebecca didn't mind him going away. She actually welcomed the peace and quiet. Sometimes she took a weekend off to visit Sarah at Leeds University or Toby at Bristol. Last time she had gone to Leeds she had treated herself and Sarah to a day at a Spa and they'd spent a lovely few hours wrapped in fluffy white towels being pampered.

That was an idea - perhaps a long weekend at a Spa would be good. Recharge her batteries, spend some time thinking about what to do next.

A car. Well Rebecca could do with a new car. Daniel had a company car, a Ford Focus which was replaced every two years and came insured and serviced and seemed perfectly acceptable to Rebecca. Daniel didn't think it was appropriate He felt he should have something that reflected his position in the company. Rebecca had refrained from pointing out that his position was that of the worst performing sales man. Her car was a little Nissan that was old and rusty but Daniel had declared it good enough.

She could buy the children cars as well, nothing over the top but something to give them some independence.

She hugged herself. What fun! What else could she buy?

She thought about a holiday and realised that Daniel would only want to go somewhere he could play golf - regardless of what Rebecca might want to do. He certainly wouldn't be interested in a weekend in Prague or New York, 'who wants to go to a city for a break, just go into Newcastle and shop instead' he would say. He wouldn't dream of going on a cruise 'surrounded by people who thought they were better than they were'. He certainly wouldn't want a couple of weeks on a tropical beach 'God knows what you'll catch and why go all that way when there's perfectly good beaches much closer to home'. And as for skiing - Rebecca could just see his face turning purple as he explained to her how many people broke their legs or even worse, their necks on the ski slope every year.

So she moved quickly on and thought about a house. But she knew that would be another problem. Daniel would want to stay in Darlington. They had moved here five years before when Daniel had decided he needed to be closer to Head Office. It made no difference as Daniel's area spread right down to the Midlands but he had decided they needed to move and that's what had happened. The move had coincided with Peter Thompson's arrival at White's. Daniel decided that the reason he hadn't been promoted and that Peter had been chosen for the job was because Daniel hadn't lived close enough to the office. Daniel had been overlooked because of his location, because he wasn't in the office every day to remind them who he was and how good he was. Rebecca was of the opinion that if Daniel had been good enough for the job they would have given it to him anyway but muttering about being held back and needing to compete, Daniel had dragged them all North.

Rebecca and the children had hated it. Rebecca had loved Leeds. She had loved the village where they lived on the outskirts of the town, she had loved her friends, the life she had grown for herself over the last 15 years. The children were appalled to be dragged out of their school and away from their friends but Daniel had gone steaming ahead. It was what he needed and as he was providing the roof over their head, they would all have to get used to a move to Darlington. They had never recovered from that move.

With 15.7 million they could buy the house of their dreams wherever they wanted. And as far as Rebecca was concerned it would be anywhere but Darlington.

She finished the brandy with a sigh. Her virtual spending wasn't exactly working out. Making a decision she jumped up and ran up the stairs to find some socks for her still cold feet, slip on some boots and grab her coat. Before leaving the house she held the lottery ticket in her hand. It had lived in her pocket throughout the previous week and had gone everywhere with her. But now that she knew it was worth so much, she was frightened at the thought of taking it out of the house. Suppose she lost it? Suppose she put it in her purse and then she had her purse stolen? If she put it back in her pocket it might fall out.

Should she leave it in the house? And if she did where did she put it? She didn't think for a moment that Daniel would start looking. He despised her for wasting her money every week on what he called a loser's game. But suppose someone broke in? Suppose the house burnt down? By now Rebecca was sweating, the back of her neck was damp and her top lip held beads of perspiration. Leslie had said it was a good idea to photocopy the ticket but where did she do that? If she took it into a print shop they would know why she wanted to copy it. She couldn't give it to Daniel and ask him to take it into work, which is what she would do with anything else she needed copying.

Making a decision she pulled her gloves out of her bag and folding the ticket as small as she could she pulled on her left glove and then pushed the ticket down until she could feel it against her palm. The ticket was going with her, she wasn't letting it out of her sight until the money was in her bank.

Tesco was quite full but Rebecca didn't mind. She grabbed a bag snorting with laughter at the thought of filling it with 15.7 million pounds of Tesco items. Ignoring the stares of other shoppers, she set off down the aisles, the ticket still held against the palm of her left hand.

A little while later she looked at the contents of her basket and smiled. Examining baskets was something she often did when queuing to pay. Out of boredom she would look down at the baskets in the queue and decide who they were shopping for. Singles were easy to spot, meals for one, bags containing two apples and one tomato. The men would have a few beers tucked in there, the women a bottle of wine. Busy working mums topping up the cupboards were easy too. Nearly always another loaf of bread, peanut butter for lunch boxes, packets of crisps, cans of pop, milk, beans. Shopping for a dinner party she could spot - fromage frais, vanilla pods or ginger stems, exotic herbs, fancy pasta, sun dried tomatoes, expensive wine, anchovies - nothing practical.

Rebecca looked down at her basket. A printer, small, compact and easy to install according to the box. A bottle of very expensive Pinot Grigio which she had once bought for a dinner party but never for herself. A pack of knickers, not the plain cotton that she usually bought but soft silky ones with lace edging and little bows and flowers embroidered along the top. A pair of slippers, soft fluffy and almost sexy. An Ideal homes magazine. A throw - pale duck egg blue with circles on that Rebecca had admired last week and thought would look lovely on her favourite chair. Having just paid the electricity bill she had stroked it and moved on but now it sat defiantly in her basket. And a salmon fillet. Ready to be poached when she got home and eaten when she opened the Pinot Grigio. What did Rebecca's basket say about her? Rebecca grinned, it certainly didn't say she had just won 15.7 million on the lottery but it definitely had an air about it. A casual carefree air. It had a whiff of the extravagant and a little touch of luxury.

Having only managed to spend £81.57 Rebecca added a selection of brochures from the little travel agent in the lobby and headed for home, where she threw some bread that was far from stale out for the robin, shooed away the cat and turned the heating up to maximum.

When Daniel returned home later that evening, Rebecca was curled up in a corner of the settee with a glass of wine in her hand. If he had concentrated he would have detected the aroma of salmon in the air, poached with a handful of herbs and served with the tiniest squeeze of lemon. Rebecca hadn't bothered to do any potatoes or vegetables with it - which is what Daniel would have insisted she make. She just had salmon and a glass of chilled white wine.

'What a bloody waste of time,' growled Daniel as he came into the living room. 'What a complete waste of time and money.'

He threw his keys and change onto the small table by the door. Rebecca had asked him more times than she could remember not to put them there. She had even bought a little wooden bowl and placed it on the hall table for Daniel to use for his bits and pieces. But he ignored her and every night he would walk past the bowl and into the living room to throw his keys and loose change onto the small cream table. She didn't bother asking him anymore and tonight his keys skidded onto the surface that was scratched and marked from the nightly onslaught.

'I had old David Murgatroyd here,' he thrust the palm of his hand in Rebecca's direction. 'Right here.' He clenched his fist, his face almost purple with rage. 'And then that silly little upstart of a son started bleating on about sustainability and environmental impact,' he spat the words out as though they were poison. 'And then he had the nerve to tell me that they had put all their business with Hanson's now.' He was quivering with anger as he spoke, 'Bloody Hanson's! I bet they didn't take him out and pay for a round of golf and dinner!'

Rebecca watched him as she took a sip of her wine. She doubted that any of the sales staff at Hanson's would be stupid enough to pay for golf and dinner. They probably just did their job properly and told David Murgatroyd and his son how the whole of their packaging plant was now geared towards packaging with a conscience, with one eye on the environment. Just like Daniel could have done if he had actually listened to anything Peter Thompson had tried to tell him over the last five years.

'What's for tea?'

Rebecca raised her eyebrows at her husband.

'Nothing - you told me that you were eating out.'

Daniel stared at her as she took another sip of her wine.

'But you always make something anyway,' he spluttered, 'and the meal at the golf club was bloody awful despite costing a packet! I was looking forward to coming home to eat something.'

Rebecca shrugged. She did always make something and Daniel always sneered at her and reminded her how he had just eaten at a first class restaurant and why would he want some of her food and what a waste of time and money both the meal and Rebecca were.

Turning on his heel Daniel went into the kitchen and Rebecca could hear the oven door slam and the microwave open and close as he checked all possibilities. She heard the fridge door open and the clink of a glass as he poured himself a glass of wine and she took another sip of her Pinot Grigio. She had gone in to the kitchen when she'd heard Daniel's car on the drive and put the bottle behind the fish fingers in the freezer. She had replaced the now empty spot in the fridge with a bottle of the cheap wine they bought each week.

Daniel came back into the living room glaring at her as he threw himself in the settee. 'I wouldn't have thought it was too much to ask,' he muttered, taking a huge drink of wine. 'I've been out working all day and you've been sat at home reading magazines.'

He kicked the Ideal homes magazine that was on the floor. 'Most women would have actually thought to make their husband something to eat.'

Rebecca wondered when she had lost the inclination to argue with Daniel. When they had first moved to Darlington she had been furious with him and they spent most of their first 12 months arguing day and night.

But one day she had watched him spluttering and pontificating about the rights and wrongs of the move, his importance in the general scheme of things, her lack of importance in anything and she suddenly just couldn't be bothered anymore. She had let him rant and moan and halfway through she had just stopped listening. And it had been pretty much that way ever since.

She took another sip of wine. Daniel hadn't offered her a top up. In a moment she would go and empty the rest of the hidden bottle into her glass before going upstairs and treating herself to the luxury of a bath before she climbed into bed. Daniel always said that baths before bed were a complete waste of time. She would have a shower in the morning, what a waste of water and gas to have a bath before bed.

'Are you listening to me?' Daniel stuck out his foot to shove her roughly on the leg and Rebecca looked up from her glass and her thoughts.

'You told me you were having something to eat,' she reminded him. 'I didn't want to waste food.'

He growled something under his breath. One of his favourite complaints was waste. If she cooked too much it was a waste of food. If she went to the shop and came home without any milk it was a waste of petrol. If she washed on a rainy day and used the tumble drier it was a waste of electricity.

'It wouldn't have been a waste if I ate it – would it?'

He pulled himself to his feet and stumbled off towards the kitchen, returning with a topped up glass, still not offering any to Rebecca.

'You just need to be a bit more thoughtful. I'm working as hard as I can to keep this roof over our head, the least you could do is support me now and then.'

Rebecca drifted off, he was starting on the supporting lecture. The one where he did everything and she barely contributed. She had heard this so many times before.

She should have bought some really nice bubble bath at Tesco. She didn't normally buy any. It was something else that Daniel thought was a waste, spending money on bubbles.

Bubbles were air, they disappeared as soon as you emptied the bath, what was the point in spending money on something whose purpose was to disappear. But she liked bubbles. One of those lovely scents that made you feel as though you had just spent the day at the Spa. She would get some tomorrow. Maybe she would splash out and buy some really expensive stuff at the little perfume shop on the corner of the parade. And some candles. Daniel laughed whenever she lit candles and would ask if the electricity had gone off. But she would get some scented candles and some expensive bath foam and not care what Daniel said.

Rebecca realised it had gone quiet and looking over she saw Daniel's glass tipping to a dangerous level as his eyes closed and a gentle snore started. Sliding off the settee Rebecca took the glass out of his hand and into the kitchen. She took the Pinot Grigio out of the freezer and emptied the last of it into her glass before wandering upstairs, humming happily to herself as she ran a bath.

Chapter 3

On Monday morning Daniel was like a bear with a sore head. He had woken on the settee in the early hours of the morning and came stumbling to bed complaining loudly about being abandoned by an uncaring wife. Rebecca, who was in the middle of a dream which involved a huge bath full of bubbles and a waiter handing her a cocktail on a silver tray, rolled over and took no notice. Rebeca was on an afternoon shift at the Deli and she held her tongue and supplied tea and toast until eventually Daniel and his complaints walked out of the front door and finally it was just Rebecca and a welcome silence. She took out the number Leslie had given her. This time she was far more focused and started by apologising for her rather emotional response the day before. Leslie laughed and assured Rebecca that it had been the expected response from someone who had just won 15.7 million pounds.

'Well I'm thinking a little clearer now,' Rebecca said, 'I'm ready to sort everything out.'

It turned out that there was far less to do than Rebecca had imagined.

'We really do make it easy for you to collect your winnings you know,' laughed Leslie.

Rebecca needed to show her ID and her ticket to a member of the lottery team and then - well she simply had to watch her bank account until it increased by the sum of 15.7 million pounds.

'Will it take long?'

'Oh heavens, no,' answered Leslie. 'You'll have the money in your account by the end of the week.'

Rebecca sat down.

'The end of this week?'

'That's right.'

'All of it?'

'All of it!'

Rebecca tried to imagine her bank statement showing over 15 million pounds but simply couldn't. It had never held more than £500.

'Are you alright Rebecca?'

Leslie's anxious voice penetrated the fog of swirling numbers and Rebecca shook herself.

'Yes, I'm fine. It's just - Oh God 15 million pounds -it's a lot isn't it?'

Leslie laughed again. 'It certainly is but you mustn't worry. We have a team of people who can advise you. Whatever you're thinking off, investments, bequests, inheritance…we can get you on the right track.'

'Right,' said Rebecca faintly. 'Well I think I may need to speak to someone.'

'Of course you will,' Leslie said firmly, 'but not right now Rebecca. Don't make any quick decisions. If you don't want to go public…'

'I don't,' interrupted Rebecca.

'I know, I know. All I was going to say is, if you're not going public tell as few people as possible. Let it sink in before you decide what to do with it all. It can be overwhelming and as soon as everyone finds out they'll all be telling you how to spend it.'

'I'm keeping it very quiet,' confirmed Rebecca. 'Very quiet.'

'Good. Right, where do you want to meet the lottery advisor? We can arrange for him to come to your home. You could meet away from the home, even at your bank if you want to make it a little bit more official.'

'Not at home! I mean, the neighbours -you know how nosey neighbours can be.'

'No problem. Have you any ideas?'

Rebecca thought for a moment. Her mind was still whirling with the thought of a bank account showing several million pounds. It was difficult to think clearly.

'Leeds,' she blurted out, 'I want to meet in Leeds.'

'Okay. Any idea where?'

Not really, Rebecca didn't have a clue what she was doing.

'Er… I'm going to be in Leeds for a couple of days this week. Can I let you know when I've booked my hotel and we could maybe meet there?'

'Absolutely no problem Rebecca. You've got my number. When you're sorted let me know. If we can meet on say Wednesday, the money will be in your bank by Friday.'

Rebecca's head was whirling again.

'15.7 million pounds?'

'That's right Rebecca - 15.7 million pounds in your bank account by Friday.

When Rebecca told them at work that she needed to take a few days off there was a little mewl of distress from Carol who owned the Deli. With flushed cheeks Rebecca lied and said that her mother wasn't very well and she needed to go to Leeds and visit her for a couple of days. At which point Carol and Susie both put their arms around Rebecca and told her it wasn't a problem at all, of course they could manage, hadn't it turned out all right the week before when Susie had been ill? She must go and not give them a second thought and even whilst Rebecca's heart turned with shame at her lies and their concern she nodded her head and let them hug her and offer her support.

'It'll do you good anyway,' offered Susie in the lovely Geordie accent that Rebecca had taken almost two years to fully understand. 'A couple of days away from Mr Nobby.'

Carol nudged Susie in her ribs but Rebecca didn't mind. They had never known Daniel as she had, when he had been relaxed and happy, when they were a young couple with two adorable children. The only Daniel they had ever met was the pompous, self-absorbed man he had become, constantly lecturing and berating, full of his own ideas with a mind that was completely closed to anyone else's thoughts or opinions. Rebecca didn't mind because she agreed with Susie, a couple of days away from Daniel was always a treat.

So Rebecca carried on with a guilty heart and a flood of emotions that had her constantly confused and resulted in several mistakes. She had only been at work for an hour when Carol gently drew her into the tiny little office at the back of the shop. This was where Rebecca had been interviewed 4 years earlier. She had worked in the local supermarket when they first arrived in Darlington. Daniel had made it clear it was time for everyone to join in supporting the Miles household and Rebecca's years of being a mother and housewife were over. Rebecca had actually quite looked forward to going back to work but she had hated the supermarket. She left after a few months and moved to a bakery. She had hated the bakery. A few months later she had seen a job offered at the small Deli and tea rooms she often popped into when doing her shopping. She had met Carol in the tiny little office which could hold two people but which struggled with three and she had fallen in love with the Deli, Carol and Susie, the flame haired, warm hearted and rather verbose assistant who already worked there. She had been offered the job on the spot. Now Carol put an arm round her sympathetically.

'Rebecca darling, I think you should go home.'

Rebecca looked startled. Was she being sacked?

'No, I'm sorry! I...'

'No,' interrupted Carol. 'You're obviously worrying about your mum and you're just not yourself. Go home and get yourself sorted for your trip. Put your feet up, have a coffee and relax, pack…do whatever you need to do but go home.'

Rebecca let herself be persuaded. She had never imagined that it would be this hard, keeping her millions a secret. Her hands were shaking and her mind kept drifting to all manner of places, houses, cars and some of the exotic locations contained in the travel brochures now secreted under the living room sofa. So she put on her coat, allowed Carol and Susie to kiss and hug her, promised to be back as soon as she could and set off to the car park and home.

The first thing she did was make a coffee, then she turned on the laptop and curled into her chair in the conservatory, the duck egg blue thrown over her legs as she researched Leeds hotels. In her hand was the credit card taken from the bottom of one of the shoe boxes at the top of her wardrobe. It was her safety net. She had applied for it two years earlier after discovering that Daniel had emptied the bank account to pay for a week of golf in Scotland, where he was convinced he would pick up enough business to put everything right. The electricity bill and the car insurance had rolled through the door within minutes of his departure and in desperation Rebecca had applied for a credit card so she could pay the bills and also to give her some security for the future. When Daniel returned they'd had one of their rare arguments as she accused him of being selfish and deluded. With his face purple with rage at being questioned he had argued back that she needed to earn more and that the responsibility of the entire household and family shouldn't be on his shoulders alone. Rebecca hadn't told him about the credit card or that the bills had been paid. She made a point of serving nothing but beans and chips for weeks, refusing to buy any wine and asking him every night, as soon as he arrived home, if he had managed to write any business as a result of his trip to Scotland. The credit card was repaid and hadn't been used since but it was still at the bottom of the shoe box, ready for the next emergency.

Normally when she went to Leeds to visit her mother and Sarah, Rebecca would go by train and stay in the Travelodge in the city centre. If she booked far enough in advance she could get a super saver room and she was close enough to the bus station to be able to travel out to the nursing home where her mother lived and was within easy reach of Sarah's student rooms.

But that was before Rebecca had won 15.7 million pounds. A few keystrokes later and she had decided on Quebecs Hotel, still in the centre of Leeds but this time in a room that was quite rightly classed as luxurious. With damask curtains, a king size bed, TV, a small sitting area and a selection of toiletries that rivalled the contents of Rebecca's complete bathroom, it was a far cry from the usual comfortable and practical room Rebecca would occupy.

She lifted the phone with a heart that was thumping and a few minutes later it was done. Rebecca was booked into the luxurious Quebecs hotel for a minimum of 3 nights with the option to extend. She put the phone down and wiped the sweat from her forehead.

If it was going to take this much out of her spending a few hundred pounds, how on earth would she cope with spending 15.7 million? She patted the credit card, probably in shock after so long in the shoe box and stretched out in her chair smiling.

It was only a few nights in a decent hotel but it was a glimpse of the life ahead and Rebecca had a feeling she was going to enjoy it.

By the time Daniel came home, slamming the door behind him in temper, Rebecca had booked a train ticket, first class of course, phoned Sarah to let her know she would be in Leeds for a couple of days and phoned her Mum at the nursing home to say she would be popping in to visit her. She had phoned Leslie and arranged to see the Lottery adviser at Quebecs hotel on Wednesday morning. The little account which was soon to hold 15.7 million pounds had been opened in Leeds many years earlier and she had also made an appointment to see her bank manager to warn him of the unexpected boost to her bank balance. She had packed a small case with a few essentials, not too many because she had every intention of visiting the shops while she was in Leeds and she was ready to leave.

Whenever Rebecca went away for a few days she would make Daniel a meal for each night she was away and put them in the freezer. She didn't think he had ever said thank you.

'Bec, where are you?'

Every night the same question, every night the same answer. Rebecca would be in the kitchen making the evening meal, even if her own shift had only finished a few minutes before Daniel came home. She heard the keys and change hit the table and heard his footsteps stamp into the kitchen.

'What's for…Bec, where are you. What's for tea? What are you doing?'

Rebecca stayed where she was in the conservatory and took a sip of her wine. Another bottle of Pinot Grigio, the bottle well hidden in the kitchen.

'I'm in here,' she sang out as Daniel loomed in the doorway.

'What's happening? What are you doing in here? Why are you drinking and what's for tea?'

His voice rose indignantly on each question as he waited for Rebecca to answer.

'I've been too busy to think about tea. There's some chicken in the freezer if you want to make something or the menu for the Chinese is next to the fridge.'

Rebecca stayed in her seat, watching with interest as Daniels face coloured from brow to neck as he watched her sitting in the chair drinking wine.

'You expect me to work hard all day and then come home and make my own tea! What's wrong with you? Don't tell me you had a bad day at the Deli,' he sneered, 'too many people wanting a pot of tea at the same time?'

Rebecca didn't answer straight away. She was watching the dull flush of colour spread across Daniel's face.

'Actually I've been packing, my mum's not well.'

For a moment she saw a little glimmer of fear in Daniel's eyes. It had been years since he had bothered to accompany Rebecca when she visited her mum but he lived in terror of the day when he might be expected to join her.

Gwen's opinion of her son in law had never been particularly high, even when Rebecca had loved him with all of her heart and he had carried the children high on his shoulders around Gwen's garden. 'Weak', she would mutter to herself but in Rebecca's hearing, 'weak chin, mark my words he'll let you down'. But Rebecca had told her mother firmly that Daniel was a good husband and Gwen, for her daughter's sake had kept her opinions mainly to herself. When Daniel began to change and a bewildered Rebecca struggled to find the old Daniel inside the dour man he had become, her mother had never said I told you so, she had merely taken her daughter in her arms and held her tight.

It was to Daniel's real chagrin that shortly after they moved to Darlington, Gwen had become increasingly more frail and a little forgetful until after a nasty fall in the shower followed by a kitchen fire, when she left a tea towel sitting next to a pan of boiling water, the decision was made that Gwen would sell her house and move into sheltered accommodation. She was there for 2 years before reluctantly having to accept that she now needed to spend most of her days in her wheelchair and she moved on again, this time into a residential home, a small private one on the outskirts of Leeds set in an old manor house with a lovely large garden at the back and security gates at the front. That such huge sums of money were spent every week on Gwen's care hurt Daniel to the core. The fact that it was Gwen's own money made no difference to Daniel. It would have come to Rebecca as an only child and now it was being eaten into on a huge scale every week, month and year that Gwen stayed there. He hated visiting her. Hated the scrutiny of her sharp, bright eyes.

'How bad is she?' he asked nervously.

'She's okay, but I need to visit her. For a couple of days. I'll see Sarah while I'm there as well.'

Daniel nodded, patently relieved that he was not included in the visit and Rebecca couldn't help the little twist of shame as she counted the lies she had told over the course of the day.

'Right,' he nodded his head in the nearest to sympathy that he seemed capable of these days. 'Well I suppose it won't hurt to get a takeaway once in a while. I'll choose shall I?' and he stalked back into the kitchen, leaving Rebecca sitting in her chair counting the hours to her 10.25 train the following morning, her first class seat and the luxurious room waiting for her at Quebecs.

Chapter 4

The train was precisely 2 minutes late and at 11.51 Rebecca arrived in Leeds station. The hotel was only a few minutes' walk away and Rebecca had very little luggage. She paused at the taxi rank before grinning to herself and continuing on her way. She had won the lottery, not lost the use of her legs and she walked past the rows of waiting taxis and set off in the direction of her hotel. Within 5 minutes she was walking through the main door, held open for her by a smiling concierge, and towards the reception desk.

'Hello, I have a room booked for later, I wondered if I could leave my bag here while l shop a little?'

Her voice little more than a whisper, Rebecca looked uncertainly at the receptionist.

'Of course, no problem.'

Taking Rebecca's name, she consulted the register, 'You're booked into the Robinson suite. Check in is at 3.00pm, we'll have your bag in your room for when you return.'

Rebecca nodded her head, 'Right. Good. Thank you. Thank you very much,' and smiling she turned to walk back through the lovely glass door and out into the bright but cold air of Leeds.

15.7 million pounds. Like a little mantra inside her head the number seemed to fit in with her footsteps as she walked towards the nearest shopping area. 15.7 million. Oh my God, she had won 15.7 million and it would soon be in her bank. Where should she start?

A few hours later Rebecca sat in a small café and sipped at a caramel macchiato as she rested her weary feet. If she was going to spend 15.7 million pounds she would have to change her tactics. Despite a first class rail ticket and a luxury hotel plus a few hours of good old fashioned shopping, Rebecca hadn't even made a dent in her new fortune. Her credit card, her trusty companion, had started to shout with glee when it was taken from her purse but even so, she had spent very little.

She had visited Boots and allowed an enthusiastic young assistant show her a selection of creams and potions especially for the 'more mature skin madam'. Rebecca had nodded in agreement when asked if she could feel the softness of the cream on the back of her hand, agreed enthusiastically when asked if she approved of the aroma and casually handed over her credit card when asked if she would like try its powers for herself. Then she had walked past Topshop, continued past Dorothy Perkins, completely ignored Primark, winced at the doorway of Harvey Nicholls, paused at the entrance of Wallis and finally spent over an hour in Debenhams designer department. She emerged laden with several bags and the beginnings of a new wardrobe including a pair of scandalously high shoes, a new handbag and a fantastic trench coat that Rebecca considered to be criminally expensive but which would certainly keep out the freezing Leeds air.

And now she was worn out and although there was a wonderful trickle of guilt travelling down her spine, when she added everything together she had hardly spent anything. Not when she had over 15 million to dispose of.

She had spoken to Sarah the previous evening.

'I'm going to hit the shops before I meet you,' she had confessed to her daughter and Sarah had laughed her lovely rich laugh.

'Oh God mum, it's about time! Make the most of it. When are you going to see Granny?'

'Well I think I'll go on Thursday, I've got a few things to do Wednesday.'

'What kind of things?'

Sarah was intrigued and Rebecca couldn't really blame her. When did Rebecca last have anything interesting to do.

'Oh nothing special. I need to go see the bank, you know what they're like these days. They want to give you a personal service and your own account manager and it must be 8 years since I stepped foot in the place.'

Sarah had chortled at the thought of her mum having a personal bank manager.

'Sounds like fun! Then we'll meet Tuesday evening, I'll treat you to a pizza.'

Rebecca had smiled, 'That would be lovely my darling but it's my treat and maybe we should go somewhere a bit more upmarket?'

'Don't be silly Mum, there is nothing more upmarket than a pizza!' and laughing they arranged to meet at their favourite restaurant on The Headrow.

Rebecca looked at her watch. It was 3.20 and she decided to go back to the hotel and deposit her shopping bags. She still had several hours before she met Sarah. Perhaps she would have a bath. If the bathroom was anything like the picture on the web site she couldn't wait.

The picture didn't do the bathroom justice and Rebecca had to hold in a little squeak as the polite young man who showed her the room threw the bathroom door open with a flourish. It was bigger than Rebecca's bedroom at home and was nothing short of palatial, full of marble, fluffy white towels, exquisitely presented toiletries and a bath that just invited her to jump in. The bedroom was large, the settee soft and plump, the bed a field of soft goose down. Rebecca simply nodded her head.

'Very nice,' she whispered then cleared her throat 'Yes, very nice thank you.'

She pushed a note into the hand of the young man and then waited until she estimated he had reached the lift before whooping and throwing herself on the bed. Is this what happened when you had 15.7 million pounds, a bed that reached up and enfolded you, making you feel that you never wanted to leave it and a bathroom that looked like a film setting? Rebecca smiled, this was going to be good.

Wednesday morning found Rebecca dressed in one of her new outfits and sitting in the hotel as she waited for the Lottery advisor to arrive. She was in a small alcove above the main reception area, away from the hustle and bustle. A superb stained glass window that stretched the height of the wall allowed a rainbow of light to dance across Rebecca's face as she waited. A small settee and a couple of large comfortable chairs were set around a table decorated with an artful arrangement of flowers. She had ordered a coffee and explained that she was expecting guests. The answer as usual was 'no problem' and an assurance that the visitors would be taken to Rebecca as soon as they arrived along with a fresh pot of coffee. If you had enough money were there ever problems wondered Rebecca? If you were staying in the lap of luxury and made a request, did there ever come a time when the staff simply shook their heads and said, 'sorry Madam, we just can't do that'?

She smiled as she thought back to last night. She and Sarah had enjoyed a lovely evening. They had met at the little Italian restaurant on The Headrow they always visited and eaten pizza as Sarah brought her mum up to date with the latest ups and downs of student life. If she had wondered why her mother could afford to be so generous she hadn't said anything as Rebecca ordered not only a bottle of wine with their meal but then insisted on treating Sarah to several cocktails before ordering a taxi home for her daughter and pushing the money to pay into her protesting hand.

She had wanted to tell Sarah what had happened. She wanted to wrap her arms around her daughter and tell her that all her problems were over. She didn't have to worry about paying back her student loan. She could resign from her job in the local pub and her job in the corner shop, both of which she kept so she didn't have to constantly ask Rebecca for help. She had wanted to tell her daughter everything, but she hadn't. How could she when she hadn't told Daniel yet? He must be told first, after all it was their money. So she had said nothing but hugged her daughter tightly and said goodbye.

'Rebecca?' A tall, thin young man stood before her, an attractive blonde woman at his side, both looking enquiringly at Rebecca as she sat lost in her daydream.

'Yes, that's me.'

Rebecca jumped to her feet nervously, almost knocking over her coffee cup, artfully rescued by the waiter who had accompanied her guests. He ushered them all into seats and then produced another pot of coffee, extra cups and a plate of pretty little cakes before smiling politely and withdrawing.

Rebecca's heart was hammering so loudly she felt sure that everyone must be able to hear. What if it had been a mistake after all? What if she had misunderstood something and there was no money, no millions about to be placed in her bank account? How would she explain the mountain of debt now sitting on her credit card? How would she manage to pay it back, what on earth would Daniel say?

'Well Rebecca, congratulations! You've won 15.7 million pounds on our lottery. Well done!'

The voice was discreet enough not to draw any attention but to Rebecca it sounded like a trumpet being blown.

'Really?' she whispered, 'I've really, really won?'

Fifteen minutes later even Rebecca had to admit that there was no mistake. Alan had examined her ID and lottery ticket, double checked her bank account details, confirmed that there was to be no publicity and finally declared that the amount of 15.7 million pounds would arrive in Rebecca's bank on Friday morning, first thing. He advised Rebecca to see her bank manager and made an appointment for her to see an investment specialist who could answer any questions she had about the handling of a large win.

Alan had also explained that people often worried about the wait, those long days before the money reached their bank account. What if something happened to them, would their family still get the money?

'And will they?' asked Rebecca curiously. 'Still get the money, I mean?'

'Oh of course! You've won the money Rebecca, we don't take it away if your circumstances change. But always remember the money is yours and until you make a will no-one is automatically entitled to any of it.'

'Mine.' Rebecca twiddled her fingers as they rested in her lap. 'Surely it belongs to my husband as well?'

'Oh no,' interrupted the blonde who had said very little up until now and whose name Rebecca couldn't remember. 'It's your money Rebecca, it's not a matrimonial asset so it's actually entirely up to you to decide what you want to do with the money.'

'Oh.' Rebecca bit her lip. 'Not that I wouldn't … well you know I'm not asking because…'

'Like I said,' the blonde added firmly, 'it's your money, entirely yours and entirely up to you what you do with it Rebecca. You and no-one else.'

They left shortly after and for a while Rebecca remained on the settee in the corner.

When the waiter arrived to ask if she wanted anything else she started to wave him away and then jumped to her feet with guilt.

'Oh I'm sorry, how much…'

'It will be added to your account Madam. No problem.'

Of course there wasn't a problem, giggled Rebecca, she had just won over 15 million pounds, what could be a problem?

After going back up to her room to splash cold water on her face and slip on her trench coat, Rebecca set off into Leeds once more. The bank was only a few streets away and she had a couple of hours to while away. She wandered along, her mind whirling as she went over and over the meeting she had just had. There was absolutely no doubt any more. No mistake, no possibility that she had gotten anything wrong. Rebecca Miles would soon have millions of pounds in her bank account.

She stopped in front of a window and stared. Five minutes later she was still staring. Could she? Could she really?

She opened the door and looked around to see if anyone was free.

'Can I help?'

An older lady, smartly dressed in a trouser suit with her hair neatly set, smiled in Rebecca's direction.

'Yes you can.' Rebecca walked over and sat at the chair in front of - she leaned forward to read her name badge - in front of Annie's desk.

'I am thinking of buying a house in this area and I would like you to show me what you have.'

Having answered a few basic questions for Annie, how many bedrooms, reception rooms etc. they had arrived at the matter of the budget.

'And how much do you have to spend?' asked Annie.

Rebecca shrugged. How much did she have to spend? 15.7 million pounds actually. Not that she would spend all of that on a house.

'I'm not sure,' she confided, 'I suppose it depends on the house.'

Annie nodded. 'Yes I understand but if you can give me a starting figure, just so I know what we're looking at?'

Rebecca chewed on her lip. How much? She had 15.7 million pounds. How much was a reasonable amount to spend on a house?

'Well, I suppose a million?' she offered nervously.

Annie stared at her for a fraction of a second and Rebecca pushed her hair behind her ears. 'Maybe a couple of million?'

Annie's eyebrows shot upwards and although her manner had been exceptionally pleasant ever since Rebecca arrived, Rebecca wondered if she detected a tiny little change in her demeanour.

'Right. A couple of million - do you mean 2 million?'

Rebecca nodded uncertainly. 'Well - yes.'

She wondered if that was enough. Obviously 2 million was enough to buy a house. It was more than enough. But was it enough to spend when you had won 15.7 million? Did people with that kind of money only spend 2 million on a house? Or did they spend less? Suddenly Rebecca wished she had waited a little longer before making this visit. She almost wished Daniel was here, at least he would be able to make a decision.

Before they left Leeds they had lived in a beautiful stone terrace north of the city. Their money had bought a lot more in Darlington and they had moved into a 4 bed executive detached which Rebecca had hated from the moment she crossed the threshold. In Leeds, although within easy reach of the city centre, they had lived in a small village surrounded by fields and good friends. The sort of friends who invited you on impulse to a Sunday afternoon barbecue. The sort of friends you could ask at the very last minute to help you out by collecting your children from school, who sat in your kitchen until late as you chatted and put the world to rights and emptied several bottles of wine.

She had friends in Darlington, she loved Carol and Susie, their neighbours Elaine and Dave were okay but it had never been the same and her heart had always ached to come back to Leeds.

'Yes 2 million,' said Rebecca firmly, 'more if you find the right house but let's start with 2 million.'

Once Annie learned that it was a cash purchase with no existing house to sell, Rebecca had quickly been upgraded to a seating area at the back of the shop where she could spread out the brochures Annie produced across the polished coffee table. A glass of champagne had even been forthcoming as Rebecca reduced the selection down to three possible houses. She made arrangements to see one tomorrow after visiting her mum and the other two on Friday morning before she left Leeds, although the thought of sitting on the train back to Darlington was already depressing Rebecca.

Having spent a few wonderful hours in the estate agents she ended up having to hurry along the busy streets to the bank, arriving with cheeks flushed from the joint effects of the champagne and the bitter wind and with the glossy brochures of three beautiful houses tucked under her arm. She was taken into a small side office for her appointment and sank into the chair opposite Luke Brady trying to catch her breath. She had never meet Luke Brady, in fact judging by his age and the spots still scattered across his chin, Luke had undoubtedly still been at school when Rebecca had opened her account several years before.

But he smiled politely and tried to look interested in the middle aged woman with the wind blown hair and red cheeks sitting opposite him.

'Hello Luke,' began Rebecca. 'I take it you are the manager here?'

'I'm your account manager,' offered Luke smoothly as he straightened his tie. 'How can I help you today Mrs Miles?'

Rebecca smiled to take the sting out of her words. 'Then I think there's been a slight misunderstanding Luke because I asked to speak to the manager.'

Luke's own smile dropped. 'Mrs Miles…'

'Luke,' interrupted Rebecca gently 'I want to speak to the manager of the bank. Today, now. That's why I've travelled from Darlington and that's why I'm here. To speak to the manager. Please get him for me.'

'I'm afraid I can't…where are you going?'

'The manager Luke. Now, or I will be taking my deposit, my multi-million-pound deposit to another bank.'

'Mrs Miles I really can't … multi-million … please wait!'

He leapt to his feet and Rebecca sank gracefully back into the chair.

'I'll just get him!' he squeaked and shot out of the door.

Five minutes later Rebecca was upstairs in a much larger office with a coffee in her hand and an older man sitting at the desk opposite. Rebecca had nothing against young men. She had nothing against young men called Luke. But she had no intention of trusting 15.7 million of her pounds into his hands.

'So I understand this is a lottery win Mrs Miles?'

'Please call me Rebecca. Yes, it's a lottery win and it should be arriving on Friday morning. It's an account I use very rarely and I just didn't want any problems, you know? 15.7 million pounds …'

'Is a lot of money and of course you did the right thing. Now,' he said efficiently, turning to the screen before him, 'you obviously won't have had time to decide what you want to do with it all yet but I imagine you'll want to make some initial purchases so we need to make sure there is an up to date debit card on the account and we'll upgrade the limit on your credit card of course and issue you with a new platinum version.'

Rebecca felt a moment of sorrow for the plain little non platinum card that had made this trip possible.

'I see that the account is in your name only, are you happy to leave it this way? You also have a joint account with us in the name of yourself and Mr Daniel Miles?'

When Rebecca had taken out the account the children had been small and she and Daniel had been happy. It had never occurred to Rebecca to open an account at a different bank.

Rebecca chewed her lip. She could imagine the conversation, the bank manager phoning and asking Daniel if he had decided what to do with the 15 million pounds in the account, Daniel wondering what he was talking about, Rebecca explaining that she hadn't told him yet because … actually Rebecca wasn't really sure why she hadn't told Daniel yet but the news needed to come from her and not the bank manager.

She cleared her throat and leant forward ever so slightly to meet the gaze of the bank manager. His name badge gave no first name.

'Mr Dickinson, I need to know that until I say otherwise the money will stay in this account. I will be moving it into our joint account, of course I will!'

Of course she would, thought Rebecca firmly. Why wouldn't she?

'But until I do I need you not to...well I don't want you discussing the money with anyone. I mean, no-one must know. If Mr Miles phones you…'

Rebecca shook her head, why on earth would Daniel suddenly take it upon himself to phone the bank and ask if there was 15 million pounds in his wife's account?

She sighed, 'I'm sorry, I'm not being clear, what I mean is…'

Fortunately, Mr Dickinson interrupted her, raising his hand and smiling reassuringly at the thoroughly confused Rebecca.

'You have our absolute assurance Mrs Miles that your account is totally confidential. No details will ever be revealed to anyone, even Mr Miles.'

Rebecca smiled and sat back in her seat. 'Good,' she said simply. 'That's good.'

She left some time later with a selection of brochures regarding investments, wills, inheritance tax and savings accounts, a vastly increased limit on her little credit card, a new card ordered and with her account upgraded to an all singing all dancing executive status.

She had seen Mr Dickinson eye the property brochures she had placed on the desk and he added a leaflet about house conveyance and legal fees. She had been escorted to the door and her hand gripped firmly as he assured her of their best attention at all times and finally Rebecca was walking back towards the hotel, the light already fading and the wind colder than ever as she pulled the trench coat around her shoulders and picked up the pace. Stopping only briefly to grab a handful of glossy magazines, the sort that Rebecca normally considered far too expensive for her purse, she was soon back in the wonderfully heated lobby of Quebecs hotel with one of the bell boys catching her eye the moment she entered the door and pressing the lift button for her floor.

Rebecca ran a bath and relaxed up to her neck in bubbles until she felt the warmth return to her bones and the stress of the day seep out of her skin. Wrapping herself in a fluffy white towel that felt like a cuddle from a loved one, she rubbed her hair dry and ran a brush through it before she gazed critically into the bathroom mirror. She had been pretty once. Now, like most 45 year olds, it was all a little loose. Her hair needed a good cut and not the trim she usually did herself over the sink. It had lost a lot of the rich auburn colour of her youth and was more of a non-descript brown at the moment. Her neck was definitely starting to sag and the laughter lines round the corners of her hazel eyes were more pronounced than they had been a few years earlier. But she wasn't too bad for her age she mused. Nothing that a visit to the hairdresser and the beauty counter at Boots couldn't sort out. She shook out all the creams and potions she had bought the day before and tried to remember the benefits of each one. She opened one pot and inhaled the contents. It smelled divine, she could feel it working its magic before it even touched her skin. It was rich and creamy and yet light as a feather. For someone who normally bought her moisturiser from the supermarket with the weekly shop, it was quite a change and closing her eyes she stroked the soft cream across her cheek and relished the feel of it sinking into her tired pores. She dabbed some serum around her eyes, a different cream on her hands and elbows and a squirt of a new perfume across the hollow of her neck. Satisfied, she wandered to the sitting area and took the room service menu from the table. A few minutes later she had ordered a bottle of excellent white wine - at least the person who took her order said it was excellent – together with a fillet steak and salad. She had been asked if she would like some strawberries to follow, the kitchen had received some fresh in that day and Rebecca had decided yes, she would very much like some strawberries to finish her meal. And when the waiter delivered it to her door what seemed like only minutes later he reported to the kitchen staff what a very pleasant lady was in the Robinson suite - and that wasn't just because she had tipped him £20.

When Rebecca's eyes were drooping, in part due to her busy day and in part due to a large glass of white wine, she had gathered all the glossy magazines and house details into a neat pile on the coffee table and slid into the bed with its turned down corner and its wonderful deep nest of a quilt and had the best night's sleep she had slept in many years.

Chapter 5

Rebecca ordered room service again for her breakfast. She was making the most of these few days and it was such a change to have her meals delivered to her door each day. She had it set down in the sitting area and then curled up on the settee tucking into her croissants as she took another glance at the estate agents brochures. She had said no to a glass and chrome house which was sleek minimalist and totally impractical. She had said no to a mock Georgian new build that looked exactly like a mock Georgian new build. She had said no to the seven bedrooms overlooking the golf course - she couldn't imagine anything worse. And she had said no to the farmhouse that came with 17 acres and several barns.

But she had said yes to the three houses before her. One in particular had caught her eye. It was further out of Leeds than she was thinking but built of the most wonderful mellow old stone. It was set down a long drive for privacy and despite the fact that it had several reception rooms and the most glorious, great big kitchen, it had a warm welcoming air to it that had immediately taken Rebecca's fancy. There seemed to be a lot of pale cream settees scattered around that Rebecca felt would not suit the average family with children and dogs and a plethora of muddy feet. But Rebecca didn't have to worry about those things anymore and although she also felt it might be a little large for just her and Daniel, she couldn't wait to visit. There were two more, similar in style that she would visit tomorrow but this was the one that interested Rebecca. She glanced at her watch. She had decided to get a taxi to her mother's residential home. It was easily reached by bus but Rebecca had elected not to wait at the bus station in the freezing cold and instead she retired to the bathroom to have another deep luxurious bubble bath as she closed her eyes and dreamt of a beautiful honey stone house within driving distance of Leeds.

When Rebecca got out of the taxi she knew Gwen had remembered her daughter was visiting that day. Rebecca opened the main door to the house and then rang the intercom on the internal glass door, standing where she could see across the lobby and into the TV lounge where Gwen was waiting, sitting with her wheelchair turned towards the main door.

Rebecca waved as one of the staff came to let her in and in seconds she had her arms around her mum breathing in the familiar perfume that Gwen hadn't changed in 30 years.

'Oh Rebecca my darling, it's so good to see you,' and then Rebecca had to submit to the inspection of half a dozen elderly ladies as they all came wandering in to say hello to Gwen's lovely daughter and stroke her cheek and say how she hadn't changed and ask after the children.

Eventually it was just her and Gwen and Rebecca wheeled her mum towards the French windows, firmly closed against the cold day but still allowing a beautiful view of the large gardens behind the house.

Gwen hadn't gone into the home unwillingly, although Rebecca often wondered if she had still been living in Leeds whether Gwen would have remained at the sheltered home for longer. They had taken a great deal of time and effort before finding Parklands but the minute Gwen arrived on an inspection visit she had turned to Rebecca and nodded, saying 'this is the one'.

It was a little faded and in need of some upkeep. The heating was a nightmare to get going and the plumbing sometimes shook the whole of the house. Everywhere was in need of a lick of paint and it had been Rebecca's long held concern that it was struggling to keep its doors open in the current financial crisis. But Parklands had kept going despite everything. If the heating played up the residents were wrapped in snuggly warm blankets with lots of hot water bottles, the plumbing may shake the building but it always eventually produced hot water and the staff looked after their charges with a care and courtesy that brought relief to Rebecca's heart every time she visited. There was an air of gentility and grace about the place which had immediately attracted Gwen. It was a lovely old house however much the paint was peeling and the residents appreciated the spacious rooms with their intricate architraves as much as the beautiful old gardens, extensively planted with sweet smelling roses.

'So how are you my darling?' Gwen grasped her daughter's hand and looked into her eyes.

Rebecca grinned back. 'Good mum, really good.'

'Hmm, you certainly seem a lot happier than the last time I saw you. Have you left him?'

'Mum!' protested Rebecca. 'Of course I haven't. But things are better.'

She couldn't tell Gwen, just as she hadn't told Sarah. She had to tell Daniel first. It was their money. She would tell Daniel and then she would tell Sarah and Toby and Gwen. And Carol and Susie. She would hand in her resignation and she would move back to Leeds. If not to the house she was going to see this afternoon, then another beautiful million-pound property somewhere in the area. She would move back to Leeds, visit her mum more and be able to see her old friends far more frequently. She smiled at her mum who was watching her shrewdly.

'Yes things are a lot better mum and I think they're going to carry on getting better.'

After several very pleasant hours with her mum, countless cups of tea and a round of ham sandwiches, Rebecca kissed Gwen, said goodbye to all the other residents, thanked the staff as she always did for their marvellous effort, noticed that Mrs Wendover the manager was looking even more tired than usual, prayed that Parklands would last a little longer for Gwen's sake and climbed into the taxi that had arrived to take her to see Beech Grange. She was meeting Annie there and she had brought the glossy brochure with her which she pulled out of her bag as they drove. The kitchen looked amazing, with a vast array of surfaces, a never ending choice of cupboards and large French doors opening into the garden. It had a huge central table, ideal for cosy meals with friends and against one wall were double glass doors that opened onto an adjoining garden room with a wood burning stove and a collection of lovely deep settees. Rebecca hugged herself, she could just imagine a day like this, with a fire crackling, the smell of casserole in the air, a bottle of wine in the fridge and her friends and family sitting round the table.

Rebecca looked around the whole house before she spoke to Annie. She looked in every bedroom and every cupboard. She checked every bathroom and looked behind every door. She even looked round the garden and the tennis court hidden behind the apple trees and the garage which was big enough for 4 large cars. She looked in the wood store and the greenhouse where the current gardener propagated the plants. She looked inside the double range oven and opened the double doors of the American fridge freezer. She flicked the switch that dimmed the lights and she flicked the switch that drew the curtains. She flicked the switch that turned on the surround sound and the one that turned on the garden lights. She looked at the state of the art alarm system and the array of switches that set the individual temperature in each room. She looked at everything that Annie showed her saying nothing more than the occasional 'that's nice' and 'oh yes I see'.

Rebecca had made up her mind seconds after stepping into the lovely hallway and seeing the warm and welcoming house stretch out before her. But she let Annie show her all these things partly because Annie was enjoying it so much and partly because it gave Rebecca's reeling senses time to organise themselves. And when they had finally done the whole tour and they were back in the hallway next to the lovely staircase that curved upwards, Annie turned to her with a slight edge of desperation to her voice and demanded, 'So, do you like it?'

Rebecca looked down the hall into the lovely bright kitchen and then turned to smile at Annie.

'Oh yes, I like it. I'll take it please.'

Annie's eyebrows shot up to lose themselves in her hairline.

'You'll take it,' she repeated.

'Yes, I'll take it,' answered Rebecca, as casually as though she had just chosen a new set of towels.

'When can I have it?'

Rebecca wondered if she should take Annie's arm, she looked very pale.

'Well, when did you want to...'

'Oh straight away. No point hanging around once you've chosen is there? How soon can these things be organised?'

'Well, I think a couple of weeks if everyone is...'

'Oh and I'd like the furniture as well.'

'The furniture?'

Poor Annie really did look as though she needed to sit down. Rebecca had realised as she followed Annie on her tour, that this house was the product of a great deal of time and effort. It was presented in a way that only the truly gifted can make a house look and although Rebecca was sure she could manage the same effect given time, why bother? She loved the whole house, pale cream settees included and had decided it would be far easier to just buy the whole thing as it stood.

'Right,' said Annie, 'well of course I'll have to ask them…'

'Oh I'll pay,' said Rebecca 'just tell them to let me know how much they want,' and smiling at Annie she walked out into the garden where she was sure the air had suddenly become a whole lot warmer.

It was Friday morning and as Rebecca opened her eyes she had trouble working out what time it was. The thick damask curtains did an excellent job of keeping out the light, weather and noise and it took Rebecca a few seconds to focus on the clock on the side table. She had overslept. It was 9.07. Another superb meal followed by another deep, luxurious bath had sent her into a long sleep ably helped by fluffy pillows and goose down quilt and Rebecca had stayed in bed long past her usual 7.30 wake up time.

She sat up, looking around the still dark room before slipping out of bed and into her dressing gown. She pulled back the curtains, enough to let in some of the hard, bright winter light and then walked over to the sitting area where she did the same, gazing down onto the street below.

It was busy. Workers still flooded the streets, buses and taxis lined the road. Everybody busy, everybody with somewhere to go. Rebecca turned back and sat by the small coffee table. It had occurred to her yesterday that she had no means of checking her bank account so she had made a quick visit to the nearest electrical shop and now a brand new laptop sat on top of the piles of brochures, magazines and leaflets that were starting to accrue.

She had asked for the password for the hotel's Wi-Fi the night before and she had checked her bank account, which showed exactly zero.

But today was Friday and the balance should be a whole lot more.

It wasn't until she had logged into her bank account and was watching the swirling circle as the page loaded that Rebecca realised she was holding her breath.

She exhaled, loud and deep just as the circle completed and on the screen came her balance.

15.7 million pounds.

It was there in black and white. She counted the noughts just to be sure but there really was no mistake. Rebecca Miles had 15.7 million in her account.

Chapter 6

It was Monday morning and Rebecca was on an early shift at the Deli. She had arrived home on Sunday afternoon, having extended her stay at Quebecs. She had met Sarah again and taken her shopping, refusing to listen to her insistence to pay her own way. She had done a little more shopping herself but had been quite restrained, after all where would she wear all these new clothes? As yet she had told no-one about her win. She was carrying on with life as normal and Rebecca's normal life did not include a wardrobe of new clothes. But she had visited a hairdresser and her hair had been cut and coloured back to the vibrant auburn tones of ten years earlier and she had been amazed at the difference it made to her face. She'd also spent a few more hours in Debenhams, wandering through the household section and visualising all the soft bath towels lined up in her bathroom, choosing the pans that would be in her kitchen, picking out a new colour scheme for her bedroom.

And she had also bought a house.

Annie had phoned her only a few hours after they had visited Beech Grange to tell Rebecca that her offer had been accepted, the house and the majority of the furniture was hers. The owners were looking for a quick sale and were delighted that Rebecca wanted to move things along so speedily. Details were exchanged, solicitors engaged and Rebecca was told that in the absence of any problems the house would be hers within the next few weeks.

She had returned to Darlington with a far bigger suitcase. The new laptop was packed under her new trousers and trench coat, the new phone she had bought on impulse tucked next to it. Rebecca had never bothered with a mobile. But with solicitors, bank managers and estate agents all now needing to keep in touch, she had wandered into a shop and departed clutching a phone that was a complete mystery to her but which now contained her new list of contacts.

The first thing on her list of things to do was to tell Daniel. He needed to know so that they could actually move on with their new lives. The holiday brochures that Rebecca had brought home from Tesco were now tucked at the bottom of her underwear drawer and even Rebecca appreciated that it would be hard to fit in a two-week luxury break on a tropical island without her husband noticing. She needed to tell him. Sooner rather than later. Especially as she seemed to have bought a house.

Except when she got home the house was empty and there was a brief note from Daniel that simply said 'golf'. There were pots in the sink and food on the surface. The takeaway menu was next to the kettle and Rebecca felt a tiny moment of guilt that she hadn't bothered to leave him any meals prepared. But it was only a tiny moment and soon disappeared as she spent the next hour cleaning the kitchen and restoring order. At least it gave her time to take her suitcase upstairs and unpack out of the way of prying eyes. Not that Daniel would have bothered to watch her unpack, he seemed to have very little desire to pry into her life these days. The laptop went onto the top shelf of the wardrobe amongst the shoe boxes, the phone went into her handbag, the clothes into the wardrobe. The toiletries and cosmetics were shared between the bathroom and her dressing table and when everything was unpacked and the suitcase put away, Rebecca went downstairs to make a cup of tea which she took to bed before falling into an exhausted sleep.

In the morning she had received a grudging apology from Daniel for his late return home before he brought her up to date with every slight and insult he felt had come his way during her absence. He was incensed that Peter had now insisted that Daniel bring himself up to date with the new practices of the business whether he wanted to or not.

How dare he! Did he not realise how much experience Daniel had in this business? Did he not understand how much Daniel knew about the packaging business? Didn't he know just how many customers Daniel had brought to White's over the years? How dare he act as though he was in charge. How dare he!

Rebecca listened as she gazed around the kitchen and thought about her new house. The kitchen alone was as big as the ground floor of their Darlington house. She couldn't wait to move.

'Are you listening to me!' Daniel was thrusting his quivering red face inches from her own.

Rebecca put down her coffee cup. 'Yes I'm listening. But Peter is in charge, isn't he Daniel?' and she walked out of the kitchen leaving Daniel, for once, silent.

So she had not told Daniel about the 15.7 million pounds in her bank account. Or the house she had arranged to buy in Leeds. She hadn't told Daniel and therefore she couldn't tell Carol and Susie so she turned up for her shift as usual that afternoon, answered all their questions about her mum and her few days in Leeds and carried on as though everything was exactly the same as normal. They admired her hair and she admitted she had decided to treat herself but she didn't wear any of her new clothes and the new perfume stayed on her dressing table. It was a normal day and half way through Rebecca began to wonder if it had all been a dream until she arrived home and checked her account online. The money was still there, the balance large, bold and real and sitting in her account. She closed the laptop and went into the kitchen to peel some potatoes.

She didn't tell Daniel that evening, or the next morning, or the next evening. She still hadn't told Daniel on Friday morning when she took a call from Leslie to arrange a meeting the following day with another Lottery advisor, followed by a call from Annie to check that all was ok and to suggest a date for the signing of the contracts and finally a call from Sarah saying what fun it had been to spend some time with her mum the previous week.

Every night Rebecca decided that she would break the news, show Daniel the ticket, show him her bank account balance on the computer. She would explain that she hadn't told him earlier because she had wanted to be absolutely sure. She would have to explain that she had already bought a house, that would be hard but initially she just needed to tell him about the money, about her win.

But it simply hadn't happened. For some reason as she sat and watched him eating his meal, listening to his usual angry rant about the state of White's since Peter Thompson took over, how humiliating they were making it for him, how they didn't know what they were doing; as she listened to the excuses why none of his deals had completed, listened to the reasons why there was no new business to be had, she just couldn't bring herself to say the words. She watched his mouth move, his words falling out. She needed to tell him. She wanted to tell him.

'I'm going to Leeds tomorrow.'

Daniel stopped mid-sentence and stared at Rebecca, his fork halfway to his mouth. 'Again!'

Rebecca didn't answer.

'But you've only just got back, why are you going again?'

'Because I want to visit mum again.'

'But you've only just visited her. Why do you need to go again so soon?'

Rebecca carried on eating, meeting Daniel's eyes across the table.

'I mean,' he grumbled, 'you are my wife. Is it too much to expect that you could stay at home with me occasionally? Look after me instead of running off to Leeds every two minutes to visit your mum. What about me?'

Rebecca thought about pointing out that this may have been the second visit in the last two weeks but she had gone months before that without traveling to Leeds because Daniel always made so much fuss about spending money on train fares when there were bills to pay. She stared at him as he shoved a forkful of vegetables in his mouth. He hadn't asked her about her mum. Hadn't asked if she had been okay. He hadn't asked about Sarah, whether Rebecca had met with her, if she was okay. He hadn't actually asked about anything, her journey, whether she had had a good time, where she had stayed.

In fact, Rebecca mused, Daniel didn't really ask her anything anymore, other than when his food would be ready. He didn't ask about her day, about her health, about what she was doing.

He complained. He complained that she hadn't done enough chips or that she had done too much rice. He complained that she hadn't put any petrol in the car or that she had forgotten to buy his favourite shaving foam. He complained that she had the heating up too high, the lights too low, the TV on too loud.

He complained a lot.

And he told her things. He told her how hard his life was, how unfairly he was treated at work. He told her constantly how hard he had to work to keep the roof over her head. He told her that things hadn't gone well, that the potential customers he had spent the weekend trying to impress had gone to another packaging firm. He told her that he was fed up with Peter Thompson, fed up with being overlooked. He told her how disappointed he was with his life, how he had been let down after all his hard work.

He told her lots of things but he never asked her anything anymore.

He was still talking. 'It's not easy you know, coming home and having to look after yourself after a hard day at work. Just having you here occasionally isn't too much to ask. Another visit so soon seems unreasonable to me. You live here!'

Now, thought Rebecca. Tell him now. Tell him that there's 15.7 million in the bank and he doesn't have to work anymore. Tell him that you've spent 2 million on a house in Leeds and you want to leave Darlington.

'Daniel…'

'What?'

'It's only for a couple of nights, you'll be fine.'

Rebecca caught the train to Leeds the next morning. She had booked into Quebecs again and was delighted to hear them say how happy they were that she was coming back and would she like the same room. She arrived early again, left her case to be taken to her room, smiled at the receptionist and then walked down to Annie's office where she was treated to a warm welcome and the offer of a coffee.

'I just wanted to catch up,' explained Annie. 'The vendors have drawn up a list of all the furniture they're prepared to leave. There are just one or two bits and pieces they want to keep but the rest is yours. Here's the itinerary.'

Rebecca took it and read through the pages of descriptions. It didn't mean a great deal. She hadn't fallen in love with the furniture because of the name or the style but because it had all looked so right, part of the home she had decided to buy.

She handed it back to Annie. 'That looks fine.'

Annie cleared her throat. 'There are some very good quality items in there Rebecca. They want an extra £50,000.'

'Okay.'

Annie looked relieved. 'That's not a problem?'

'Of course not Annie, I said I would buy the furniture, I didn't expect them to give it to me.'

'Right,' suddenly looking a lot brighter, Annie topped up Rebecca's coffee.

'Well, all is going to plan. They'd already had all the surveys done and now it's just a case of waiting for the conveyancing. As there's only the two of you in the chain it looks as though it will be yours on 19th April.'

Just over two weeks away. She really must tell Daniel. And soon.

Rebecca left a smiling Annie and walked back to the hotel just in time to see a middle aged woman arrive at the reception desk and ask for Rebecca Miles.

Rebecca shook her hand and asked the receptionist if there was somewhere they could talk privately. Two minutes later they were in a small side room, obviously used for such meetings and decked out with a small table with chairs on either side and a pot of coffee.

It was a long drawn out affair, especially for someone like Rebecca who hadn't ever been involved in investments and savings before but the woman, Joyce McCrindle, had been efficient and clear.

Basically Rebecca discovered that the large amount of money sitting in her bank account was entirely hers to dispose of. When Joyce McCrindle heard that Rebecca wanted to provide for her children but not overwhelm them, she suggested setting up trust funds for them both together with monthly allowances. When she heard that Rebecca's elderly mother was in a home and living from the sale of her house, she suggested a separate account that would meet the cost of Gwen's care, her resident's fees and perhaps give her a small monthly allowance too, saving Gwen's remaining assets.

When Joyce McCrindle failed to find out anything at all about Rebecca's husband, she advised Rebecca that the money was not actually a shared asset. Rebecca had come by it independently and it was actually nothing to do with Daniel. When Rebecca protested that of course it would involve Daniel, Mrs McCrindle put her hand on Rebecca's arm and repeated that it was entirely Rebecca's decision what she did with her winnings.

Complete with brochures, leaflets and a better understanding of what was needed to keep control of such a large sum of money Rebecca went back into reception to collect her key. Arriving back in The Robinson suite was like arriving home. Rebecca sank onto one of the overstuffed settees and put her collection of brochures onto the table. She probably felt more at home here than in Darlington, which was a sad thought.

She thought about her new house. Only two weeks and it would be hers. She could live in Leeds again in her beautiful new home. She just needed to tell Daniel.

Unpacking and slipping on her trench coat, Rebecca took to the shops and over the next few hours she all but emptied Debenhams and House of Fraser as she chose huge fluffy bath towels, colour co-ordinated bed linen for every bedroom including a luxurious rich red brocade and velvet throw for her own room, a top of the range selection of pans and kitchen accessories, cushions, toiletries, glass vases, silver photo frames, heavy cathedral candles - and anything else that she could think of. All for her new home and left at the store for delivery once Beech Grange was officially hers. Then Rebecca did a little more personal shopping, this time walking confidently into Harvey Nichols before eventually wandering back to the hotel with her arms full of bags.

It seemed so much easier to shop this week. She didn't have the same feeling of being a fake and as she walked around the shops she was overwhelmed with the knowledge that she could afford just about anything that she wanted. Instead of chewing her lip and wondering if she was being ridiculous, Rebecca was full of a confidence that she hadn't known for years.

She had phoned Sarah earlier who was amazed that her mum had returned to Leeds again so soon and had said she couldn't meet her mum that night. They arranged to go the Parklands together the next day and then on for Sunday lunch somewhere.

'We'll take Granny,' Rebecca had announced and when Sarah had questioned how, Rebecca announced airily that they would book a special taxi, one that could take wheelchairs.

So the next day she and Sarah were driven to Parklands where they spent a lovely hour. Rebecca wore a new pair of trousers with a top in a rich bronze colour that brought out the tone of her hair and made her hazel eyes sparkle. They sat in the TV lounge, drank tea and listened to the chatter all around them. Rebecca wondered again at how pale and tired Mrs Wendover looked and planned to have a word as soon as she could. Maybe the home was in trouble, maybe they needed some help. Rebecca was certainly in a position to do just that and she had to make sure it survived for her mother.

When lunch time came so did the special taxi organised by Mrs Wendover and Rebecca, Sarah and Gwen travelled the few miles to a local pub that Rebecca remembered well from their time living nearby. The Sunday lunches were famed and there was a table waiting for them close to a roaring fire. Gwen got slightly squiffy on sweet sherry much to Sarah's amusement and Rebecca probably drank more wine than she should have done but the afternoon was magical, only spoilt somewhat by Sarah taking her hand in the taxi going back to Leeds and asking, 'Have you left Dad?'

'What!'

'Have you left him?'

'Of course I haven't,' said Rebecca in amazement, 'what on earth gave you that idea?'

'Well, this is your second visit in as many weeks. You look amazing, happier than I've seen you look for years. You're spending money on yourself - about time too. And, I don't know, you just look different.'

'And you think that's all because I've left your father?'

'Well I could see how leaving him would cause all of those things to happen, yes.'

'Well I haven't, silly girl. I've just missed being in Leeds, I've decided to spend more time here, visiting mum and you. I'll go down to Bristol as well and visit Toby more.'

Sarah looked doubtful. 'It's okay, you can tell me you know.'

Rebecca leant forward and smoothed her daughter's hair out of her eyes. 'I would tell you sweetheart. I would tell you if I had left your father. I wouldn't keep something like that a secret from you.'

Just 15.7 million pounds.

Sarah smiled and squeezed her mother's hand. 'Well as long as you know, I would be alright with it mum.'

Sarah wanted to drop Rebecca off at her hotel. 'Is it the Travelodge Mum?'

Rebecca didn't actually answer, saying they would drop Sarah off first although she felt the taxi driver staring at her as he eventually dropped her outside Quebecs.

Sitting in the room that she had grown so fond off, she put her feet up. That morning on impulse she'd decided to postpone her journey home until tomorrow. She'd originally booked the last train back on Sunday night but decided instead to catch the early morning train on Monday instead. She would still be back in time for her afternoon shift at the deli and she'd had such a wonderful day that she couldn't bear the thought of going back now and bringing it to an end.

So she phoned down to reception to order a meal, checked the train times and then left Daniel a message on the house phone before putting on her fluffy dressing gown and flicking on the TV with a deep sigh of bliss.

Chapter 7

Rebecca decided on the train journey back that she needed to do something about work. In a little over two weeks she would be collecting the keys for her house in Leeds. She obviously couldn't keep working at the Deli. She needed to let them know as soon as possible that she was leaving, but of course she couldn't tell them the truth.

So that afternoon when she arrived at work she took Carol to one side, well aware that Susie was listening in, and told her she was resigning.

A loud wail from Susie blocked out anything Carol was saying but the look on her face was enough.

'No! Oh Rebecca - no. Why? Are you going to work somewhere else, where are you going?'

Rebecca laughed putting her arm around Carol and turning to face Susie. 'I'm not going anywhere, I would never leave you two to work somewhere else. I just need to leave. I-I'm…'

She had won 15.7 million on the lottery and was moving to Leeds.

'I just need to spend more time in Leeds, my mum…'

She trailed of and felt a sliver of guilt as both Carol and Susie immediately nodded sympathetically.

'Poor you,' offered Carol. 'Is she no better?'

Rebecca hated using her mother as an excuse, it was a little like tempting fate but it was either that or the truth and the truth seemed to be something that was becoming more difficult by the day.

'She's okay but I - worry.'

Susie was looking at her through narrowed eyes. An easy going, generous and loud person she was also razor sharp.

'Have you left Mr Nobby?' she demanded.

Carol dug her in the ribs and Rebecca looked shocked.

'Of course I haven't!'

'Susie!' berated Carol. 'Why would you say that?'

'Well she looks so much happier! Look at her, she's glowing, she's had her hair done, she's wearing a new top, she keeps going to Leeds - Oh My God! You're having an affair aren't you?'

'Susie!' Carol's voice was even louder and Rebecca felt her cheeks flushing.

'Of course not Susie! What a thing to say.'

Susie wasn't convinced and for the rest of the afternoon she kept a watchful eye on Rebecca much to Carol's amusement.

The problem of her replacement wasn't really a problem. The young girl who covered the weekends had already made it clear she would love to do more hours and so it was agreed that Rebecca would leave at the end of the following week.

'But you're still coming to my party aren't you?' asked Susie plaintively.

It was Susie's wedding anniversary and she had been planning the party to end all parties for months. Rebecca felt a brief regret that it meant a weekend she would be unable to visit Leeds.

'Of course I'll be there,' she said hugging her friend. 'It's the day after I'm leaving Susie, I won't have forgotten you by then!'

At home the evening meal was as silent and strained as ever. Daniel was wallowing in self-pity at having been abandoned over the weekend and Rebecca felt herself caring even less than usual. She had put away all her new clothes, her new shoes, her new perfume. But she refused to revert to the downtrodden woman of only a few weeks earlier and she put on a new pair of trousers, ones which fitted neatly at the waist and narrowed at the ankle, a pair of shoes with much higher heels that her usual flat courts and one of her new tops. She felt good about herself for the first time in many years. It was amazing the difference new clothes could make and as she carried a plate from the kitchen and placed it in front of Daniel she felt she did it with a certain flair.

He didn't notice. 'It's going to be a very hard week for me,' he started. 'Peter is on my case non-stop. He's jealous of course. He knows I'm the better sales man, he's doing everything possible to stop me.'

He carried on as Rebecca ate her food and poured herself a glass of wine. The Pinot Grigio had become a permanent fixture in the fridge and she hadn't bothered to hide it for some time. She looked around the boring dining room and thought fondly of her bedroom at Quebecs.

'And I suppose you'll be back there this weekend?'

Rebecca stared down at her fork. She hadn't said it out loud but she knew inside, she had known since the moment she climbed on the train bringing her back to Darlington.

'Yes, I am.'

Daniel's face darkened. 'Again!' he exploded. 'You really need to go again?'

He threw his knife and fork on the table.

'This is just too much Rebecca. This can't go on. You are my wife, I deserve some consideration, I deserve to know what's going on!'

Rebecca met his eyes, waiting until the storm had finished. He was right, he did deserve to know what was going on.

'I don't have to go,' offered Rebecca watching Daniel's tense jaw relax a little.

'Well, I should think so. I…'

'Mum could come here for the weekend instead.'

She actually saw his life flash before him. She saw him weigh up the idea of having Gwen in his house for the weekend. The cancellation of his golf as he helped get Gwen in and out of the car. His involvement in the general organisation of where she would sleep, how they would get her up the stairs.

'Well…' He was sweating. He tugged at the collar of his shirt which wasn't at all tight and puffed his cheeks. 'Well… I suppose... I mean it's not that I don't want her to visit...'

'Or I could go to Leeds and visit her?'

He was gritting his teeth. He didn't want to be beaten. He didn't want to give in. But neither did he want Gwen in the house.

'Probably for the best,' he grunted. 'I suppose.'

The week took a long time to pass for Rebecca. Daniel all but ignored her, which actually suited her very well. He made no comment on the dramatic improvement in her appearance although she thought she caught a few questioning glances her way.

The best part of the day was either during the morning of a late shift at the Deli, or an afternoon following an early shift. Then it was just Rebecca and her thoughts. She would come home, turn the heating up full, make a cup of coffee in her new coffee machine and look through the growing pile of glossy magazines and brochures. She would make plans, decide where she would put all her new purchases once Beech Grange was hers, how she would put her own personal touch on the already beautiful house. Occasionally she would check her bank account and look at the numbers. The money for the house hadn't been transferred yet and the shopping Rebecca had done so far was a drop in the ocean. The figure had hardly moved. At work she was the same old Rebecca, albeit better dressed and happier. At home she was still Bec, in the kitchen making the evening meal for when Daniel came home. But for those few hours she snatched to herself each day she was a lottery winner with millions in the bank.

She ordered a new bed to be delivered once the contracts had been exchanged. She narrowed a choice of holidays down to an all exclusive resort in Mexico or a beach hut in the Seychelles. She knew Daniel would not want to go on either. She bought a plasma screen TV for her new lounge. She also looked into the problems of running a residential home, the average costs and investment needed and made an appointment to meet Mrs Wendover the following Saturday. She donated money to the local dog's home and pledged monthly amounts to almost every charity that advertised on the TV. She read through the documents left by the investment Lottery people and worked out some rough figures as to how much she should put in trust for the children and how much to put away for her mother's continuing care. She read the report the bank manager had sent her and had to pour herself a brandy as she read how much interest she was earning on a monthly basis and she tried to learn a little more about stocks, shares, interest rates and other financial matters.

The only thing she didn't do was tell Daniel. Each evening he came home and told her how hard his life was, how hard he had to work. And Rebecca did what she had been doing for years, nodding in the right places, serving his meal and waiting for him to shut up so blessed peace would reign in the house.

It was a tactic she had adopted after realising that arguing, discussing, trying to reason - all just prolonged the agony. Daniel never listened, never welcomed her opinion, never changed his mind. If she shared in the conversation it just made it last longer. So now she kept quiet. And even though every morning she decided that she had to tell Daniel the good news and show him her bank balance, each evening came to an end with Daniel none the wiser.

When Friday came, Rebecca woke up feeling relaxed and happy. She was working the early shift and had decided to go to Leeds at tea time and not on Saturday morning. There was a play at the Leeds Grand that night and she had booked a ticket. She had thought about asking Sarah but decided that her daughter probably enjoyed spending weekends with her friends not her mum so she booked one ticket and said nothing. She was meeting Mrs Wendover on the Saturday and had also booked herself a couple of hours at the Spa.

She couldn't stop smiling at the Deli and Carol had stopped berating Susie so loudly whenever she brought up the possibility of Rebecca of having an affair. But Rebecca ignored them both and when her shift was over she walked to her rusty old car and drove to the train station, only slightly guilty about the note she had left Daniel explaining her early departure as she jumped into the first class carriage.

Her suite was waiting for her, like an old friend. The play was wonderful, the meal she had in the hotel restaurant glorious, the new dress she wore for the occasion looked fantastic and by the time Rebecca fell into bed she was exhausted but so happy that for almost the first time since she won, she forgot to fret about the fact she hadn't told her husband anything about her new life and she drifted to sleep without a thought of Daniel in her head.

Saturday she met with Mrs Wendover who although a little confused by Rebecca's sudden interest, presumed that she was worrying about Gwen's long term plans. She admitted that the home was in difficulties. People just couldn't afford the cost of private care at the moment, she confided in Rebecca. Few could now treat themselves to the luxury of a home like Parklands. Bookings had gone down and a few of the residents were actually having trouble paying their bills. Delicately Rebecca asked how much a home like Parklands sold for these days and wasn't really surprised to find that it would be well over 3 million. The house and grounds were large and in a prime location regardless of added value of the business. Rebecca had patted Mrs Wendover's arm, told her she thought everything would work out okay and then had tea and sandwiches with Gwen before leaving to spend the afternoon at the Spa.

On Monday, arriving back in Darlington, she felt as though she had been on holiday with her batteries fully charged. It was her last week at the Deli and on Saturday it was Susie's party which meant Rebecca couldn't go to Leeds. But then she was a free person, nothing to tie her to Darlington, nothing to stop her going to Leeds permanently. Nothing except Daniel of course.

She had skirted around the subject at work but eventually Carol and Susie realised that Rebecca didn't want them to mention anything about her leaving work to Daniel. And it was only a few short guesses after that to work out that Rebecca hadn't actually told Daniel she was leaving the Deli which sent Susie into overdrive with her affair theory. But they both agreed to keep Rebecca's news to themselves, in fact Susie relished the thought that finally Rebecca was defying her husband and loved the idea that she knew something Daniel did not.

Friday was an emotional day, all three of them sniffed their way through Rebecca's last shift, weeping into pots of tea and sobbing over the scones. Finally, Rebecca took off her apron for the last time, hugged both her friends and said goodbye. She walked across the precinct towards her car hugging her body, partly against the cold night air and partly to hold in the sobs. She was leaving because she had won 15.7 million, she should be happy. On the drive home Rebecca wondered what it would have been like if she'd been able to tell them the real reason she was leaving. They would have been pleased for her she was sure of it. They would have whooped and screamed and would have wanted to hear all about her plans. She could have shown them pictures of her house, taken her new clothes into work, described the hotel - which Susie would have loved and the night at the theatre - which Carol would have loved and for the first time since her win Rebecca felt lonely. What was the point of having a windfall like hers if you couldn't share it with people, tell them all about it, how you felt, what your plans were? She decided to tell Daniel that very night. She would show him the bank account, tell him she had won and then they could go to Susie's party the following evening and share their news with everybody.

She didn't. She made something to eat, listened to the evening tirade, cleared away and sat on the settee to read a book that she'd bought herself on the way home, a hard back that had cost £12.99. She waited for Daniel to notice and ask her what she was doing wasting money and why she hadn't waited for the paperback version; but he never did and he went to bed still none the wiser about the large amount of money in his wife's bank account or the fact that she was shortly to become the owner of a house in Leeds.

As Saturday arrived Daniel started to present the reasons why he couldn't escort Rebecca to Susie's party. Rebecca didn't bother to answer. She cleaned the kitchen and put in some washing as he described how he needed to go through some figures that evening and it might be best if he stayed at home and how tired he was anyway after such a hard week. And when he had finished she turned and smiled pleasantly as she said, 'We need to leave at 7.30pm Daniel.'

A couple of hours later Rebecca nursed her glass as she looked around the room. Susie had greeted them at the door, already giggling and unsteady on her feet courtesy of the champagne she was liberally pouring for everyone. She looked amazing in a corset style dress that made the most of her natural assets and took the eye away from her slightly expanding middle. Her bright red hair tumbled onto her shoulders and she looked exactly what she was, a vivacious confident woman, comfortable in her own skin and happy to celebrate her 25th wedding anniversary with a man she still loved. As Susie embraced them on the doorstep, Rebecca saw Daniel's sneer at her dress, her rough manner, the tiny mid terrace house and she resisted the urge to slap his mocking face. As they walked into the kitchen Rebecca grabbed a champagne flute and walked quickly back towards the little living room already packed with guests.

'You can drive tonight Daniel, I'm having a drink,' and she was gone leaving him no time to protest or argue.

It had been the final insult as far as Daniel was concerned. He was there under sufferance and now he was being deprived of the pleasure of drowning his sorrows and in a rage he had grabbed a soft drink and retired to a corner of the room to sulk. Rebecca glanced over at him now as he stood, stiff as a board, clutching a warm orange squash, his face radiating displeasure as he gazed out of the window visibly ignoring the chatter around him. Turning away her glance rested on Carol and her husband. Tim was older than Carol; a wonderfully pleasant and old fashioned man, he was a gentleman through and through. Daniel despised him as weak and ineffectual, Rebecca loved spending time in his company. The tales he told were dry and witty, educational and amusing. A real contrast to

Daniel's pompous lectures and one sided opinions. Rebecca smiled as she watched Tim slide a piece of stray hair behind Carol's ear and drop a kiss on her nose. It was the sort of gesture that Daniel would have made only a few years before. What had gone wrong she wondered? What on earth had she done to destroy that tenderness?

'How are you Rebecca?'

'I'm well thanks Tim, very well.'

Tim smiled, 'Carol tells me that you've left the Deli?'

Rebecca shot a nervous glance in Daniel's direction. This was her one worry about tonight, that an unwary comment might let Daniel know that she had resigned her job.

'Oh don't worry!' Tim leaned into her a little and she realised that his voice was deliberately low. 'Carol did tell me not to mention it in front of Daniel.'

Rebecca sipped at her drink.

'Strange though, if you don't mind me saying. Stopping work and not telling your husband? He's going to find out some time.'

Rebecca stiffened as she met Tim's eyes. There was no recrimination there, just a gentle curiosity. He was, of course, right. How on earth did she think she could keep this from Daniel? How could she continue to hide any of this from Daniel - in fact, why did she want to? He was her husband. She had just won the lottery - a huge amount of money that could solve all their problems and bring back some joy and love into their lives. Why on earth hadn't she just told him?

'It's difficult,' she muttered, her eyes fixed on the carpet. 'I can't really… I mean it's something that … I…'

A hand came to rest gently on her own. 'I'm sorry Rebecca. How rude, it's absolutely nothing to do with me.'

Rebecca sent a wary smile in his direction. 'It's just...'

'No! Please, I shouldn't have mentioned it, what happens between you and your husband is nothing to do with me. Now, let me get you another drink and we'll change the subject,' and taking Rebecca's glass from her he gave her a warm smile before walking across the room, stopping briefly to chat to someone she didn't recognise and to twirl his wife around on the tiny area marked for dancing.

What was she doing? Why hadn't she told Daniel? Why hadn't she told the children, her mother, her friends? How wonderful to have given Susie a whopping great cheque instead of a pretty crystal vase. To give Carol enough money to pay of the small but ever present loan on the Deli, to let her mother know she needn't worry about Parklands closing, to pay off the children's student loans, buy them cars, give them an allowance.

She hadn't told them because it all revolved around telling Daniel first and Rebecca had to admit that the longer she delayed telling him the harder it was becoming. Why hadn't she let him know that first weekend? They could have met the lottery people together, watched the money arrive in their account and chosen a house together. What on earth was she thinking?

'Here we go, a fresh, cold glass of champagne!' and Rebecca's anguish was cut short as Tim thrust a glass into her hand and Carol appeared by their side, closely followed by Susie who had smudges of mascara under her eyes and very pink cheeks but who couldn't stop smiling.

For the next few hours Rebecca ignored Daniel's increasingly desperate attempts to persuade her to leave as she joined in the fun. These were friends, they were good people and she felt a very real guilt at the pretence she was carrying out and the lies she was telling.

Eventually it was time to leave and as Daniel stalked back towards their car in a rage Rebecca wandered slowly in his wake, smiling at the memories of the evening and ignoring her husband's stiff shoulders.

‘How could you,’ he hissed as they got in the car, ‘how could you?’

He was glaring at her with such ferocity that Rebecca was horrified to think somehow in the course of the evening her secret had come out.

‘W-what do you mean?’ she whispered.

‘Getting drunk! Partying with those…common people. Making me stay there until all hours speaking to wretched people who haven’t got an original thought in their head! That’s what I mean Rebecca!’

The relief kept her silent, but not so Daniel. He complained all the way home, complained as they parked the car and went into the house and continued to complain for a good half hour after they got into bed. In the end Rebecca, who now had a pounding headache and just wanted some respite, rolled over and pressed her hand none too gently across his lips.

‘Enough Daniel. Enough.’

‘No,’ she added crossly as he started again. ‘Those were my friends and I enjoyed their company. Now shut up!’

And much to her surprise he did, rolling on to his side with a grunt and within seconds he was snoring.

Rebecca laid back. The bed was hard because Daniel liked hard beds. Rebecca preferred the soft snugly mattress of Quebecs hotel. But Daniel hadn’t consulted her when he bought a new mattress, it had just arrived one day, a hard, orthopedic mattress that he declared would let both of them sleep better. In the dim light of the street lamps she could see the plain magnolia walls of the bedroom. Their house in Leeds had been warm and inviting, each room having its own character and charm. When they moved here Daniel had arranged for the decorators to come in and paint everything magnolia; made the rooms look clean and calm he said. Rebecca hated magnolia. She hated the house, magnolia or not. Her flair for decorating hadn’t moved from Leeds to

Darlington. She had looked around at the magnolia walls and decided it wasn't worth the effort or the arguments.

She would tell him tomorrow she decided. Absolutely. She would show him her bank balance tomorrow and tell him she had won. Tomorrow they would clear the air and they could both start again.

Chapter 8

Rebecca slept late that morning and was woken by the slam of the door. Sitting up, still half asleep she reached out. 'Daniel?'

She knew what she would find before she even went downstairs. He needed revenge, he needed to teach her a lesson. The message was short and to the point. GOLF.

She made a cup of tea and wandered through to the conservatory. She had less than a week to go. Then Beech Grange would be hers. If she wanted to live there she had to tell Daniel. She had to tell him she had won the lottery, left her job and bought a house in Leeds.

The phone rang and Rebecca reached out to grab the receiver.

'Hello Rebecca?'

Rebecca didn't recognise the voice for a moment.

'Yes. Speaking.'

'Rebecca, it's Mrs Wendover at Parklands. I'm so sorry Rebecca but your Mum's had a nasty fall. She's in hospital.'

A cold hand of fear clutched Rebecca's heart. This was her fault. She had brought this on her mother through all the lies she had been telling. For the last three weeks she had used

Gwen as an excuse for her trips to Leeds. She had lied to everyone she knew, she had told them all that her mother was ill and this was the result.

'Is she okay?' whispered Rebecca.

'Oh I'm sure she'll be fine. We think she's broken her wrist, nothing more serious but at her age we can't be too careful so we sent her straight to the hospital. She was trying to get from her bed to her wheelchair by herself and fell. Please don't worry my dear, I had to let you know but it's nothing serious, I'm sure.'

Was it Rebecca's imagination or was there an element of doubt in Mrs Wendover's voice.

'I'm coming down,' said Rebecca, leaping out of her chair. 'I'll be there as soon as I can.'

'I thought you might dear but you really don't have to…'

But Rebecca was already gone, running up the stairs with tears pouring down her cheeks as she went over every lie she had told, every occasion she had used her 'sick' mother as an excuse, all the sympathy she had received, all the best wishes. It was her fault. All her fault.

She threw some things in an overnight bag and without even bothering to check the train times drove at breakneck speed to the station. She had left Daniel an explanation on the bottom of his own terse note. Mother in hospital. Gone to Leeds. She had written down the number of the mobile she had bought weeks ago so she could keep in touch with the lottery people, the bank, Annie, the hotel. So many people had come into her life over the last few weeks, people that Daniel knew nothing about.

She was fortunate, there was a train just about to depart and she was soon in a taxi on her way to the hospital. Running up several flights of steps to her mother's ward, Rebecca stood panting in the doorway. Her mother was sat up in bed dressed in her favourite nightgown and a delicate crocheted bed jacket.

She had one wrist in a pot and was nibbling at a biscuit. Mrs Wendover sat at her side drinking a cup of tea and they were both laughing at something the lady in the next bed had just said.

'Mum?'

'Rebecca my darling girl! Mrs Wendover said you were coming. There really wasn't any need you know. I am quite alright. Oh whatever is the matter?'

Because Rebecca had burst into loud noisy sobs and would have fallen to the floor if a passing nurse hadn't held out a supporting hand and whisked a chair under Rebecca's shaking legs.

Shock, declared the nurse and for the next few minutes everything was a flurry of activity as tissues were produced, hot sweet tea poured and Rebecca was fussed over as though she was the invalid.

'Rebecca darling, it's a broken wrist, I'm absolutely fine otherwise.'

'I was just so worried Mum, I was sure that… you see I told people... I came to visit and said that you were ill and I didn't mean it to happen and it did!'

Gwen and Mrs Wendover exchanged a sympathetic glance.

'Rebecca you're in shock my dear. You mustn't feel guilty. I know you can't come down any more than you do. You have your own life in Darlington. You can't be down here every weekend.'

Rebecca stared at her mother. At the grey wavy hair that she kept perfectly groomed despite everything. At the bed jacket she had crocheted years ago and was her 'best'.

'But I can Mum. I can be down here all the time, I can come and visit you as often as I want to. Because I'm moving to Leeds. I'm coming back to live in Leeds!'

Gwen's eyebrows shot upwards into her grey curls while Mrs Wendover clapped her hands in delight.

'Oh how lovely for you both. I'm so pleased for you Rebecca.'

'Coming back to live in Leeds? Well that's lovely darling. Has Daniel moved back to the Leeds office?'

'Not exactly,' offered Rebecca, 'I mean he may do, but it's not been decided if he will, he doesn't actually need to.'

Gwen smiled, her shrewd eyes looking directly into Rebecca's own. 'So are you coming to Leeds on your own?' she asked softly.

'Oh no! Of course not. It's just that I'm definitely coming, I mean **we** will be coming I…we just haven't sorted out all the details yet.'

Refusing to meet Gwen's eyes, Rebecca turned instead to Mrs Wendover. 'Have they said when Mum can go back to Parklands yet?'

'Well, probably tomorrow. It's just a simple break. We'll have to keep an eye on it of course, make sure it heals properly, that sort of thing, but nothing we can't cope with at Parklands.'

'Thank you for being here with Mum,' Rebecca reached out and took Mrs Wendover's hand in hers. 'It's meant a lot to me over the years knowing that you've been there to look after her.'

'Oh it's nothing.' Mrs Wendover flapped her hands dismissing Rebecca's gratitude even as her eyes looked suspiciously watery. 'All part of the service. Anyway, I should get back. I'll no doubt see you both tomorrow,' and collecting her coat, hat and gloves she left waving a fond farewell in Gwen's direction.

There was a moments silence and then Gwen took Rebecca's hand in her one free hand.

'What's going on darling?'

There was no accusation in the voice, just a world of love and for a moment all Rebecca wanted was to climb onto the bed and snuggle into her mother's side as she had done as a small child.

But she couldn't tell Gwen because she hadn't told Daniel. It was bad enough that she had left it so long but if he found out others knew before Rebecca had told him he would be mortified.

So she squeezed her mother's hand instead and tried to smile a reassuring smile.

'It's nothing bad Mum. Truly it isn't. But it is a bit complicated and I can't tell you all the details right now. But I can tell you that it will all work out and I will be happy.'

Gwen looked into her daughter's eyes for a moment then patted her hand.

'When you're ready my darling, when you're ready.'

Rebecca hadn't had time to make a reservation before she left Darlington, so some hours later she left her mum at the hospital and caught a taxi asking the driver to take her to Quebecs Hotel but wait for her outside for a moment.

Walking into the lobby she felt an over-whelming feeling of coming home. How strange she thought, that a hotel could do that to her but not the house she had lived in for the last 5 years.

'I haven't made a reservation but I was hoping...'

'Mrs Miles, how wonderful to see you again. No problem at all, your usual room?'

Within minutes the taxi had been paid and dismissed, Rebecca's bag had been carried up to her room, the bed turned down and a complimentary bottle of wine left in a cooler on the table. Rebecca sank onto the settee, the lovely comfortable over stuffed settee and leant back closing her eyes.

Her mother was okay and she was back in Leeds at Quebecs. Although unplanned she couldn't deny it was a blessed relief. She would stay a few days, just until her mother was back at Parklands and everything was back to normal and then she would go back to Darlington and stop this farce. She would show Daniel the bank account and the ludicrous amount of money it held, tell him about the house, tell him everything. It was finally time.

Rebecca had a troubled night's sleep and woke feeling leaden and heavy. Even the soft squishy pillows and the all-encompassing quilt hadn't helped her in her quest for sleep. She slid out of bed and wandered to her handbag to rescue her mobile. She checked to see if she had missed any calls in the trauma of the previous day but there was nothing. Daniel had made no attempt to contact her. She had left a message for him that her mother was in hospital and he hadn't so much as sent a text. She wondered whether she should ring him, bring him up to date, see if he wanted to come down and join her before realising what a ridiculous idea that was. She phoned the hospital and spoke to the ward sister who told her that Gwen was not quite as perky as she had been the day before. 'I think the anesthetic has worn off and she's feeling a little more pain today.'

The hospital decided to keep her on the ward that day, just to keep a close eye on her and then would let her return to Parklands the following morning if all was still well.

Rebecca phoned Mrs Wendover to update her on the news, followed by a call to Sarah who didn't answer. Rebecca smiled, Sarah could be in a lecture or still in bed. She left her a message explaining that Gwen was in hospital and that Rebecca was in Leeds followed by a similar message for Toby who she also promised to go and visit in a few weeks. She gazed down at her phone again. Should she phone Daniel? Did he care? Had he even noticed that she wasn't there? Snapping the phone closed Rebecca reached out instead for the telephone sitting on the coffee table and phoned down to reception, ordering a continental breakfast to be brought to her room and a taxi to take her to the hospital and then headed for the power shower.

Rebecca spent as long as she was allowed with Gwen during the course of the day. Her mother was looking pale and a little shaky and the nurse said it was quite possibly delayed shock. But she was still smiling and desperate to get back to her room at Parklands and her friends. Rebecca took her a pile of magazines, some lemon barley water and a great bowl of fruit which Gwen promptly shared out amongst the rest of the ward and the staff.

Sarah phoned, full of concern for her grandmother. Toby sent a text. Annie phoned counting down the hours until the next day when the house sale would complete. The bank manager phoned to clarify the final details for the cash payment of 2,050,000. Susie phoned to see how Rebecca was enjoying her first day without work and was horrified to find that Gwen was in hospital. But Rebecca heard nothing from Daniel. No call, no text. Half a dozen times her fingers hovered over his work's number only to snap the phone shut again. In the afternoon while Gwen slept, Rebecca caught a taxi back into Leeds and did a little shopping for her mother's return to Parklands. Gwen may be reliant on her wheelchair but she still had high standards of personal care and with a few weeks of bed rest facing her, Rebecca wanted to make sure that she was well prepared. So she bought three new nightgowns, the sort her mother loved, delicate, flowery affairs that buttoned up to her neck and kept her legs warm. She bought a new bed jacket. Gwen loved the crocheted one she had worn for years but she might need a change and Rebecca also added a beautifully soft mohair shawl that Gwen could throw around her shoulders when the heating at Parklands went through one of its difficult phases. She stocked up on yet more magazines and a couple of the historical romance books that she knew Gwen loved to read before she went to sleep. In the basket went some delicious smelling hand cream, a bottle of Gwen's favourite perfume and a lavender plant in a pretty little pot for next to Gwen's bed. Jumping in another taxi Rebecca made a quick visit to Parklands to arrange the items in Gwen's room, had a cup of tea with Mrs Wendover who was looking more tired and worried than ever and then back to the hospital to see Gwen one last time before making her way back to the hotel.

Her knees sagging with tiredness, Rebecca asked for a salad to be brought to her room, she really couldn't face eating anything that required more effort. The minute room service left she threw off her clothes and slid into a lovely deep hot bath full of delicious scented bubbles.

It was only a few weeks ago that Rebecca had used this bath for the very first time and been awed at the range of toiletries provided. So much seemed to have happened since then. The toiletries she still appreciated but she now had a huge selection in her own bathroom albeit kept in her bathroom drawer away from Daniel's eyes. She had bought a house, she had left work, she was moving back to Leeds.

But she still hadn't told Daniel. That hadn't changed at all and it was growing into a monumental problem for Rebecca who had to acknowledge that the delay had become quite unreasonable. How did you explain that you had won 15.7 million on the lottery and hadn't told your husband after four weeks!

Sighing Rebecca finished her bath and wrapping herself in a huge fluffy bathrobe she sat on the settee to pour herself a glass of wine and eat her salad. Her phone sat on the arm of the settee, silent. Still nothing. Shouldn't he have at least phoned to see if Gwen was alive? Rebecca tried to remember what she had written in her distressed state. Mum had accident, in hospital, going to Leeds. That was clear enough, he knew that Gwen was in hospital but had no idea how serious it all was. Sighing again Rebecca pushed the salad away and finished her glass of wine. She was exhausted and just needed a good night's sleep and leaving the phone on the settee she climbed into bed and was asleep within minutes.

Waking the next morning Rebecca's first thought was for Gwen but she couldn't quite place the frisson of excitement that was gathering in her stomach. Then she remembered, today was the day Beech Grange became her own. Rebecca Miles with a 2 million pound house. In the worry and guilt of Gwen's accident she had almost forgotten all about it!

She leapt out of bed and phoned the hospital, relieved to hear that Gwen was much better and would be allowed home around lunchtime. Then she flicked open the laptop which she had picked up automatically as she fled the house on Sunday. The balance in her account hadn't changed, the house wasn't hers yet. Just then her phone rang.

'Hello?'

'Rebecca, it's Annie! Are you all set, today's the day!'

Rebecca had to laugh at Annie's enthusiasm even as she explained about Gwen and how busy she would be that day.

'Oh what rotten luck and what terrible timing. But don't worry, I'll be around to help.'

'When will it happen exactly?' asked Rebecca who had never been actively involved in any of the house moves she and Daniel had made together.

'It's impossible to say. It could be in the next hour; it could be this afternoon. As soon as the vendor's solicitor confirms that the money has transferred over he authorises the release of the keys. If you've got your hands full I can collect those for you no problem.'

They agreed that Annie would liaise with the solicitor, collect the keys, phone Rebecca once it was all finalised and they would meet at Beech Grange when Rebecca felt that she could leave Gwen.

'Thank you so much Annie, you've been wonderfully helpful.'

'Rebecca darling,' laughed Annie, 'you've bought a 2 million pound house from me. I should be thanking you, you've saved me from a truly terrible start to the year!'

Rebecca couldn't help but laugh at Annie's honesty and the genuine friendship in her voice.

'Well I'm still grateful,' she insisted and the two women said goodbye until later.

Grabbing a quick breakfast and shower Rebecca spent the morning with Gwen, waiting as the ward rounds completed and Gwen was finally discharged. She ordered a taxi, something she was becoming quite proficient at she thought to herself, and a short time later she and her mother were in Gwen's room at Parklands, Gwen wearing one of her new nightgowns with the mohair shawl around her shoulders.

Rebecca's phone rang and glancing down at the screen she saw Annie's name flashing. Her heart pounding, she stood up and wandered towards the window leaving Gwen chatting to the two friends who were sitting with her.

'Hello Annie.'

'Rebecca - I've got the keys, the house is yours!'

For a moment all that Rebecca could hear was the beating of her own heart as she stood mute, staring out of the window at the beautiful rose garden.

'Rebecca, did you hear me. It's done, I've got the keys, the house is yours Rebecca, all yours.'

It took a while before Rebecca could leave Parklands. There were lots of hugs and kisses - from Gwen's friends who had all come trooping into her room to keep her company, from the staff who had brought them both up some lunch, from Mrs Wendover who was delighted that Gwen was back and who promised to keep Rebecca updated with any changes in Gwen's health and Gwen herself who hugged her daughter and thanked her for dashing to her side. Finally Rebecca was standing outside the door on a bitterly cold dark April evening, watching a taxi pull into the driveway, a taxi that was going to take her to her new house and with a heart that was beating so loudly she felt sure the taxi driver must be able to hear it, she jumped in and gave him the address.

Half an hour later Rebecca stood in her new kitchen. The cream cupboards hugged the wall and the black granite surface twinkled in the light, stretching for what seemed like miles. The huge table would seat her entire family plus everyone she knew and the two small settees that sat by the French windows invited Rebecca to curl up on the lovely raspberry and green check seats. It was dark outside until Annie flicked a switch and then the whole garden lit up showing graceful trees blowing in the wind and borders curving around the lawn and down towards the tennis court. Immediately outside the French windows was a delightful courtyard where Rebecca fully intended to sit on a morning with a cappuccino from the space age style coffee machine on the kitchen surface and maybe a chocolate croissant warmed up in the huge cream range that took pride of place in its own alcove. Meanwhile, until the summer came she would curl up on one of the raspberry settees or sit in the garden room with its blazing wood burner and wait for the sun to emerge and the garden to flower.

She felt a gentle touch on her arm and swung round to see Annie smiling at her.

'Pleased?'

Rebecca grinned, 'Oh Yes, Annie. I'm pleased!'

And with a shout of joy she hugged the woman who had just handed Rebecca the keys to her new dream home.

'I know how busy you've been today,' said Annie when she was finally released from Rebecca's arms, 'so I thought this might help a little.'

She picked up a box from the floor and put it on the table so Rebecca could peer inside. 'Sorry about the presentation, I suppose really it should have been a wicker hamper with a great big bow wrapped round it but I just grabbed a few things to help you out.'

Milk, tea, croissants, jam, bread butter, bacon, eggs …

'Oh Annie, thank you so much!'

'And of course,' twinkled Annie, 'the obligatory celebration bottle!'

And she produced a bottle of champagne from behind her back which was soon opened and fizzing into the glasses she'd also brought and under the soft lighting of the kitchen the two woman toasted Rebecca's new house.

Annie didn't stay long. She gave Rebecca a quick reminder of where the vital switches were, handed her an envelope left by the previous owners which explained alarms etc., hugged Rebecca one last time and promised to come and visit in a few weeks when Rebecca was settled. Which left Rebecca alone in her new house. Her glorious, big, new house.

She wandered through all the rooms. It was only the second time she had been in the house and there were so many things she had forgotten. Like how gracious the living space was with yet more French windows opening onto the garden, the large stone fireplace and the beautiful cream settees that Rebecca had fallen in love with. The majority of the rooms were still furnished but there were gaps that needed filling, particularly upstairs. New beds had already been ordered and would arrive tomorrow and all the things Rebecca had bought on her previous visits to Leeds could now be delivered. There was still a lot to buy, mused Rebecca. The kitchen cupboards beautiful as they looked, were empty. She could spend the next few days organising the house as she kept an eye on Gwen.

And then she would tell Daniel.

Sipping at the champagne in her hand, Rebecca spent the next few hours wandering around her new home, familiarising herself with every nook and cranny as she planned how it would look, how she would use the space, which were her favourite parts, what she needed. She ended up back in the kitchen curled up on one of the raspberry settees, contentment pouring out of her as she looked around. She had loved the kitchen in their old house on Greyshott Road. It hadn't been anything like this in size but it had had the same welcome feel, a room where a family could gather. She would cook the evening meal as the children did their homework at the pine table and when they had finished and disappeared to do something more interesting, she would turn on the little TV tucked into the corner of the pine dresser, pour herself a glass of wine and enjoy the smell of the evening meal as she waited for Daniel to come home. She had hated the kitchen in Darlington. It was long and narrow, soulless and bland and just couldn't provide them with the family space they had previously enjoyed. The children would come home and go straight to their bedrooms. Rebecca would prepare the evening meal but then sit in the conservatory, far away from the comforting smell of a chicken casserole and wait for the slam of the door which told her Daniel was home and the evening complaints were about to commence.

Things would be different in this kitchen she decided, things would be very different.

Despite Annie's thoughtful gesture Rebecca knew she couldn't stay in the house that night, not unless she wanted to sleep on the settee, so reluctantly she rinsed her glass in the sink, pulled out her mobile to tap in the number of the taxi firm, a number she now knew by heart and put the food in the fridge ready for tomorrow before returning to Quebecs for another night of blissful sleep on their fluffy cloud of a bed.

Chapter 9

Rebecca was up bright and early the next morning leaping out of bed and into the shower before dressing and ordering breakfast.

She picked up her little phone and dialled Parklands to be told that Gwen was still asleep but had passed a comfortable night and seemed as well as could be expected.

Then she phoned to check that her new beds would be delivered as promised later that day and that her purchases from Debenhams and House of Fraser would also arrive that afternoon. She sent a quick message to both children keeping them updated with Gwen's progress and then checked for any missed calls. There were none. Daniel still hadn't called, left a message or sent a text. Nothing. Again Rebecca's fingers hovered over the house number. Should she phone him, let him know that Gwen was OK and that she was still in Leeds. Did he care? He certainly hadn't bothered to phone and ask. Rebecca sighed and phoned instead for a taxi. Maybe she should think about getting a car? She couldn't rely on taxis for ever. She remembered reading that the first purchase of many lottery winners was a car but Rebecca had never bought a car in her life. She had shared Gwen's battered little Fiesta for many years and after she met Daniel he took sole responsibility for any car buying. It all seemed so complicated. He would speak of performance, horse power, consumption, emissions. They would spend hours in show rooms looking at cars that all seemed much the same to Rebecca until finally he would make a decision and the next family car would be unveiled. Rebecca really didn't think that she knew enough about cars to just go out and buy one. Maybe this was the sort of decision best left to Daniel.

Half an hour later she was at Parklands and went upstairs to find Gwen not only awake but looking bright and cheerful. Her close friend in the home, Betty, was sitting next to her knitting and chatting away and Mrs Wendover was giving the room a quick tidy as she cleared away Gwen's breakfast tray.

'Oh darling you look so much better, come in!' said Gwen as she spotted Rebecca popping her head around the door.

Rebecca laughed, 'It's you we're worried about Mum, not me!'

'Well, maybe but it's still nice to see you looking so well and happy.'

Rebecca smiled, it was easy to look happy when you had millions in the bank.

'How are you Mum?'

'I'm fine my darling absolutely fine which is why I don't want you to stay today.'

Rebecca's eyebrows shot under her fringe. 'You don't want me to visit?'

'I don't mean that. It's lovely to see so much of you even if it is in less than happy circumstances,' Gwen half lifted her arm with the cast on. 'But you can't spend the whole day hovering over me. Enjoy yourself, make the most of being back in Leeds!'

'But mum I…'

'No. You can pop in and see me later but go make the most of your day, I'm absolutely fine here with Betty and Mrs Wendover.'

'But mum...'

Mrs Wendover bustled over, picking up Gwen's tray as she headed for the door. 'Your mother's quite right Rebecca. Go make the most of a day in Leeds. We all know how much you miss the place. I'll phone you straight away if there's any change at all with your mother, she's in good hands.'

And so Rebecca was gently shooed away, finding herself outside the front door on a bitterly cold April morning watching as yet another taxi pulled into the driveway to collect her.

She opened the door and jumped in to escape from the biting, cold wind.

'Where to love?'

She looked at her watch. She had just over 3 hours before she needed to be at the house to take delivery of her new beds.

Rebecca sat back and smiled at the cheerful face looking at her in the rear view mirror.

'Leeds please - I'm going shopping!'

Exactly two hours later the same taxi driver helped Rebecca carry the last of the bags and bags and bags of shopping into the kitchen loading them all onto the table.

He looked around approvingly. 'Nice place you've got here love, very nice.'

Rebecca smiled. She realised that this was the only person apart from Annie who had seen her new house. In fact, apart from Annie, her solicitor and bank manager, he was the only person who knew she had a new house.

'Well, I like it,' she grinned and took out her purse to pay him, including a very large tip.

Protesting at first but then taking the proffered notes with a happy smile the taxi driver left, leaving Rebecca to walk back into the kitchen and her piles of shopping. Her house, her lovely house. How good it felt to be able to show someone this beautiful house and say, this is my home.

It took Rebecca a while to get to grips with the central heating but she soon had it working and turned up high so that every room felt cosy and warm. She unpacked the bags which were full of the bits and pieces that turned a house into a home. Enough toiletries to rival Quebecs now sat in the bathrooms; the living room had some ruby red and gold cushions sprawling across the cream sofas along with a deep red throw that Rebecca could imagine snuggling under while watching TV tonight. A pile of books sat on the glass topped coffee table and a basket of DVDs sat in the space where the TV would go. The sort of DVDs that Rebecca loved, Pretty Woman, Wuthering Heights, Miss Congeniality, Bridget Jones. Tonight she wouldn't watch a single programme about cars being rescued.

More bags were unpacked in the kitchen from the beautiful, such as the delicate crystal champagne goblets that had caught Rebecca's eye, to the practical such as the state of the art spice rack that held every spice she could possibly need and more.

She boiled the kettle, a stainless steel retro version that had made Rebecca gasp when she saw the price and filled the cream ceramic caddy full of teabags before making herself a cup in one of the pretty new china mugs. Daniel always said china was a waste of time, too hard to keep clean, too easy to chip and break, pretty but pointless. Rebecca had always loved the feel of proper china and now a selection of pretty flowered mugs sat in one of the cupboards.

Curling up on one of the raspberry settees she held the mug of steaming tea in her hands and gazed out onto the garden. It was far too cold to go out and explore and she hadn't really seen much of it when she first viewed the house with Annie. Perhaps she should ask the gardener to stay on. She liked gardening but there were trees to prune and grass to cut, it might be too much for her to keep on top off herself. Her daydreams were stopped short by the ringing of the doorbell and for the next few hours Rebecca didn't have time to think about anything as she directed beds to various rooms, made copious cups of tea for various shivering delivery drivers and unpacked feverishly as box after box of items arrived at the door. It was 5.00pm before she finally stopped. Her back was aching, her knees sore, her shoulders tight but Rebecca was probably the happiest she had been in years. It was dark outside, the sun had barely made it out all day and now it had disappeared altogether and Rebecca could hear the wind howling through the trees. But the house was aglow with warmth and light. She had figured out the lighting system along with the switches that closed the curtains but for now she was happy to leave the windows uncovered. The contrast between her beautiful warm house and the cold April evening was one she was enjoying. The bedrooms were finished. Beds, quilts, mountains of soft down pillows, warm cuddly throws, all were in place. The new TV stood in the living room and the kitchen cupboards were full of pans of every size and shape and an entire new dinner service. Rebecca stood at the foot of the staircase and looked down the hallway towards the living room at one end of the house and then towards the sprawling kitchen in the other direction before heaving a sigh of ecstatic relief.

She had done it. There was lots more to do and buy but Rebecca already felt at home in a way she had never been in Darlington. And she never wanted to leave.

But leave she had to and wrapping herself up tightly she called another taxi, she would seriously have to address the issue of buying a car for when she was in Leeds, and went first to Quebecs where she packed up her belongings, paid her bill and said a sincere thank you to the staff and then to Parklands to visit Gwen. Her mother was still in her bed and this time Carol had joined her and the two were chatting happily as Rebecca entered the room.

'Oh I can feel the cold air on you,' Gwen declared. 'Come in and get warm.'

Rebecca shrugged off her coat and scarf, thinking that the room was nowhere near as warm as it should have been.

'Are they having trouble with the heating again Mum?'

'Yes,' sighed Gwen. 'Poor Mrs Wendover has been poking and banging at that boiler all afternoon but it's not making much difference.'

Just then one of the other staff members appeared at the door with a little portable radiator. Parklands had a supply which they wheeled out whenever the heating let them down.

'Here you go Gwen my love,' said Rita cheerfully, 'an extra radiator, a hot water bottle and an extra blanket. Don't want you getting cold! I've just left the same in your room Carol love.'

Rebecca plugged in the radiator, threw the blanket over Gwen's legs and passed her the hot water bottle. Perhaps she needed to speak to Mrs Wendover sooner than she had planned.

'Are you OK?' she asked Gwen who was arranging the hot water bottle by her feet.

'Oh I'm fine. Warm as toast now and feeling much better. The doctor came this afternoon and said everything looks good and the pain killers he left me are all I need when it starts aching. You look tired darling, have you had a busy afternoon?'

Rebecca smiled and flopped on the edge of Gwen's bed. 'I've had a very busy day Mum, in a nice way and I'll tell you all about it as soon as I can it's just that…'

Gwen waved her good arm in the air, 'Oh I wasn't prying! I know you'll tell me when you're ready and I'm sure it will be worth the wait.'

Rebecca smiled tiredly 'I think it might Mum, I think it might. Do you mind if I don't stay? I've actually got a taxi waiting downstairs for me and I …'

‘Of course not! Why didn’t you say. Go, go and I’ll see you later.’

And Rebecca kissed Gwen goodnight, said goodbye to Carol and to Rita who was still delivering blankets along the hall, grabbed her coat and went out into the cold air for the last time as the taxi took her home.

She had a wonderful evening. Not caring about heating bills she had the house toasty warm. There were logs left behind so she lit a fire in the vast grate and after a couple of failed efforts had a blazing fire going. She took out the rest of the champagne Annie had left and made herself a meal of smoked salmon and ciabatta and curled up under the red throw, watching Bridget Jones Diary in absolute peace and contentment. Eventually as her eyes grew heavy, she turned down the heating, turned off all the lights, finally drawing the curtains and then made her way upstairs. She was thrilled with her room. A lovely sales lady had watched her struggling at the vast choice before her and had helped Rebecca put together a bedroom full of colour and warmth which echoed the colours in the lounge. Spread across the bed was a luxurious duvet cover in a soft champagne colour and a throw of red velvet decorated with gold. Rebecca contemplated having a bath but decided she was just too tired and instead she slid into her very own nest of goose down and Egyptian cotton sheets and fell asleep almost before her head had hit the deep, fluffy pillows.

It was Thursday and Rebecca hadn’t spoken to Daniel since Saturday night. Other than the brief notes they had left for each other on the Sunday there had been no communication between them at all. Rebecca stared at her phone. Perhaps he didn’t want to speak to her. Perhaps he would never contact her again. She could stay in Leeds and she never had to tell him about the money, the house, the lies. She would just never hear from him again. She would have to tell Gwen and the children of course, how else could she explain living in a grand house such as Beech Grange but she didn't have to tell Daniel if he wasn't speaking to her.

Sighing Rebecca put down the phone. It wouldn't work, she had to go home and confront him. But not today, not right now and she pushed aside the feeling of dread and turned on the range cooker to warm up her croissant and spent 15 minutes trying to understand the amazingly complicated coffee machine that eventually produced a cappuccino that tasted exactly as though she had bought it from a café.

After using the rain shower in her ensuite, Rebecca dressed and went downstairs, padding into the kitchen which never failed to give her a shot of happiness.

She decided to phone Helen. She hadn't spoken to her for a few weeks. In fact, Rebecca worked out, she had last spoken to her the Friday she had bought the winning lottery ticket. Helen had lived in the house opposite Rebecca and Daniel in Greyshott Lane. She and Rebecca had hit it off the moment they met and with children almost the same age they found their lives matched each other's in more ways than one. Helen had been devastated when Rebecca moved, almost as upset as Rebecca herself and the two had stayed in touch and met whenever they could. Helen had fallen pregnant unexpectedly a year before Rebecca had moved away which curtailed her freedom to visit Rebecca quite as much as she would have liked but the two friends always tried to fit in a lunch every few months.

'Hi Helen, it's Rebecca.'

'Rebecca,' squealed Helen. 'I was just thinking about you. Your old house has just come up for sale again and it reminded me of how much I cried the day you moved out!'

Rebecca felt her heart jump. Her old house. Her beloved old house where her children had grown up and she and

Daniel had actually been happy. Maybe she had been wrong to go for a big expensive house. Maybe she should have just gone back to the old village and picked up the life she had enjoyed so much. But did that work, going back? Was it ever the same?

'Where are they going?'

'Oh somewhere bigger and better,' answered Helen dismissively.

Rebecca's old house had been bought by a young couple who had children almost the exact age as Toby and Sarah and Rebecca had convinced herself that pretty soon Helen would have a new best friend in Greyshott Lane. But although there was nothing wrong with the new couple, Helen had never really taken to them and they seemed happy to keep themselves to themselves.

'I wonder who we'll get next. Shame it couldn't be you!' laughed Helen.

Rebecca's heart was still fluttering. What would Helen say if she told her it could actually be Rebecca. That Rebecca had won 15.7 million on the lottery and had just bought a new house back in Leeds. That Rebecca could, if she wanted, buy her old house in Greyshott Lane.

'Actually,' she started then brought herself up short. Not yet, not until Daniel knew.

'Actually what?'

'We might come back to Leeds, in fact I'm certain that I - we're coming back to Leeds. Not Greyshott lane but we are coming back.'

Helen's squeals almost deafened Rebecca and she had to hold the phone away from her ear laughing.

'Oh Bec that would be absolutely wonderful! Really? Really! I never thought Daniel would give in and let you come back but how fantastic! Do you know where you'll be living? Oh don't make it too far away Bec.'

Rebecca thought about where she was standing, less than 4 miles from Helen's house.

'I'll make sure it's not too far away,' she promised wondering when she had become so adept at lying, 'don't worry!'

Helen brought her up to date on all the news, including that their other great friend Emma was currently on holiday.

'In the Dominican Republic would you believe!' said Helen. 'How the other half live.'

Rebecca thought of all the brochures she still had secreted around the house in Darlington. There were a few there for the Dominican Republic.

Emma's husband had been promoted over and over again at the small law firm where he worked in Harrogate and as a result he and Emma had moved out of their house on Greyshott Lane a few years ago and into a bigger house, a wonderful old property full of charm and character but still almost within walking distance of the old village and their friends. Emma wasn't at all changed by the improvement in her circumstances and spent her husband's money freely and with a smile on her face. Helen would openly admit to both Emma and Rebecca how jealous she was.

They chatted for a good half hour before Helen had to go and still smiling Rebecca put down the phone. What a relief it would be when she could stop pretending and tell her friends of her good fortune. Helen may be jealous of Emma and she would undoubtedly envy Rebecca her good fortune but she would still be delighted for her and Rebecca had every intention of sending some of her money in the direction of her friends once everything was in the open.

She stretched out on the settee. She would be able to invite all her friends around for Sunday lunch. They could all sit around the huge kitchen table and inhale the smell of roasting beef while they drank wine and laughed and chatted. Rebecca couldn't wait.

Chapter 10

Rebecca spent the next few days visiting Gwen, thinking about buying a car and doing yet more shopping. She had wandered around each room of Beech Grange making a mental note of what she needed. It hadn't occurred to her that a lot of the things she was planning to buy she could have collected from the Darlington house. Or rather, it did but she disregarded the idea. She didn't want anything from that house. She wanted to start again with bright, new things, nothing to remind her of the unhappy years of her life. She intended to go back on the Saturday morning train. She couldn't bear the thought of leaving her house but she knew that she had run out of time. To move on with her exciting new life it was time to tell Daniel. He had to know everything, about the money and the house.

So come Saturday morning she made sure that everything was secure, that the alarm was on and she called for a taxi to take her to the train station.

It was almost lunch time when Rebecca opened the front door of the house she no longer thought of as home. Her heart was hammering and her throat was dry but she was determined that this time she would tell her husband.

The house was quiet. Walking into the kitchen Rebecca could tell Daniel had been living on takeaways by the countless empty boxes that were stacked next to the bin. The sink was full of plates and cups were all over the work surface interspersed with beer cans. Daniel didn't actually tidy up after himself at all. He always expected to come home to a clean kitchen and Rebecca had noticed years ago that he just presumed that she would clear away his mess. If he buttered a piece of toast the knife covered in butter would be left on the surface, as would the crumbs from the toast. When Rebecca suggested that he use a bread board, he had shrugged and taken no notice.

The door slammed and with a thumping heart Rebecca turned around as Daniel came bursting into the kitchen.

'Bec! Where on earth have you been?' and then he brushed passed her to pick up the post that Rebecca had brought in and placed next to the kettle.

Rebecca stared at him open mouthed. 'Where have I been? You know where I've been, I left a note and you haven't bothered...'

Daniel waved his hands in the air impatiently. 'Yes, yes. I know where you've been but why have you been so long? I expected you home days ago.'

Rebecca watched as he flicked through the post not even sparing her a second glance. Her anger started to boil over.

'I've been with my mother,' she snapped. 'My mother who was taken into hospital and you didn't....'

'Yes!' Daniel almost yelled. 'I know all that. But why have you been away so long? Gwen's fine and I expected you to come back days ago.'

'Yes she is fine but…' Rebecca stopped. 'How do you know she's fine you never rang me to see how she was.'

Daniel seemed inordinately interested in the post but having finally looked at every envelope and finding nothing he flung it down on the surface amongst a pile of crumbs and for the first time looked Rebecca in the eye.

'I phoned the hospital of course. They told me what had happened. Then I phoned the next day and they said she was ok. I phoned Parklands on Wednesday when you didn't come home and they said Gwen was fine so I've been expecting you ever since. Is that a new coat?'

Rebecca shook her head. It was whirling and her heart was still pounding, partly in anger and partly in confusion.

'You phoned the hospital? But why didn't you phone me? I left you my mobile number.'

Daniel stared. 'That was your number? I didn't even know you had a mobile and you didn't tell me where you were staying. The coat?'

Rebecca looked down. She was wearing the trench coat she had bought the week after winning her money.

'Er, yes it's new. It was cold in Leeds.' she said defensively.

'Nice.' Daniel said and then walked out of the kitchen to the living room.

Rebecca wondered if she was dreaming. This was not the conversation she had been expecting.

She followed him into the living room.

'Daniel I need to tell you…'

'I wanted you to come home because I've got some news,' said Daniel.

'News? OK well I have some too and I need to tell you...'

'It couldn't be better news really Bec.'

Daniel was smiling. Actually smiling and Rebecca realised that she hadn't looked at her husband properly since she arrived back. His eyes were bright, his face relaxed, he looked almost cheerful.

'News?' she asked.

'Great news Bec. Our problems are over! It's a new life for us, no more money worries. No more worries in general.' He was grinning as he spoke, watching Rebecca for her reaction as he rubbed his hands in glee.

Rebecca grabbed the back of the settee to stop herself falling. Oh dear God, was Daniel about to tell her he had won the lottery?

‘What is it?’ she asked faintly.

‘Peter sodding Thompson that’s what Bec,’ he paused to make sure he had her full attention. ‘He’s leaving!’

Rebecca was struggling. She was trying to tell Daniel that she had won over 15 million pounds on the lottery. She was trying to tell him that their lives had changed for ever and he was telling her about Peter Thompson.

‘Right,’ said Rebecca uncertainly. ‘Well that’s news but Daniel I have something really important to …’

Daniel reached out and grabbed Rebecca’s shoulders. ‘Listen to me Bec! Peter Thompson is leaving.’

Rebecca wriggled free. ‘I know Daniel but…’

‘He’s left his job. The job he stole from me. He’s left.’

‘Yes Daniel but I need…’

‘And who do you think is going to replace him Bec?’

Rebecca stopped struggling and stood very still.

‘What?’

‘He took my job Bec, everybody knows it. That was my job and I didn’t get it because I was in the wrong place at the wrong time. But now he’s going and I’m in the right place at the right time, Bec. This time I’m here when I need to be.’

Rebecca sank onto the settee pulling at the trench coat still wrapped tightly round her body.

‘Where’s Peter going?’ she asked

‘Peter! Who cares where that little shit’s going!’ Daniel raked his hand through his hair. ‘He’s got some fancy job down South somewhere, what does it matter. The fact is - he’s going!’

His face was ablaze with excitement. More excitement than Rebecca had seen in a long, long time. His eyes were bright and his mouth was grinning as he looked at her.

‘And they’ve offered you the job?’

‘Yes! Well, not officially, not yet. But the thing is,’ Daniel couldn’t stop laughing now, ‘I heard them talking. Old man

White was going on about how this time they would recruit from within. This time they didn't need to go elsewhere to find someone for the role. This time,' Daniel reached forward and grabbed Rebecca's hand, 'this time they had someone right in their midst who was perfect for the job.'

Rebecca stared at him. 'And you think...'

'I don't think, Bec! I know! This time the job is mine!'

And he laughed, throwing his head back and laughing out loud with pure joy.

Rebecca was in a dilemma. Standing up she pulled off her coat throwing it carelessly over the back of the chair. There was no doubt that Daniel was convinced he had the job, although Rebecca couldn't imagine in a million years that White's would actually want Daniel for the role. Peter Thompson hadn't stolen Daniel's place. Although it was a subject that was never discussed, Peter lived in Harrogate, only a few miles north of where Rebecca and Daniel had lived. He had been given the job on his merits and he had done a superb job, taking White's Packaging Corporation forward and developing a reputation for them as an innovative and eco minded packaging company. He had re-educated the sales force, put a whole new spin on their advertising and improved their sales figures by a record amount. And the sales team had taken on board Peter's new direction with enthusiasm and confidence as evidenced by the increased amount in their pay packets each month.

All, that was, apart from Daniel. He had been adamant that he would have been offered the job had he lived closer to head office. He had refused to support Peter in any initiative he had launched. He had refused to be re-educated and insisted on sticking to his old and tired marketing routing with a determination and misguided self-belief that wouldn't be shaken, even as his own pay packet dwindled and dwindled with every month that rolled by. He was bombastic and deliberately high handed in all his dealings with Peter and so determined to prove that Peter was wrong going down the eco route that Daniel made a point of doing the exact opposite. Of course, everything Daniel did actually proved Peter right and that's why Rebecca was now struggling to believe that with Peter's departure White's would be rushing to offer Daniel the job.

'Have they actually offered you the job? I mean have they actually said that you will replace Peter?'

'They didn't need to - it's someone in house, who else could they possibly offer it to?'

Just about anyone in the sales department, thought Rebecca.

'But they haven't actually said it will be you?'

Daniel's smile disappeared.

'What is wrong with you Rebecca? I've told you that I'm getting the job. Why do you have to make such a fuss over everything? Why can't you just be pleased for me. Why…'

Rebecca jumped up, putting her hand gently on Daniel's arm to stop the tirade. 'I'm sorry Daniel! It's just, well I think it must be the shock!'

The smile came back, stretching into a grin. 'It is a bit of a shocker isn't it! And things round here will change, no doubt about that.'

Rebecca stiffened. 'Change?'

'Well I've done a bit of digging and you wouldn't believe how much that waste of space was stealing from the company. The wage they were paying him to write sob stories about trees and the environment - it's bloody criminal! Anyway, it will mean a huge increase in my wage,' Daniel said smugly. 'We'll be much better off.'

'I see.' Rebecca answered slowly.

'So it'll be a new car, a new house - I think we should even have a holiday don't you?'

Rebecca closed her eyes and sank back onto the settee as a whistling Daniel wandered into the kitchen to make a cup of tea.

More money, a new car, a new house, a holiday. If only Daniel knew. She chewed her lip. He was so happy, so confident. There was a little glimmer of the old Daniel in his eyes. He needed this, he really needed this.

She was still sitting there when Daniel came back into the living room a few minutes later carrying tea and biscuits. He had put a handful of digestives on a cracked plate and Rebecca stared at them with tears in her eyes as he placed it on the small coffee table.

It was the most considerate thing he'd done in the last 5 years.

'Thought you might need one,' offered Daniel gruffly. 'You look done in.'

And at that point Rebecca realised that she couldn't tell him about the millions sitting in her bank. Not right now, at this minute. How could she look him in the eye and explain that it didn't matter about the job that he wanted so badly and the extra money he would be earning, because weeks ago she had won millions of pounds but just hadn't gotten around to telling him? So Rebecca said nothing. She said nothing and instead she smiled, sipped her tea and ate one of the digestives from the chipped plate.

Later that day as Rebecca finished cleaning the kitchen, she heard the door slam to signal Daniel's return. He had told her he needed to pop out and desperate for some time to herself Rebecca had been quite relieved and told him to be as long as he needed.

She put some washing in, vacuumed the living room floor, ran a duster over the conservatory and cleaned the kitchen. And all the time her mind whirled with Daniel's news.

Why would White's give Daniel the job she wondered? They had a team of excellent sales men, all trained and groomed by Peter Thompson to understand the new direction that packaging plants needed to follow. Only Daniel had refused to take Peter's instruction on board and as a result he was by far the worst performing sales man at White's. But Daniel seemed so sure about the job. And not just sure but so positive and so like his old self that Rebecca just couldn't bring herself to burst the bubble. She had to let him enjoy his moment.

'Bec,' he yelled as he walked into the living room. 'Come and see what I've got.'

He was grinning from ear to ear as he guided her onto the settee.

'I know you've never really liked it here Bec. It was all a bit of a rush, the move and everything and you didn't really get chance to choose exactly what you wanted.'

A bit of a rush! Daniel had come home one evening and announced that their house had been sold and they were moving in four weeks. As Rebecca had stared at him open mouthed he had thrown details of two houses in her direction and told her she could make the final decision. Neither were houses that Rebecca and the children wanted to live in and they had eventually chosen the one closest to the new school the children had just discovered they would be attending.

'We'll be able to buy a new house now Bec so I thought you might like to start looking.'

Rebecca looked down at the pile of glossy A4 leaflets on her knee. Houses, houses and more houses. Several looked identical to the one they were sitting in, a couple had mock Tudor fronts, some had stone stuck to the front and one seemed to have a field for a garden. But the theme was the same. They were moving from a 4 bed executive detached into a luxury 4 bed executive detached. And every last one of them was in Darlington.

Rebecca flicked through them slowly.

'Do we have to stay in Darlington?' she eventually asked, looking up at Daniel who was hovering in front of her.

He stared at her in disbelief.

'Stay in Darlington? Of course we bloody well have to stay in Darlington!' he puffed. 'Are you mad? Why would they give me the job if I didn't live in Darlington? I need to be close to Head Office that's the whole bloody point. If I lived somewhere else the whole bloody saga would start again. Of course I need to ...'

'Peter didn't live in Darlington.'

The silence in the room was heavy, Rebecca dropped her eyes back to the leaflets.

'I need to stay in Darlington,' ground out Daniel his hands shaking with anger. 'I'm offering to buy you a new house and all you can go on about is moving back to Leeds. Listen carefully Rebecca. We are not moving back to Leeds. Not now, not next year and not the year after. We are staying in Darlington.'

Neither of them spoke for a few minutes until Daniel made a visible effort to regain control.

'Anyway,' he added with something of a forced smile, 'you can have a look through those and this time you can decide which one we'll have, eh?' and he left the room.

Rebecca sat very still. Was this why she hadn't told him about the money she wondered? Because she knew that he would have his own ideas about where to live, what to do with it. Maybe she had been trying to avoid this all along. What was Daniel going to say when she finally broke the news, not only that she had won millions of pounds and neglected to tell him but that the first thing she had done was buy a new house, in Leeds?

The weekend seemed never ending. Daniel's good mood soon returned and he even insisted on giving Rebecca a break from cooking after her traumatic week and they went to the local pub and had a lovely meal. He could barely contain his excitement as he spoke about how he would change things for White's, how he would improve sales figures, make them the number one in the area.

Rebecca smiled and nodded and tried to be encouraging.

On Sunday she discovered that she was not the only one with hidden stashes of magazines as she opened the drawers of the sideboard to find dozens of brochures for new cars. Great big 4X4 cars. Cars that seated 7 people, that could go up and down mountains, that could switch in a moment to allow driving in fields and across lakes.

'Great aren't they?' asked Daniel grinning as he found her looking through them.

'But won't you still get a company car?'

'Of course! These aren't for me. About time we got rid of that rust bucket of a car you're driving round in. These are for you!'

'Me!' Rebecca looked down in alarm. 'But I don't want anything as big as this Daniel. I've actually been thinking about a new car and I'd like one of those new Fiats. They look a bit retro and so sweet and…'

'Rubbish,' declared Daniel. 'You'll be much happier in one of these.'

And the conversation was over.

The next batch of brochures were all for holidays. And every one of them featured golf.

'No point doing without,' declared Daniel stroking the front of one of the brochures. 'We need a holiday.'

'We could go to somewhere exotic, where we can just relax all day, maybe snorkel, walk along the beach. Maybe be in one of those little huts on the edge of the sea.'

Daniel stared at her. 'Don't be ridiculous,' he said as though she had lost her mind. 'Who wants to do that? We'll go to the Algarve and I'll play golf and you can…read.'

And that was another conversation finished.

By Sunday evening all Rebecca wanted was to be back in the quiet, peaceful luxury of her new house. She longed to curl up on one of the kitchen settees with a cup of tea as she watched the rain pour outside. She watched TV with Daniel, another programme about cars being rescued and made to look like something completely different and she thought about which of her DVDs she would watch if she were at home. She would curl up under the rich red throw with a glass of wine and the heating turned up. It was no good, she had to go back.

'Daniel.'

'Mmm?'

He didn't take his eyes from the TV and Rebecca waited a few more minutes until the adverts came on.'

'Daniel.'

This time he half turned in her direction although his eyes were still fixed on the TV.

'What?'

Rebecca took a deep breath. 'The thing is Daniel I do have something important to tell you. If you remember I tried to tell you yesterday when I came home but you had your own news. Daniel!' and in exasperation Rebecca snatched at the remote control and flicked off the TV.

Now she had his attention.

'Bec! What are you doing?'

'Daniel please listen to me for a minute. I have something really important to tell you.'

Grumpily he turned to face her.

'Well make it quick, I don't want to miss the rest of the programme.'

Rebecca stretched out her fingers, trying to stop them shaking.

'The thing is Daniel…'

'Oh my God this isn't going to be one of those I need to tell you how I feel chats is it?' Daniel's nose was turned up in disgust. 'Can't it wait Bec. I am in the middle of watching something.'

'Well if you'd stop interrupting I could tell you and you could get on with watching whatever you wanted,' snapped Rebecca.

'I need to tell you that… well I need to stay in Leeds for a few weeks.'

Daniel stared at her. 'What the hell for?'

'Because there's a problem with Parklands. I think it might be on the verge of closing. And if it does we need to find somewhere else for Mum to stay.'

'It's closing?'

'Well it's not official, not yet. But they're struggling and I don't think it will be much longer.'

'Then wait until it closes and then find somewhere for Gwen,' offered Daniel with a shrug.

Rebecca tightened her hands into fists.

'But you know how long it took us to find somewhere she liked the first time round. If Parklands suddenly closes and we can't find anywhere for Gwen, well... she'll have to come and live with us for a while.'

'What! But surely…'

'Daniel, it took 6 months of looking before we found Parklands. Mum can stay with us for 6 months, that's not a problem but the sooner we start looking the quicker we find somewhere.'

Daniel rubbed his face. There was a definite glimmer of panic in his eyes. 'Well how long are you going to be there, where will you stay? I haven't got the job yet you know, we can't afford hotel bills while you wander round Leeds for weeks on end.'

'Don't worry, I can stay with Sarah, or maybe even at Parklands or...maybe with- well I don't know but I'll find somewhere.' Rebecca had been about to mention Helen or Emma but Daniel hated the fact that she kept in touch with her old friends to the point where he would actively try and stop her from meeting with them. Rebecca had long ago stopped telling him when she was going to Leeds for lunch with her two friends.

He was still looking unsure.

'And I'll come home at weekends of course,' offered Rebecca reluctantly. 'So you can bring me up to date on what's happening with the job.'

Daniel sighed. 'I suppose, but what about your job?'

Rebecca stared at him. Of course he didn't know that she had already left the Deli.

'Well, I can ask Carol for time off,' began Rebecca. 'I'll explain that…'

'Why don't you just hand in your notice?' said Daniel unexpectedly.

Rebecca stared at him open mouthed.

'I don't like you working with those common women anyway. Susie!' he spat out, shivering in disgust. 'You won't need a job soon, take some holiday and then tell them I've been promoted and you're leaving.'

And that was another conversation ended as he turned the TV back on and was soon immersed back in the mechanics of car repairs.

Chapter 11

Rebecca parked her small cream coloured Fiat by the front door and started unloading the shopping bags into the hallway. The weather had improved marginally. The rain had stopped and the sun was making more of an effort to make an appearance during the day but even as the month rolled into May it was still cold and miserable.

Inside was warm and cosy. The heating was rarely off and in the evenings Rebecca would light the fire in the corner of the living room and watch the flames flicker. She carried the bags through to the kitchen. Stocking up a house from scratch was a long business she had realised and today had involved a visit to the supermarket to stock up the freezer and her kitchen cupboards. She flicked on the coffee machine smiling as she remembered how long it had taken her to produce her first cappuccino and started to unload the bags.

She had spent the last 3 weeks dividing her time between Leeds and Darlington. The weekends were long and full of Daniel pontificating about Peter Thompson's failures, the failure of White's not to give the job to Daniel in the first place, the failure of the sales team to allow themselves to be taken in by Peter Thompson. But he was happy. Happier than

Rebecca had seen him in a long time so she smiled and agreed and nodded and waited for the final announcement which was going to take place at any moment.

And then? Her mind veered away from the next step. Of course, once Daniel knew that he had the job, he might welcome Rebecca's news. It may be that being offered the job was enough and he didn't actually need to say yes. Maybe he would still want to accept their offer but wouldn't feel the need to stay in Darlington. Rebecca really couldn't think any further than the present and she lived one day at a time trying to minimise the number of lies she was telling as she lived her double life.

As far as Daniel was concerned she was in Leeds looking for a replacement home for Gwen. The same story had been offered to Carol and Susie, although Rebecca could tell from the glance they shared that they still felt Rebecca was hiding something. Little did they know just how much.

In Leeds the story Rebecca gave Gwen, Mrs Wendover, Helen and Emma was that she and Daniel had decided to move back to Leeds and that she was staying in the area partly because she wanted to keep an eye on Gwen and partly because she was looking for just the right place to buy.

She couldn't tell the children the same story because they would know instantly it was a lie. They knew of Daniel's absolute refusal to even consider moving back to Leeds. And although Sarah and Toby rarely spoke to their father these days, it wasn't beyond the bounds of possibility that they would pick up the phone to say hello and then hear his version of Rebecca's absence. So Rebecca stuck to the Parklands story for them both and Toby, knowing that their father would do anything to avoid having Gwen stay with them for any length of time, had accepted the reasons for Rebecca's extended stay in Leeds.

Sarah was slightly more problematical. More than once Rebecca caught her staring and she had asked Rebecca outright again if she and Daniel had split up.

'I'm a big girl Mum, I can take the news,' she had declared after confronting her mum outside the pizza restaurant.

'Don't be silly! Of course we haven't. I would tell you.'

'But you look so different. Happy, relaxed. And you're spending money, on yourself. Not that I think that's wrong, in fact it's been far too long coming if you ask me. You've done without ever since we moved to Darlington whereas it had no impact on Dad at all!'

Rebecca had explained about Daniel's new job and the increase in pay but Sarah was still suspicious.

'But he hasn't got the job yet has he? And Dad is always cautious about money, particularly about anyone else spending it. How come he's OK with you being down here staying in hotels etc. before he's got the first pay cheque? I presume you are staying in a hotel?' And Rebecca had to work hard, reassuring Sarah that all was okay, avoiding telling her exactly where she was staying whilst convincing her that there was no secret being kept.

The lying was undoubtedly the worse thing she had decided. It was exhausting and unpleasant.

She really just wanted to tell them all the truth, let family and friends share in her good fortune and let them all know that any money worries they had were now over. And she would, once she had broken the news to Daniel.

Helen had asked why Rebecca didn't look at her old house and Rebecca had to constantly invent new reasons: that they had already found another house they loved, they were on the verge of making an offer, they both felt a different house would be better. Helen had surprisingly agreed that it probably wouldn't be a good idea to come back to the same street they had left 5 years before.

A bonus to being back in Leeds was the time she could spend with Helen and Emma, who was now back from her exotic holiday.

They met regularly, had lunch and generally caught up on 5 years of gossip.

'I really didn't think Daniel would ever let you back to Leeds you know,' Emma had announced cheerfully one day. 'But I'm glad the miserable old bastard finally realised he couldn't keep you away for ever.'

They were sitting in Emma's lovely living room with its polished wooden floor and huge leather sofas. Rebecca caught the admonishing glance Helen threw at their friend but she shrugged it off. She didn't care what they thought of Daniel. She didn't care that Susie thought she was having an affair or that Emma thought Daniel was a controlling miserable man. She was back where she belonged, that was the main thing.

Rebecca also met up with Annie again, taking her out for lunch as a thank you for her help with the house exchange and the two women sat and chatted for a long time as they talked furnishings and gardens and lampshades and locations.

And in an effort to validate the lies as much as possible, Rebecca had rung Mrs Wendover and they'd had another chat about Parklands. Mrs Wendover, who asked Rebecca to call her Brenda, hadn't take exception at all to Rebecca's rather direct questions about how much longer Parklands was likely to stay open and instead, she had poured them both a cup of tea and admitted that she really didn't know.

She'd explained that the home was actually owned by a Mr Hammond who had bought it several years earlier. He left its management entirely to Brenda and as long as he could take a profit from the business at the end of every month, he left her pretty much to her own devices. But the profit had been getting smaller and harder to come by. Repairs and renovation were needed. The central heating needed updating, the plumbing needed work, decoration was necessary.

'And,' sighed Brenda, 'as I told you before some of the residents are getting a little behind with their payments. Dolly for example, she's been here for years and when she sold her house there was no question that the money would be enough to keep her somewhere comfortably for the rest of her life.'

But with a steady increase in rates over the last few years Brenda knew that Dolly's money had now run out and her family couldn't afford to keep her at Parklands.

'Dolly has been her for over 20 years. She's 93, I can't evict a 93-year-old woman and tell her to spend the last few years of her life somewhere else, without her friends and the room she thinks of as her home.'

Rebecca sipped at her tea.

'What do you think will happen?'

'Oh I don't know,' replied Brenda tiredly. 'Well actually, I do, I just don't like to think about it. Sooner or later, and I think it may be sooner, Mr Hammond is going to decide that the profit simply isn't there anymore and he'll sell Parklands. Then new owners will come along and 'renovate'. They'll probably sell off the gardens to a developer, they'll cut the size of the bedrooms in half, cover everything in easy clean plastic, get twice as many residents in, reduce the number of staff and make sure the place turns a profit. That's what's going to happen.'

When Rebecca had left Mrs Wendover she'd thought long and hard about Parklands. The very reason Gwen had chosen it was because of the gracious, almost old fashioned living it offered. The original architecture was still present in most of the rooms, the huge bedrooms were more like suites and the large bay windows gave the residents a view of the beautifully kept gardens. They all had their own bathroom and the communal rooms would not have been out of place in the local manor house. How sad if the sale did happen. How sad if people like Dolly were evicted at a time of their life when continuity and routine was paramount to their wellbeing.

And the news hadn't improved. Since Rebecca's last conversation about Parklands, Mr Hammond had actually had the business valued, which had further convinced Brenda Wendover that he was about to sell. The house itself had a worth, in addition to the business and the valuation had come in at 3.8 million pounds.

It was a lot of money thought Rebecca, but there again she had a lot of money. But this wasn't an investment. The lottery people had explained to her that she needed to put her money in an investment plan so that it could produce even more money. They had talked to her of high risk and low risk, of commodities, stocks and shares and bonds. About how she had to be careful not use all her capital without getting some kind of return for her investment. A lot of what had been said had gone over Rebecca's head, but she didn't need a team of trained investment specialists to tell her that buying Parklands was not an investment. It wouldn't be a case of making money, simply spending money to make people happy. She could carry out all the work Mrs Wendover had listed, put in place a grant for residents like Dolly and make sure that Gwen and her friends didn't have to worry about their home closing. But there would be no profit to be made.

So Rebecca chewed on the problem of Parklands and felt better about the lies she told to Daniel because now she'd had her suspicions confirmed that Parklands was about to close and she would have to find Gwen a new home. Or Rebecca could spend a considerable amount of her money making sure that Parklands would survive.

Rebecca went home at the weekend, as reluctant as ever to leave the warm comfortable house that she had fallen in love with. She didn't bother to catch the train this time, now she had a reliable new car to drive. But of course she couldn't go home and park it on the driveway so she made her way to Darlington train station and parked the Fiat there before hailing a taxi to take her home. She took very little with her. She had of course shopped like a professional over the last weeks and the wardrobe of clothes she left behind in Leeds each Saturday morning reflected the amount of money in her bank account. In Darlington she was a different person. The downtrodden wife of a grumpy, belligerent man. It was getting harder and harder to play the role when she returned. The confidence that had crept back into Rebecca's life when she had the ability to make her own decisions again, wasn't easily hidden when she opened the door of her 4 bed executive house. She knew that Susie was convinced Rebecca was having an affair. Maybe she was right in a way. Rebecca was giddy with the excitement of being her own person again.

The house was relatively tidy, Daniel was making more of an effort than normal and the over whelming feeling of guilt that Rebecca carried with her had prompted a return to making him meals for every day she was away.

Daniel was in the living room when she arrived, just packing his small golf bag.

He looked up guiltily when she walked through the door.

'I know you've been away all week and I should be happy that you're back but I need to set up some meetings over the next few weeks, start getting everybody back on side.'

Rebecca held up her hand smiling from the feeling of utter relief of not having to spend a day with Daniel and listening to his long term business plans yet again.

'Go! Go on - don't worry. I need a few hours to relax anyway.'

Relieved, Daniel could afford to be generous. 'Well I'll try not to be too late and perhaps we can go out for a meal, go round to the pub again? Or I'll bring a take away home?'

Rebecca agreed and shooed him gently out of the house closing the door behind him with a soft click.

She wandered back into the living room. There really was nothing about this house that she liked and nothing that she wanted to take with her. When they had moved she had been so angry with Daniel for taking the decision away from her that she simply refused to engage with him, about the house or the move. She shrugged when he suggested the choice of wall colour, ignored him when he talked about a new bathroom suite and refused to let him take her around Darlington so that she could get to know it better.

If she'd at least met him half way maybe they would have had a better life, thought Rebecca. She had taken such pride in the house they had left behind in Leeds. There wasn't a corner of their old home that wasn't designed and decorated exactly as she wanted. She could have done the same here, she could have tried to be happy.

Then she shrugged. It wasn't really the house. That was just a symptom of how bad things had become between Daniel and herself. No, the real problem had been the complete and utter change in Daniel's character. He had transformed almost overnight from a loving husband, a good father and a capable provider to a bad tempered, over bearing man, obsessed with his job and what he saw as a lost opportunity. He no longer seemed to see Rebecca as his best friend and wife, just someone who was supposed to keep his life in order while he struggled with the injustice of a system that gave Peter Thompson the job Daniel Miles should have had.

Rebecca sighed and made her way upstairs. Opening the wardrobe door, she unearthed the glossy brochures she had collected the day she checked her lottery numbers. Exotic holidays on deserted beaches with nothing to do but lay in a hammock or drink a cocktail by the sea. Exactly the sort of holiday that Daniel had said he didn't want to have. She threw them on the bed. She would get rid of them later, before Daniel came across them and they had another row. Reaching onto the top shelf she pulled out the boxes of photos and albums. Their wedding day, albums of the children's early years, it was all there and Rebecca wanted to have them with her in Leeds. She put them in a pile on the bed before flicking through her clothes. Most of them she put back in the wardrobe, just one or two items joined the photos and she did the same with each of her drawers. In the end there was a small pile of photos, very few clothes and a selection of bits and pieces such as the mother's day cards that the children had made at school, the pottery pencil holder that Toby had made and which Daniel said was like deformed whale and the badly stitched handkerchief that Sarah had spent weeks finishing.

Collecting an empty box from the utility room, Rebecca packed up the few possessions and put them back in the bottom of the wardrobe. The brochures she put in a plastic bag.

Then brushing her hair and throwing a scarf round her neck she went into town to visit Carol and Susie at the Deli, taking the plastic bag of brochures with her and dropping them in a bin as she went.

True to his word Daniel came home at a reasonable time clutching a bag full of Chinese take away. Rebecca was glad they weren't going out. If they did they would have to talk to each other whereas this way they could sit on the settee, Daniel could watch TV and Rebecca could retreat into her own world. Which she did until Monday morning finally came and she waited for Daniel to leave before calling a taxi to take Rebecca and her single box of possession to the train station and to her small cream car.

Within a couple of hours she was back in her own house, sighing with relief as she kicked the door shut behind her and feeling a whole new persona begin to cloak her shoulders.

This was the Rebecca she loved. This was the real Rebecca.

Chapter 12

The week passed as the previous ones had. There was little to shop for now, the house was almost as Rebecca wanted it to be. She had wondered if she would get bored when shopping was no longer a day to day necessity but the truth was that Rebecca just felt content. The pile of books on her coffee table grew as did the DVDs and Rebecca was at her happiest on an evening when she could snuggle down and lose herself in a good story. She met with Gwen, Sarah, Helen and Emma. She met Annie again for coffee. The rain had stopped and the weather was almost verging on the spring like and Rebecca spent a wonderful afternoon wandering around her new garden and getting to know what lived there. She decided a gardener would be necessary. She loved gardening and had every intention of planting herbs in the courtyard by the kitchen and maybe even vegetables down the side of the house. But there were some large trees that would need cutting back and lots and lots of grass to cut.

She re-organised all the photos, choosing a few to put out on display in the lounge and on the hall table. She went to the market and bought armfuls of fresh flowers to put in every room. A waste of time Daniel always said of fresh flowers but Rebecca loved the welcoming scent every time she entered a room.

She also went to visit her bank manager and spoke to him about trusts for the children. Probably the hardest part about keeping quiet thought Rebecca was not being able to put Toby and Sarah's minds at rest. She knew Sarah was already having sleepless nights about the growing total of her student loan and to be able to tell them that they needn't worry was a moment Rebecca couldn't wait to happen.

'How much do you want to give them?' asked the bank manager as they sat in his office.

'Well, started Rebecca uncertainly, 'I must admit I'm not really sure. You see, I want them to have some of the money, I just don't want to spoil what is a really important part of their lives. I mean - if I give them a couple of million pounds tomorrow will they even finish university? Will they feel the need to get a job and plan the rest of their lives? Do you understand?'

The bank manager understood perfectly. He had two sons both at university and he knew exactly the quandary that Rebecca found herself facing. They had a long, pleasant chat and he suggested figures for Rebecca to think about. He proposed that initially Rebecca could pay off their student loans and give them a monthly allowance so their day to day lives would be easier but without the responsibility of a large amount of money. He suggested a trust that provided them with a cash amount when they were 25, followed by a larger amount when they were 30. It gives them time to find their own course he had suggested and Rebecca had agreed. 'So what amount in total are you going to give them, have you decided?'

'Maybe a million each? Maybe a bit more. Of course they'll get even more when I've… well you know, later. But for now…... Is that enough do you think?'

The bank manager nodded. 'You do need to be careful about spending too much of the capital of course Rebecca. You don't want to run out.'

Rebecca laughed. She threw back her head and laughed until she realised that he was serious.

'Run out! I won 15.7 million pounds, how could I possibly run out?' she asked shocked.

He shrugged. 'Easier than you might think actually. Oh people think that it will last forever but if you keep spending the actual money rather than the interest, it can go surprisingly quickly. You've spend 2 million on a house. A house like that needs money to maintain it, your average utility bills are going to be high. You will probably buy another car,' he waved his hand at Rebecca's protests. 'Oh I know you're happy with the one you've got but I bet you'll have another one within a couple of months. Bequests to friends and family, investments, good and bad. You're earning a very healthy rate of interest but all you need to spend is a few million here and a couple of million there and suddenly it's gone.'

Rebecca had left his office feeling almost depressed. Arriving home she flicked open the computer and looked at the balance in her account. There was still over 13 million there. Even if she put two or three million aside for the children and gave money to her friends, even if she decided to buy Parklands it still left her with over 5 million pounds! Surely that would see her through the rest of her life!

She shrugged her shoulders and decided it was good advice but not relevant to her and rolling up her sleeves, the house was soon full of the smells of baking as she produced several trays of scones to take around to Parklands that afternoon.

The week passed as they all did, in a haze of contentment and all too soon it was time to turn on the alarm and head back to Darlington. Arriving at the train station she parked the little Fiat and hailed a taxi to take her home.

As soon as Rebecca opened the door she sensed disaster. It was nothing that she could put her finger on, just an all pervading feeling of bad will. It hung in the air, creeping around her shoulders until she shivered.

'Daniel? Are you home?' She hung her coat in the hallway and walked slowly to the living room. He hadn't answered but she knew he was there.

'Daniel?'

Pushing the door open she walked inside.

'Oh you're back are you. Nice of you to come home once in a while. It's not like you live here is it? Not like I should expect you to be here when I get home in the evening is it?' Daniel sneered.

He was drunk. The bottle of whisky sitting next to him was almost empty and from the dishevelled state of him and the blood shot eyes Rebecca guessed he had drunk most of it as he'd sat in the living room.

She didn't need to ask what was the matter.

'Daniel I'm so sorry. I...'

'Sorry!' he shouted trying to pull himself to his feet and lurching sideways into the coffee table. 'Sorry! I don't think you're sorry at all. You never thought I would get that job did you. Be honest, you never really thought that they'd give it to me. You just sat there smirking and agreeing and not giving a shit.'

The bottle of whisky tipped over, rolling around as the last dregs dripped onto the carpet.

'You didn't believe in me, you didn't think I was good enough. You didn't…' he waved his arms in the air before turning to flop back into the chair. 'You didn't think…' but he was running out of steam and his voice tailed off as he put both hands over his face. 'You didn't care,' he whispered.

Rebecca took a hesitant step forward reaching out her hand. 'That's not true Daniel. Of course I care, of course I believe in you.'

But it was another lie and even to Rebecca's ears it sounded thin and unconvincing.

'No.' Tiredly Daniel shook his head. 'No, you didn't think it was mine. You didn't think I had it.'

Rebecca let her hand fall to her side and said nothing. She stood there and stared out onto the bleak garden that never got any sun. She looked down at the whisky that was soaking into the carpet and she knew that he was right. It had never occurred to her for a minute that Daniel would get the job at White's. She had gone along with the idea because it had made her life easier not because she thought Daniel would succeed. She stood there and watched as his head fell back onto the chair, his eyes closing as his breathing changed and he fell asleep. She stood there and struggled with her guilt, knowing that she could have saved all this from happening if she had told Daniel the truth the moment she found out she had won.

Eventually she went to get a cloth from the kitchen and soaked up the spilt alcohol as best she could. The room stank of whisky. She got a throw from the back of the settee and threw it over Daniel's legs. She moved the glass from his side and turned up the heating. It was so cold that the windows were misting over from their breath. Then she sat curled up on the settee opposite and waited for him to recover.

It wasn't long before the whole story came out. That the job had indeed gone to an existing member of the sales team. Joshua, who was only 34 but consistently the highest earning sales man at White's. It had been announced at the previous day's sales meeting. He was thrilled to be offered the job, thanked the management team sincerely and told the sales team how he would carry on with Peter Thompson's magnificent sales strategies.

Shocked beyond words Daniel had gone straight home, opened the whisky bottle and not stopped since.

Rebecca tried to console him but he wanted nothing from her. She tried to commiserate but he looked at her as though she had deliberately gone out of her way to humiliate him. She tried to suggest that maybe it was time to leave White's and look for another job but he told her to shut up. She decided not to suggest leaving Darlington behind and starting again, she didn't think he was ready for that just yet. She didn't tell him that it was irrelevant that they hadn't offered him the job because she had money anyway. She didn't think he was ready for that either. And she didn't tell him about the beautiful new home that was paid for and which they could live in without either of them having to work again. She definitely didn't think he was ready for that.

So they spent the weekend in total misery with Daniel more obnoxious than ever and blaming the entire sorry saga on Rebecca's lack of faith.

'If you don't believe in me,' he had snarled, 'how can anybody else be expected to.'

Come Monday morning Rebecca wasn't sure what would happen but Daniel got up at the usual time, put on his suit, made a cup of tea and picked up his briefcase, albeit with the air of a man who was about to walk into the hangman's noose.

'Are you going to Leeds again?' he demanded as he stood in the doorway.

Rebecca hadn't been sure what to do. She really couldn't bear the thought of spending any more time with Daniel in this mood. But to go to Leeds when he needed her?

'You might as well go, you're no bloody use here.'

Rebecca's head shot up. 'Then I'll go,' she said quietly.

'Any luck finding somewhere for your mother? You've been looking for long enough.'

Rebecca shook her head. Daniel had been so preoccupied with the possibility of a new job he hadn't given a second thought to her long absences. This was the first time he had asked about any progress she had made.

'There can't be that many places to look round.'

Was it her imagination or was he looking at her strangely. There again he had been looking at her strangely all weekend.

'No there aren't many more options,' said Rebecca truthfully. 'I think I need to make a decision this week.'

Daniel nodded. 'About time,' he said gruffly. 'I'll see you at the end of the week.'

And he was gone leaving Rebecca slumped against the closed door with her heart hammering against her chest.

Chapter 13

She drove back to Leeds less than half an hour later, desperate to get back to the peace and tranquillity of the house she now thought of as home. Closing the door behind her Rebecca looked round the hallway with desperate eyes. She couldn't keep this going any longer. She couldn't keep up the pretence and the lies. And whatever he might think, Daniel actually needed her at the moment. She should be sharing her new life with him.

The week began its usual pattern, Rebecca filled the fridge, spoke to Sarah, started her herb garden and visited Gwen. She arranged to have lunch with Helen and Emma on Wednesday and asked the bank manager to make arrangements to draw up a trust for the children. They would each receive £250,000 on their 25th birthdays and a further one million each on their 30th birthday. As soon as she had told Daniel about the money she would also make arrangements to transfer some to her close friends. She wanted Carol and Susie to have something, they had made her life bearable in Darlington with their friendship and support. And she wanted Helen and Emma to have something. Emma maybe didn't really need it but Rebecca knew that Helen and her husband were in a constant battle with their finances.

So she made plans, wrote down figures and smiled happily as she went about her day to day business. On Wednesday morning she went to visit Gwen first thing only to find her in tears. She was no longer confined to bed and had joined her friends downstairs in the communal room.

'Dotty has to leave,' she told Rebecca, tears rolling down her cheeks. 'She's run out of money and Mr Hammond said she pays or goes. Her family can't afford to keep her here, she's moving to some new build place on the other side of Leeds.'

Rebecca consoled Gwen and went over to kneel down by Dotty who sat silently in her favourite chair by the window.

'Oh Dotty, don't worry. I'm sure the new place will be lovely.'

But Dotty just shook her head mutely and as her eyes met Rebecca's own, Rebecca was shocked to see that there was no sign of any life or happiness left in them.

Rebecca left and drove home her head whirling with the possibility of buying Parklands. The bank manger's words echoed in her head. A couple of million here, a couple of million there and it's soon gone. But even if she bought Parklands, still gave the planned donations and set up the trust for the children she would have millions left. That would be enough, surely. How many millions did you need to live comfortably for the rest of your life?

She parked the cream Fiat outside the front door and went inside to turn on the coffee machine. She had been planning on driving straight to Helen's house but in the end had cut short her visit to Parklands and decided to call home first instead. All she could see was the dead despair in Dotty's eyes.

The doorbell rang and with a sigh Rebecca made her way into the hallway, still racked with indccision.

She opened the door and at first she couldn't make sense of what she was seeing. It was wrong, out of place and for a moment she just stared until Daniel put his hand through the doorway and pushed her to one side so he could enter the house. Stumbling against the doorframe Rebecca put out a hand to steady herself and then gasped in pain as Daniel grabbed at it, twisting her towards him so he could meet her eyes.

'Well, well,' he said in a quiet but vicious voice. 'Look what we've got here,' and with a grunt he threw her away from him so that she fell backwards, cracking her elbow against the still open door.

'Daniel,' she gasped. 'Daniel I …'

'Where is he then?' asked Daniel, unnaturally calm as he thrust his hands in his pockets and walked slowly across the hall. He stopped to look at the photos gathered on the hall table, photographs of his own children and his face darkened with fury.

'Where is the man you've been shacking up with all these weeks?'

Rebecca stared at him shaking her head as the tears started rolling down her face.

'M-man? There is no man Daniel. This house is…'

'Don't lie to me!' he thundered, his voice echoing around the hall. 'No more lies you bitch. Where is he?'

Rebecca pushed the door shut and tried to stand tall, pulling back her shoulders as she met her husband's gaze.

'Daniel you must listen to me, please let me explain. There is no man, there's no affair, this is my house and….'

He laughed. An unpleasant laugh that reached out and slapped her across the face.

His voice was quiet but dripping with venom, his body was rigid and his hands clenched into fists. His eyes were wild with rage and, was that fear?

'You're lying,' he thundered, suddenly lunging in her direction and terrified Rebecca couldn't help herself as she whimpered and tried to step backwards.

He grabbed at her and pulled her to within inches of his face, his mouth contorting as he spoke, spitting in her face as his words launched at her.

'You fucking slut! All this time. All this time you've been shagging someone else. Pretending to be such a good little wife, such a supportive little wife. Well I'm not stupid Rebecca. I could tell there was something going on now you need to tell me, WHERE IS HE?'

Rebecca sobbed as he shouted the last words so loudly it hurt her ears.

'Please Daniel, please just listen to me. I'm not… there is no-one. I need to tell you…'

'Stop lying you stupid, stupid woman. Did you really think I would fall for your pathetic stories? Did you think I wouldn't know what you were doing? How long did you think you would get away with it Rebecca? Just how long did you think you'd be able to pull the wool over my eyes?'

'No - no,' sobbed Rebecca, 'I haven't…'

'SHUT UP! The only thing I want to know is - who he is? No one with any taste that's for sure!' He laughed unpleasantly. 'I mean come on Rebecca. Who in their right mind would give you a second look.'

Rebecca stayed silent as Daniel circled her like a shark, looking her up and down with a contemptuous expression on his face, his lips twisted in disgust.

'Let's face it Becs old girl, you're hardly the sort a man would lose his head over. A bit past it, a bit wrinkly, not really got it any more have you?'

He turned to whistle appreciatively at the beautiful wooden staircase curving toward the upper floor. 'Now this guy, whoever he is, he's got it. He's got money hasn't he Becs? Is that why you're with him, because he's got money? I understand that, you know, I really do. I can see why you would want to be with him. What I can't work out is why the hell he's with you. Is that how he gets his kicks, taking in desperate old housewives who will do anything he tells them for a handful of notes?'

'Please stop,' whispered Rebecca as Daniel came full circle to stand in front of her again. 'Please, please stop Daniel and let me tell you what this is all about. You really have got the wrong end of the stick.'

Daniel snorted. 'Well go ahead *Rebecca*, I can't wait to hear whatever little story you've concocted. Just how are you going to explain this set up *Rebecca*?' He poked her hard on the shoulder each time he ground out her name.

'So come on *Rebecca*.' Another hard poke to her shoulder, 'start talking.'

Rebecca took a step back, out of range.

'Let's go in the kitchen,' she suggested and turned away to walk down the hallway.

'Oh well let's be civilised about this by all means,' and almost knocking her out of the way Daniel strode down the hall pushing the kitchen door open so violently it almost flew off its hinges.

'There's no-one else here Daniel,' offered Rebecca, 'I've told you, there is no man.'

She watched as Daniel looked round the room. It couldn't fail to impress anyone who saw it for the first time.

Rebecca walked over to the huge wooden table and sat down waiting to see if Daniel followed her lead.

He didn't. He strolled round the kitchen, letting his hand trail along the edge of the black granite work surface, deliberately banging each of stainless steel pans that hung in perfect order over the range cooker before turning to glare in Rebecca's direction again.

Well go on then,' he snapped. 'I can't wait to hear this one.'

Rebecca took a deep breath. This was going to be every bit as difficult as she had imagined.

'There's something I haven't told you Daniel,' she ignored his snort of derision and carried on. 'I should have let you know weeks ago but I didn't. I just didn't know how to tell you. At first I just wanted to be sure, absolutely sure before I told you anything and then it got difficult… the longer I left it the harder it became.'

She sighed, rubbing her forehead with one hand. 'No, no excuses. I should have told you Daniel and I didn't. You thought you were going to get the job you see…' she trailed off.

Daniel's face had gone almost purple with anger. 'Anyway,' she carried on hastily, 'that made me decide to wait, I decided to let you have your moment and I just didn't think you would want to…

Rebecca jumped as Daniel's fist slammed violently onto the table.

'Who is he?' he shouted. Spit landing on her cheek.

'There is no-one Daniel. I haven't been having an affair, I haven't been coming down to Leeds because there's another man in my life. I'm here because a few weeks ago I won over 15 million pounds on the lottery. I'm here because this is my house. This is the house I bought with my lottery winnings Daniel. There is no man, this is mine.'

Rebecca had expected a huge feeling of relief to descend upon her once she told Daniel. It wasn't there. She could stop lying now and that felt good. But the relief, it simply wasn't there. And suddenly Rebecca knew why she hadn't told Daniel. She hadn't told him because quite simply, she hadn't wanted him to know. This was something that had happened to Rebecca. It was her moment. It had brought joy into her life and she just hadn't want to share that with Daniel. Not right away. But she would have told him eventually, of course she would she told herself fervently.

She looked up to see him staring at her with disbelief emblazoned across his face.

'You expect me to believe that. You expect me to ...'

'It's the truth Daniel,' said Rebecca firmly. 'I can prove it, you have to believe me. It's the truth.'

Daniel pulled out a chair slumping onto it as he stared at Rebecca.

'But why wouldn't you tell me if you had won the lottery?'

Oh why indeed, thought Rebecca.

'I told you the timing was never right, I was going to, when it seemed the right time.'

'I don't believe you.'

He said it flatly, decisively. 'You're lying. It's a smoke screen to stop me finding out about the affair…'

Rebecca cut him short, reaching out for the laptop that sat on the table and flipping it open so that Daniel could see the page. It showed her bank account. A bank account with a balance of over 13 million pounds.

Daniel stared. He stared at the laptop and then he stared at Rebecca before turning his gaze back to the laptop.

'But you didn't tell me.'

Rebecca bit her lip. 'You were so excited about the job I thought it would spoil things for you. You tell me you're about to get the promotion you've always wanted and I say it doesn't matter. I couldn't do that to you, so I waited.'

Daniel nodded. Rebecca could see his mind playing over the events of the last few weeks.

'When did you win?'

The question Rebecca had been dreading.

'I'm not actually sure,' she said with a nervous laugh. 'I didn't check my ticket for a week or so and then all of a sudden I found out I'd won.'

Daniel was in shock. He took both hands out of his pocket and laid them on the table.

'And this house…?'

Again Rebecca felt her heart fluttering.

‘One of those things. You know how it is. I was in Leeds to meet the lottery people to check the ticket, get the money and everything and I saw the house and I... well I bought it.’

He was staring at her as though she had gone mad. Of course he didn’t know how it was, he hadn’t just won 15.7 million pounds.

‘Right. So the money that’s here,’ he waved his hand towards the computer screen, ‘that’s what’s left?’

Rebecca nodded mutely. She thought about telling him of the trust funds she was organising for the children, about her plans to give money away to her friends, the possibility that she might spend nearly 4 million on a nursing home that was unlikely to make any money. But instead she nodded and left it at that.

Daniel’s shoulders had started to relax a little and he pulled the laptop towards him to look at the balance again.

‘Why did you put it in this account?’ he asked, suddenly realising that the account was in the name of Rebecca Miles and wasn’t their joint account.

‘Only account details I could remember off the top of my head,’ lied Rebecca.

Daniel nodded again. There was a long silence as he stared at the screen.

Rebecca’s mobile rang and she stood up quickly and retrieved it from the counter top.

‘Hello? Oh hello Helen. What? Oh I’m so sorry, I completely lost track of time, I’ll be there in half an hour. Sorry’

Rebecca put down the phone and turned to see Daniel staring at her.

‘Helen? You’re meeting Helen?’ he asked darkly.

‘Mm,’ said Rebecca, ‘And I’m late!’

‘I thought I told you I didn’t want you to see her any more. And Emma. Trouble causers the pair of them.’

Rebecca shrugged impatiently. She really didn't understand why Daniel had suddenly developed such a violent objection to Helen and Emma. When they had all been neighbours Daniel had gotten on like a house on fire with both women.

'And I've told you Daniel they are my friends and I will carry on seeing them.'

'Well at least call and cancel now. You can't tell me something like this and then walk out.'

Rebecca struggled with her conscience. If she were truthful she would like a little distance between herself and Daniel right now. She needed some time to think, to clear her head.

'I can't cancel Daniel. Helen has made lunch for us both and it would be rude not to go.'

'Rude?' Daniel spat out in disbelief. 'Not half as rude as not telling your husband you'd won 15 million pounds. Now that's rude!'

That made Rebecca's decision for her. 'I must go. It will do you good to have a bit of time to think about it all. I know it's a bit of a shock. I remember when I found out…' she trailed off.

'Anyway, you have a chance to clear your head while I'm out and we can talk when I get back. You can stay here, obviously. There's food in the fridge and…'

Daniel was looking at her if she were some two headed monster and Rebecca had to admit she was being a coward, telling him then fleeing the scene.

'I suppose you've told them all?' His voice was bitter.

'No. Actually I haven't told anyone. Not a single soul, apart from the bank manager. I didn't want anyone to know until I'd told you Daniel.'

He didn't look impressed but a little of the anger left his face.

'I'll be off then. I won't stay long,' and Rebecca was out of the house, almost running in her haste and holding her breath until the Fiat had started and she was pulling out of the drive.

Her legs were shaking so much she had to pull into a lay-by only a few minutes later, dropping her head onto the steering wheel until the trembling had stopped.

What had she expected she asked herself angrily? What did she think he would say? *'That's okay Rebecca, never mind.'*

True to her word she didn't stay too long at Helen's. It was obvious to her friends that there was something wrong as she sat in a daydream, not hearing their questions and blindly staring out of the window.

'Is it Daniel?' Helen had asked, sympathetically.

'Daniel?' Rebecca looked up. What made them ask she wondered, had they heard something?

'Er no, not really. Why do you ask?'

Helen and Emma exchanged a glance and Emma shrugged her shoulders. 'Well you know, we just wondered if he had changed his mind about moving back to Leeds.'

Perhaps her friends knew her husband better than she did. Despite every lie that Rebecca had told them, they didn't believe that Daniel would agree to a return to their old life. What had made Rebecca think that he would?

The awkward conversation stopped and Rebecca left not long after. She was tempted to visit Parklands before she went home. She wanted to check if Gwen was okay after her distress of the morning. And if she were honest she really just wanted to delay her return to the house.

But there had been enough prevaricating Rebecca decided so she squared her shoulders and drove back, albeit very slowly. She pulled up outside the front door, next to Daniel's car and with a sigh climbed out of her car and into the house.

He was in the living room sitting in one of the large cream chairs. His fingers formed a steeple underneath his chin and he had obviously been thinking.

Rebecca crossed the floor and sat opposite him.

'How did you know where I was?' she asked curiously.

Daniel didn't answer for a moment and then he put down his hands and turned to face her. 'I phoned the nursing home. I said I was checking on Gwen and asked if you were there. I've phoned up a few times this week but I've never got the timing right. Today Mrs Wendover told me you'd just arrived so I drove straight down. I watched you leave and followed you here.'

Rebecca nodded. If only Daniel was as imaginative in the rest of his life.

'I've been looking round the house. Very nice.' commented Daniel.

Rebecca didn't answer.

'How come you've managed to get it looking like this so quickly?'

Rebecca shrugged. 'I bought the furniture as well. Seemed the easiest thing to do.'

Daniel nodded.

'Have you told the children?'

Rebecca shook her head, 'I told you, I haven't told anyone. Not until I told you Daniel.'

'Have you told Gwen?'

'No-one Daniel. I have told no-one.'

He stood up. 'There's no beer in the house,' he said and walked into the kitchen to pour himself a glass of wine instead.

Rebecca followed, standing in the doorway and watching him open all the cupboard doors until he found a glass.

'I'm sorry Daniel, I'm so sorry. But I would have told you, I was just waiting for the right time. Once the whole job thing was… sorted, I was going to tell you. Of course I was.'

Daniel poured the wine. Watching the pale liquid fill up his glass, he took a long drink then topped it up again. Rebecca could see his reflection in the glass of the patio doors, could tell from the stiffness of his back how tightly he was hanging onto his emotions.

A moment passed and then slowly he reached into the cupboard and pulled out another glass, filling it to the brim before turning and pushing it in Rebecca's direction as she stood hovering in the doorway.

'Of course you were Rebecca, of course you were.'

The evening was long and tortuous. Rebecca cooked them some pasta and chicken. Daniel emptied the bottle of wine. She felt riddled with guilt and Daniel was still taking in the news, asking questions, spending long periods in silence. Somewhere around midnight he decided to forgive her. Rebecca could see the emotions in his face, had watched him go through feelings of betrayal and anger through to eventual reconciliation and forgiveness. Because as Rebecca had already worked out, if he didn't believe that she intended to tell him about the win, where on earth did that leave Daniel and Rebecca Miles?

Rebecca showed him to one of the spare rooms. She didn't care how he took it but she couldn't sleep with him next to her. She wouldn't be able to rest feeling his anger bubbling throughout the night.

'Very nice,' was his only comment as he looked around the room decorated in duck egg blue. And closing the door slowly behind her Rebecca escaped to her own room, trembling with fear and self-loathing.

She found it difficult to sleep. She tossed and turned and even her wonderful nest of goose down and the best of linen didn't soothe her. In fact, was it her imagination or had the whole house suddenly become slightly tainted by Daniel's presence?

She over slept and made her way downstairs the following morning with a thick head and a heavy heart. Pulling her dressing gown around her she recognised the smell of bacon half way down the stairs and made her way warily into the kitchen.

Daniel was cooking. He had a glass of orange on the table and the coffee machine was glugging away beside him He had obviously worked it out a lot quicker than Rebecca had. He was whistling softly as he added an egg to the pan and just at that moment some bread threw itself out of the toaster.

Hearing Rebecca he turned and smiled at her as she stood in the doorway.

'I've made enough for two,' he said. 'It will be ready in a few minutes.'

Rebecca sat down heavily at the kitchen table staring as Daniel buttered toast, poured coffee and then distributed the food across the two plates he had standing ready.

'I have to say Bec, this is a wonderful house. The kitchen is superb,' and he slid a plate in her direction as he sat down to tuck in.

Rebecca had no appetite but neither did she want an argument so she forced down the toast and a little egg but passed on the bacon.

Eventually Daniel finished and pushed his plate away with a sigh of satisfaction.

'Right,' he said in a matter of fact tone. 'I suppose we need to have a discussion.'

'About?' asked Rebecca carefully.

'Well about the money, what we're going to do with it, how we're going to spend it, what a difference it will make to our lives - all that sort of thing,' smiled Daniel.

Rebecca stared down at her plate.

'I've been thinking,' he went on and Rebecca tensed as she waited to hear where those thoughts had taken him. 'This has obviously all been a huge misunderstanding, bad timing and all that. But we need to get over it and move on.'

She was watching him speaking although she couldn't quite believe it was Daniel saying the words. He actually sounded excited. He looked like the cat that had swallowed the cream. He looked exultant.

'I appreciate what you were trying to do regarding the promotion Bec and it was…considerate of you. But I suppose it has all worked out for the best hasn't it?'

Rebecca wanted to run. She wanted to leave the kitchen and find another house, one that no-one else knew about and where she could pick up that contented life she had enjoyed so much over the last few weeks.

'Let's face it, I don't need the job at White's now do I?'

Daniel could hardly contain himself. His eyes glittered and his hand shook with excitement as he lifted up his coffee cup.

'I don't need the job Rebecca because I can go one better than that. I'm going to buy White's, I'm going to buy it lock stock and barrel.'

Chapter 14

Rebecca showered and dressed, made her bed and still the shaking hadn't stopped. Daniel was outside looking at her new car and she walked back into the kitchen and automatically started to clean up the mess left from breakfast.

Daniel wanted to buy White's Packaging. He wanted to buy it because that way he truly would be in charge. He could eradicate the thought of Peter Thompson and the humiliation of being passed over for the job by actually buying the place and putting himself in charge.

He had described his plans to Rebecca, how the first person he would sack would be Joshua who had taken his coveted sales manager role. Then old Mr White himself who clearly didn't recognise good staff when he saw them. He described how he would take White's back to the glorious company it had been when Daniel was the top sales man, forget all this eco rubbish and new wave thinking that had seeped into the soul of White's over the last few years and run it how it was meant to be run.

Rebecca had listened and nodded. She wasn't required to participate. Daniel didn't ask for her opinion, he didn't even ask if she agreed, he simply told her that he was going to buy White's Packaging Corporation. With her money.

'What on earth where you thinking buying that little car?' demanded Daniel as he came back in. 'You don't want a silly little thing like that, I've already chosen a good car for you. Don't worry, we'll use the Fiat as part exchange.'

'I don't want a 4X4 Daniel, I've already told you that. I like my little car.'

'Rubbish,' said Daniel. 'You need something bigger, stronger. I'll take you to see the car I'm thinking of later in the week.'

Rebecca gritted her teeth. She was keeping her little car. He wandered to the window looking out into the garden.

'I'm going to have to go back to Darlington today. Start putting things in motion for White's. You need to come with me.'

Rebecca stiffened.

'It looks bad, us living in two separate places. Looks like the money has come between us.'

Did Rebecca sense a warning tone in Daniel's voice?

'No!' The last thing Rebecca wanted was to go back but she had no more excuses. Not now the truth was out.

'No,' she said again a little calmer. 'I can't go back right now.'

'Why not?' Daniel was blunt and to the point and Rebecca desperately searched for reasons.

'Well now that you know I need to tell Mum, Sarah and Toby. I need to organise things.'

'What kind of things?'

He was unrelenting, staring her down as her mind raced.

'Well there's lots I haven't done because I was waiting until you knew and now I can do them,' Rebecca finished weakly.

Daniel turned and walked to the door. 'You can have today, then I want you back in Darlington.'

And he left, getting in his car and driving away.

Rebecca clutched at her stomach, the toast and eggs churning. She had the distinct feeling that her joy at winning the money was about to disappear altogether now that Daniel finally knew.

She phoned Toby and broke the news to him that she had won several million pounds on the lottery. He was half asleep and more than a little hung over and it took a while to sink in but eventually his brain connected and Rebecca could hear the whoops of joy echoing around his room.

He promised to come and visit as soon as he could and when Rebecca told him that she had already bought a house in Leeds he promised to come up even sooner. Toby had hated Darlington even more than Rebecca had. Next she spoke to Sarah who wept with joy at the thought of having her student loan disappear.

'Is that what the big secret has been Mum? Why on earth didn't you tell me sooner?'

But she was too excited to really take Rebecca to task and she was easily fobbed off with stories about how it took time etc.

Next she drove to Parklands and broke the news to Gwen, who was at first very confused and had to be reminded what the national lottery was but when she realised that Rebecca had become very rich overnight she clutched her daughter's hand.

'You can do whatever you want now my darling,' she said meaningfully, looking deep into Rebecca's eyes, 'whatever you want.'

Everyone around her was so happy for her good fortune that the tea tray came round loaded with biscuits as they all drank to her health.

Rebecca was exhausted with the sheer emotion of the last 24 hours and the excitement that had kept her going all these weeks had disappeared with barely a trace. She hadn't told Helen and Emma yet but she planned to break the news to them later that afternoon. And when she got to Darlington she would go visit Carol and Susie.

And then they would all know. There would be no mores secrets, no more double lives and yet as Rebecca sat with a cup of tea in her hand gazing out onto the courtyard she couldn't stop the tears from rolling down her face.

She spent the rest of the day preparing her house for an absence that she hoped wouldn't last very long. She eventually phoned Helen and Emma and listened to their shrieks of excitement before she had one last evening, tucked up on her settee with the red throw over her knees. She didn't put on a film, she didn't read a book. She just sat there with her head resting on the back of the settee and revisited in her mind every glorious, wonderful moment that she had experienced over the last 8 weeks. Her life had changed forever. The old life was over, she was about to start a whole new one so why did it feel like a bereavement, like it was all about to end.

There didn't seem any point in putting off the inevitable so Rebecca drove back to Darlington first thing Friday morning and this time parked her little Fiat on the driveway.

She could feel Daniel's energy the minute she walked in the house. He was walking around the living room floor talking to someone on his mobile. His voice was loud, confident. Maybe a little too confident, he sounded brash and threatening to Rebecca. His shirt sleeves were rolled up and there were countless cups of half-drunk coffee spread on every available surface.

He stopped the call shortly after she arrived and threw the phone onto one of the chairs.

'I'm glad you're here,' he announced pushing past her to pick up a file from the coffee table.

Rebecca smiled. There was no point doing this with a bad grace.

'I said I would come.'

'We need to move the money.'

Her smile froze in place.

'W - what?'

'The money!' Daniel exclaimed impatiently. 'What on earth possessed you to put it in your account?'

Rebecca stood very still in the middle of the room.

'Do you know that snotty little bank manager refused to move it for me!' he carried on indignantly. 'Said it was your money and he didn't have the authority to move it into any account without your say so! Little shit. How dare he stop me using my money?'

He was shuffling through the papers, ignoring Rebecca even as he regaled her with the faults of the bank manager.

'Well he'll regret that attitude. I've told him we're moving the account. I've made a few calls already, you tell a bank you want to open an account with 13 million and they can't do enough for you.'

'Did he move any of it?' asked Rebecca.

'What? I've already told you, he refused. Anyway you need to phone him up and tell the idiot to get that money in our joint account straight away. I'm putting together the deal of a life time here and I won't be held up by some pompous git who thinks he can control my money!'

Rebecca left the room as Daniel's mobile rang again. She walked upstairs into the bedroom and closed the door tightly before taking out her own phone and ringing the bank manager whose private number she now had.

'Richard?' she asked as he answered the phone, 'Richard it's Rebecca Miles.'

‘Ah, I was hoping you’d phone.’

‘Richard I am so sorry. But this is really important, you won’t move any money will you? I mean, I may ask you to move some and if I do then that’s okay but if Daniel, Mr Miles should ring you won’t...’

‘Rebecca,’ interrupted Richard Dickinson calmly, ‘do you remember the very first conversation we had? This is your money and yours alone. It is in your bank account and it will stay there until you personally tell me otherwise. No-one else has a right to it Rebecca not even your husband. Please don’t worry.’

Rebecca apologised again. She could imagine his conversation with Daniel had been far from pleasant and then she went back downstairs. Daniel was shouting into the phone still and she slipped into the kitchen and put on the kettle.

‘Why is everyone so bloody inept,’ he growled following her. ‘If you want anything doing, do it your bloody self, that’s what I always say!’ and then he stalked back out.

Rebecca took him a cup of tea.

‘The valuation has come in!’ Daniel looked up at her his eyes blazing with barely contained excitement. ‘4.8 million!’

‘What!’ Rebecca put Daniels cup down on the coffee table before she dropped it.

‘But that’s so much money, 4.8 million. We can’t afford that!’

Daniel snorted. ‘That’s why people like you shouldn’t be allowed to have large amounts of money,’ he stated pompously, ‘you really have no idea how to invest it wisely.’

Rebecca’s head was whirling.

With the money she had already paid for the house the car, the furniture etc. she still had over 13 million in the bank. But she had arranged trust funds for the children and was arranging to pay off all their student loans and buy them a little car each. She was still undecided on whether to invest in Parklands and if she did that would be another 3.8 million. There were bequests to friends. With Daniels potential investment of 4.8 million that would still leave her with over 2 million in her bank account but she couldn't help but remember what the bank manager had said, a couple of million here, a couple there and soon it's all gone. She had a house to maintain and children to look after, she wanted to live a comfortable life. It was all disappearing rather faster than she had wanted.

'Oh by the way, I've told those so called friend of yours about the win.'

Rebecca looked puzzled. 'Which so called friends?'

'Carol and that bloody tart Susie, I called in earlier this week to see if they knew where you were staying. I said that I'd lost your address in Leeds. That smug faced bitch Susie, I could tell she thought you were having an affair so I went back and put her straight. Told her we'd won millions and you were in Leeds taking it easy. That shut her up.'

Rebecca's eyes blazed. 'You told my friends?'

But Daniel had lost interest and had pulled out his calculator to add up a row of figures.

With a yelp of anger Rebecca pulled it out of his hands and threw it to the floor, ignoring the look of absolute surprise and shock on Daniels face.

'You told my friends?' she demanded.

'Yes I did,' Daniel snapped back. 'I thought the secret was over.'

Rebecca was so angry she wanted to punch him in his smug face. She had told so many lies, in particular to Carol and Susie and the one thing she had needed to do was tell them the truth herself, try and explain why.

'How dare you,' she ground out, 'how dare you interfere.'

'Interfere! Oh excuse me. My wife had disappeared and I went to see her friends to see if I could track her down!'

'But you went back Daniel - you went back and you didn't have to.'

Daniel sniffed. 'Serves her right,' he snapped. 'Uppity bitch. Thought she knew all about you. I put her right, you should have seen the look on her face.'

And he pushed Rebecca to one side so he could rescue his calculator before turning his back on her and resuming his tapping.

Resisting the desire to throw his tea in his face, Rebecca clenched her fists and stormed from the room. Grabbing her coat and her car keys she flew outside, jumped into her car and screeched out of the drive.

Arriving outside the Deli she found a parking space and almost ran to the shop. There were three people at the counter and one couple who were just putting on their coats and leaving their table after an afternoon tea.

Susie and Carol both looked up as Rebecca came in and although they smiled it seemed to Rebecca that they were tight, uncertain smiles. She waited patiently by the door until the couple had paid and left along with their mountain of plastic shopping bags and the last customer at the counter had been served.

'Hello,' she said softly, walking towards her two friends.

They both nodded, Susie wiping her hands and staring down at the counter as Carol met Rebecca's eyes with a confused look.

'I know Daniel came in,' started Rebecca, wondering how she could explain to her friends why she had lied to them for so long. 'I had wanted to tell you myself.'

'Is it true?' asked Susie with wide eyes, 'Have you won the lottery?'

Carol nudged her friends arm and Rebecca smiled.

'Yes, it's true. I won 15.7 million pounds.'

Carol gasped and Susie squealed. '15.7 million!' she screamed. 'Crikey Rebecca, 15.7 million pounds!'

Rebecca carried on smiling, how could she not. After all she had won millions of pounds.

'We were a bit confused,' said Carol coming from behind the counter and giving Rebecca a hug. 'Daniel said he needed to know where you were staying in Leeds. He seemed so angry and desperate. Then he came back and told us you'd won the lottery and you were staying in Leeds for a bit. He said that's why you were leaving work. We didn't tell him you'd left weeks ago.'

Rebecca smile slipped and she slumped into the nearest chair. Carol leant over and flipped the shop sign to closed and Susie came round and sat next to Rebecca.

'The thing is I won almost 2 months ago.'

Susie's jaw dropped open.

'No!' she gasped.

Rebecca continued. 'I won the money, I bought a house in Leeds and I've been living there during the week.'

She could see the confusion in both their eyes.

'You see, when I won the money I didn't tell Daniel!'

There was a moment of stunned silence in the room.

'Oh my God!' yelled Susie, 'You did what?'

'I won millions of pounds, left work and moved to Leeds without telling my husband.'

Rebecca looked up at the shocked faces before her.

'I lied to you about Mum being ill and needing to visit her. I lied to you about leaving work because I needed to spend more time with her. I didn't want to, believe me I wanted to tell you both what had happened. But I couldn't. Not until I told Daniel and I just... didn't tell him.'

Carol was still silent but a smile had started to spread across Susie's face.

'Oh this is wonderful Rebecca. This is priceless! I take it you've left the miserable old bugger now?'

'No!' insisted Rebecca. 'Of course not!'

'But you didn't tell him about the money!'

Rebecca twisted her fingers together. Susie was right. It didn't look good.

'But not because I was going to leave him,' insisted Rebecca. 'It was just hard finding the right time and place.'

'Not really,' reasoned Susie. 'I mean if I won I'd just go home and say to my old man 'guess what, I've won the lottery'. It's pretty easy really.'

Rebecca saw Carol nudge Susie hard and Susie stopped talking.

'I'm so sorry about the lies Carol, I'm so sorry but I had to keep it a secret until Daniel found out.'

Rebecca looked beseechingly into her friend's eyes and Carol nodded reassuringly.

'It's okay Rebecca, don't worry. It sounds - complicated.'

Susie couldn't keep quiet for long and she leant towards Rebecca with her eyes shining.

'So when did he find out?' she asked curiously.

Rebecca sighed, thinking back to the moment when Daniel had come bursting through the door.

She told the two women the whole story accompanied by gasps of horror from Carol and excitement from Susie. They ignored the rattle of the locked shop door and as Rebecca paused for breath, Carol rescued a bottle of wine from the fridge and poured them all a glass.

'It's like something from Dynasty,' breathed Susie when Rebecca finally finished and they all looked at each other and burst into laughter.

'So you've really won all that money.'

It was a statement not a question and as Rebecca nodded they fell quiet and all gazed into the future.

'It must feel absolutely fantastic,' said Susie with a tinge of envy.

Rebecca didn't answer. It had felt fantastic. At first, when she was in Leeds and no-one else knew. Now it felt more complicated. Now it was a struggle.

'I should go,' said Rebecca standing up abruptly. She had suddenly remembered Daniel pacing their lounge spending over 4 million pounds with no consultation.

They all hugged and Carol assured Rebecca that there were no ill feelings regarding the lies and Susie couldn't stop the giggles that kept erupting at the thought of Daniel not having a clue about his wife's fortune.

'I'll see you both soon. There's a lot going on at the moment as you can imagine,' Carole nudged Susie before she made any comment. 'But I'll be in to see you both soon. After all, we need to go on a shopping spree to end all shopping sprees!' and Rebecca grinned from ear to ear blowing a kiss to them both and returning to her car to drive back to Daniel.

Chapter 15

Daniel was still in the living room when she returned. The tea had been replaced by a whisky and he still had his mobile clamped to his ear. Rebecca was exhausted. She wasn't going to cook tonight she decided, they would have a take away. They could afford it. She looked in the fridge and found half a bottle of white wine. She took out the biggest glass she could find and poured in most of the contents of the bottle. She couldn't bear to listen to Daniel, he sounded so thoroughly obnoxious as he banged on to the sales broker about how money was no object, how he expected that the staff would be delighted when they found out he would be taking White's back into number one position, how someone had to make up for the mistakes of Peter Thompson.

She slipped into the conservatory and curled up in her chair to watch the darkening skies and sip her wine.

Eventually he came to find her, rubbing his hands with glee.

'I think it will be in the bag pretty soon,' he gloated his face smug. 'We've had a valuation done and made an offer. Just have to wait for them to accept now.'

He threw himself in the chair opposite Rebecca sighing with happiness.

'What fantastic timing, they screw me over on the job and I win enough money to buy them out! Priceless.'

Rebecca had to work hard to remind Daniel that he hadn't won anything. She, on the other hand, had won 15.7 million.

'What's for tea?'

Rebecca stared at him.

'Oh, shall we have a take away then? By the way did you speak to the bank manager?'

Rebecca shrugged, sipping more wine. 'Not yet.'

'You need to do it straight away Rebecca! We can't have the money festering in that silly little bank account of yours. I might need to move quickly, next week the money needs to be available.'

Rebecca didn't answer.

'And besides, I can't use any of it when it's in your bank account. I mean how ridiculous is that? I've won over 15 million pounds and I can't spend any of it.'

How long did guilt last wondered Rebecca? How long would she feel so deeply and profoundly guilty?

'Shall we have a Chinese or a curry?' she asked and ignoring Daniel's glare of disapproval she went to find the menus.

'Monday Rebecca, speak to him on Monday. I need to have access to the money - I can't actually afford to pay for a curry for God's sake. I've just won all that money and I can't even afford a curry!'

'And will you bring back another bottle of wine,' asked Rebecca. 'A decent bottle not that house plonk, it tastes like vinegar.'

It was Monday and Rebecca woke with an overwhelming need to pack a bag and travel down to Leeds. Daniel was already up and she could hear him whistling as he wandered around downstairs. She laid in bed staring at the ceiling. He would be busy planning his new empire, there was no reason why she couldn't go to Leeds. She hadn't seen Gwen in days and when she had last visited there had been a great deal of general upset about Dotty leaving. That reminded Rebecca that she still hadn't really made any decision about Parklands. It was pretty much off the cards anyway if Daniel went ahead with his plans to buy out White's. It would leave them struggling to afford the lifestyle they were busy buying. But she could still go to Leeds. There was no reason why she couldn't go back to her house. Daniel knew everything now. He could phone her there. He could visit her there. In fact, she could stay in Leeds permanently now it was all in the open. It was up to Daniel when, or if, he came down to visit.

She slipped out of bed and pulled on her dressing gown. Daniel was just making a coffee.

'Slept in eh? All that money making you lazy!'

He laughed at his own joke and took out a cup for Rebecca. 'Don't forget you need to phone the bank manager this morning.'

Rebecca didn't know how she could possibly forget. He had reminded her every hour on the hour all over the weekend. When he had gone to put petrol in the car he bemoaned that he didn't have access to 'his' winnings. When he had gone for a paper and to get some milk from the local shop he reminded her that he couldn't just dip into a bank account holding millions like she could.

'I may have to go see him,' said Rebecca casually.

Daniel stiffened. 'Why would you need to do that?'

Rebecca raised her eyebrows and snorted derisively. 'Daniel! This is a bank account holding millions of pounds, do you think they'll take a phone call and just transfer it all into another account!'

Daniel flushed a little.

'I thought you had more business sense than that Daniel,' and she left the room her sense of guilt in overplay but her satisfaction levels riding rapidly.

She was halfway up the stairs, her step suddenly a lot lighter.

'I'll come with you'

She stopped, turning and looking at him standing at the foot of the staircase.

‘I’ll come with you, we can sort out the bank together.’

Rebecca gripped the coffee tightly.

‘No need.’

‘I know but we haven’t spent much time together lately and let’s face it, now we’ve got all the time in the world!

Showered and dressed, Rebecca refused to share a car with Daniel as they drove to her house. She might want to visit Gwen whilst they were there and Daniel wouldn’t want to join her, she reasoned. So they took two cars which gave Rebecca some time to think and as she pulled into the drive of her beloved house she had a proposal for Daniel.

‘Why don’t we stay here for a few days, a week, a few weeks?’ she asked as she unlocked the door and led him inside.

‘What for?’ asked Daniel grumpily. He had driven much faster than Rebecca and had been waiting in the drive a good 20 minutes.

‘Because it’s a beautiful house. Because we can afford it. Because... because why not?’

Daniel didn’t reply for a moment. The entrance hall of the house was particularly attractive. The walls curved around a wonderful wooden staircase that rose upwards against an exposed wall of rich honey stone. The polished floor stretched to either side, the multi paned windows on each side of the door flooded the area with light together with the slight scent of honeysuckle that grew above the front door. It was rich and welcoming.

‘I suppose,’ began Daniel reluctantly, ‘it could …’

‘Good,’ interrupted Rebecca briskly. ‘You had a good look round last week but if you want to know where anything is…’ and she left Daniel standing slightly bemused with the door still open to the elements as she strode off in the direction of the kitchen.

She had always known that eventually she would be sharing the house with Daniel. Maybe once he had spent some time in Beech Grange he would stop being so resistant to the idea of moving to Leeds. For now she was just thankful to be living in her home without any pretence.

Within minutes Daniel was ensconced in the study, his mobile to his ear and his chest puffed with importance. Rebecca took him in a cup of coffee.

'Just a minute,' he demanded to whoever was at the other end of the phone, 'Rebecca, when are we going to see the bank manager?'

Rebecca paused by the door and then turned to give Daniel an amused look. 'Pop in and see him? Ask him to move millions of pounds? I think you'll find we need to make an appointment Daniel,' and then quickly left the room before he could reply.

Standing in the kitchen with the fridge door open she decided to go to the supermarket and writing a quick note rather than risk another conversation with her husband, she slipped out of the house and back into her car.

Shopping bags full, Rebecca sat in the car park of Tesco for 10 minutes staring out across the nearby fields that were finally beginning to show signs of spring after the horrendously cold weather of the last few months.

Then starting the car she pulled out of the car park and in minutes was on the A61 heading into Leeds.

'I don't have an appointment,' she explained to the woman on reception, 'but I could really do with speaking to Mr Dickinson if he's available. My name is Rebecca Miles.'

The woman smiled and spoke softly into a phone before waving Rebecca onwards and within minutes she was sitting in Richard Dickinson's office with a fresh cup of coffee in her hand.

'Rebecca, good to see you.'

Strangely Rebecca felt he actually meant it and gave him a slightly strained smile.

'Richard, thank you so much for seeing me. It's a bit… delicate.' She cleared her throat nervously. 'I mean it's just that I need to, well I…'

'Is it about your husband and the transfer?' asked Richard Dickinson taking pity on her.

Rebecca looked down at the highly polished desk. 'Yes.'

'Okay,' he leant forward, steepling his fingers under his chin. 'Well, let me start by just reminding you of a few facts.'

Rebecca put her cup and saucer down on his desk. He had a very smooth and efficient tone that immediately relaxed her.

'The money is yours and yours entirely Rebecca. You have placed it in the account of your choice. Whether you move that money is your decision and yours entirely. If you choose to move the money into your joint bank account, then tell me and I'll do so immediately. If you feel that you would have more - control over the money by keeping it in your own account, then I have to say that is a decision that I would applaud.'

Rebecca twisted the fingers that lay in her lap. 'I don't want you to think that I don't want him to have any…'

Richard held up a hand to stop her. 'It's not up to anyone else to judge what you do with your money and believe me I only have you and your best interests at heart.'

He leant in a little closer. 'Rebecca you have a considerable amount of money, carry on being as careful as you are before sharing it out amongst anyone else including your husband.'

Rebecca stayed a little longer and they chatted about anything that had nothing to do with money and husbands before Rebecca thanked him and drove back to the house.

Daniel was pacing the floor in the living room when she returned, shooting into the hall as he heard the door slamming.

'Where the hell have you been?'

It was funny thought Rebecca she didn't remember Daniel caring at all where she was at any point over the last 5 years. In fact, Rebecca did remember spending most of her weekends alone as he went to play golf, entertain business prospects and generally ignore her. But there again, she thought, she didn't have over 13 million pounds in her bank account then.

She pointed to the shopping bags gathered in the hall.

'Shopping,' was her only reply as she gathered them together and made her way into the kitchen.

'You've been a long time,' he accused, not attempting to help carry any bags.

Rebecca shrugged.

'Did you go to meet Helen?'

Rebecca stared at him.

'I told you, I went to the supermarket. Why on earth would I call in and see Helen?'

'Well I don't know but you need to watch that one, especially now the word is out about the money. I never really trusted her.'

Rebecca looked at him in amazement. Never trusted Helen? For years Helen and Steve had been their closest friends. They'd spent most weekends together, had shared numerous bottles of wine, put the world to rights over the kitchen table, helped each other out with babysitting, garden tools, lifts to the airport. Daniel had always got on with Helen.

'What on earth are you talking about Daniel? Not trust Helen? Are you mad?'

Daniel turned away, his shoulder's stiff. 'Just saying, that's all. Did you phone the bank, make an appointment for us to see that useless bank manager?'

Rebecca paused in her stacking of the fridge.

'No,' she said casually. 'I actually called in on my way back from the shop.'

She didn't mention that the bank was nowhere near the shop, she didn't have to really. She was sure Daniel could work it out.

'You did what? I thought you said you need an appointment? What did he say, why the hell did you go without me?'

Rebecca looked into the fridge. It was still early but she pulled out a bottle of wine. She had a feeling she would need it.

'I just thought I would try on the off chance that he could see me.'

'Yes, well I suppose that was - good thinking. But you should have waited until I was with you. Anyway what did he say, when is he moving the money.'

The only sound in the kitchen was the gentle ripple of wine hitting the bottom of a glass.

'He's not.'

Rebecca took a deep drink. There was nothing like cold, cold Chardonnay.

'What? What do you mean he's not? I told you he was useless!'

Daniel snatched the bottle from Rebecca's hand and slopped some into another glass.

'You shouldn't have gone without me Rebecca. You don't have what it takes to handle this kind of money. You have no experience with high finance, with business.' He drained the glass and slopped in some more spilling some on the kitchen counter where Rebecca watch it pool against the side of the bottle.

He turned on her, waving his free hand in the air.

'You know nothing Bec, nothing about handling money and negotiation. You should have told me right at the beginning and then you wouldn't have ended up with a silly little car and a great, big house miles away from where we live.

The money would be in the right account where I could access it and not stuck in your savings account.'

His voice was getting louder and louder, his face an unpleasant shade of purple.

Rebecca briefly considered letting him believe that the bank had simply refused to let her access her money. He would phone and shout at them but they wouldn't transfer the money, Richard Dickinson had promised her that.

'Daniel,' he paused in his ranting, glaring at her as she turned to face him full on. 'Daniel, I told the bank not to transfer any money. Not for the moment.'

They stared at each other.

'You did what?'

Rebecca took a step towards him but he pushed a chair in her way, holding up his hand as though to ward her away.

'Daniel please don't think that I am trying to keep the money away from you. Of course I'm not.' She ignored the snort that erupted from his throat.

'It's just that, it's a lot of money and it needs ... planning and controlling. I don't want to move millions into another bank account without really thinking about whether we want to go ahead with this White's thing.'

'Planning and controlling!' yelled Daniel with such ferocity that Rebecca winced.

'What the hell would you know about planning and controlling, you stupid woman.'

'Daniel...'

'Shut up! Just shut up.' He threw his glass in the sink and Rebecca watched as it shattered, the glass flying across the sink and surface. What a shame to destroy such a lovely crystal glass. She would buy another so she still had a full set.

'And tell me please,' he started sarcastically, 'just what plans and control did you have in mind?'

Rebecca shook her head wearily.

'Daniel it's just that we need to take it slowly. Work out all the things that we need to do, the things we want to buy, how we want to live- before we just spend millions buying a company.'

'Like you thought carefully before buying this place?' demanded Daniel nastily. 'Did you plan and control the millions you wasted here. Spent without even telling me. Moving in WITHOUT EVEN TELLING ME!'

Rebecca closed her eyes. The guilt was back, as painful as ever but she had to be strong.

'I'm not saying we won't buy White's,' she said choosing her words carefully, 'I'm just saying that we need to do things a little more slowly. When I... when the moment is right of course I'll transfer the money and then we'll…'

But Daniel had gone, the kitchen door slamming behind him and his footsteps thundering down the hallway.

Rebecca started to clear up the broken glass. She could just give in, transfer the money, let him buy White's, change her own plans if necessary to make it affordable and just get on with life. Why didn't she?

She didn't see much of Daniel for the next few hours. The house was big enough to lose the two of them. She heard him in the study. She heard him in the small snug room listening to the TV. She heard him upstairs, in the guest room she'd shown him to the previous week. But she managed not to bump into him at all until early evening when he appeared in the doorway of the kitchen.

'The solicitor has put the offer to White's. They'll give us an answer within 72 hours,' he spoke coldly, stiffly. 'I hope that your - planning has been completed by then. When they accept I'll expect the money to be in the account to complete the sale Bec,' and he walked out, his back stiff and radiating disapproval and a few minutes later she heard his car wheels screeching down the drive.

Rebecca spent the rest of the evening with great waves of guilt and confusion flooding her every moment. She decided to transfer the money. She would phone Daniel and apologise, let him buy whatever he wanted so they could move on with the rest of their lives in some semblance of peace. Then she shook her head. No, she would stand firm and hang on a little longer. Make a decision about Parklands, think objectively about the benefits of buying White's. She would transfer the money when she felt they had made a sensible decision about any investment.

She wondered if Daniel would come back to the house and finally she gave up waiting and went to bed at 12.30. She heard Daniel come in shortly after and could tell from the staggering steps in the hallway that he was drunk. She waited until his bedroom door had slammed and then she slipped downstairs to lock the front door. She had also worried that he might come into her room but that seemed far from his mind at the moment and as Rebecca paused outside his bedroom door, she could hear the sounds of his snoring already filling the room before she went back to bed and tossed and turned the night away.

The next morning Rebecca dreaded getting out of bed but eventually she did to find the downstairs empty of Daniel's angry presence. It was almost like the weeks before Daniel arrival, when she'd had the house to herself and relaxing a little she made herself a coffee and a croissant and curled up on the raspberry settee as she looked out onto the garden and the fields beyond. She made the most of the peace and quiet but all too soon she heard footsteps in the hall and a hung over Daniel put his head round the kitchen door just as the phone rang.

'Helen,' said Rebecca as she watched Daniel's progress to the coffee machine. 'Lunch? Sorry, just hang on a minute Helen.'

'What?' she said to Daniel who was waving his arms around to catch her attention.

'Don't go with Helen,' he said as Rebecca stood with the phone in her hand her eyebrows raised questioningly.

'It's just that I thought, well it would be good, nice if we spent some time together. You know, try and get over all this… business.'

Rebecca stared at him for a moment and then raised the phone to her ear.

'Sorry about that Helen, no I can't make it today, I'm having lunch with Daniel. But I'll call you later shall I?' and she rang off.

She looked at Daniel slumped over the kitchen table, clutching his head.

'Are you sure you're up to going out?' she asked.

'Yes, yes,' he waved his hand in the direction of the coffee machine, 'I just need a coffee, maybe two, that's all.'

An hour later he was in the same position and Rebecca who had showered, dressed and cleaned the kitchen sat down opposite him.

'Daniel you're clearly not up to it. We'll go out another day shall we, I'll phone Helen and…'

'No!'

Rebecca raised her eyebrows and Daniel continued in a quieter tone. 'No, don't do that I'm sorry - I'll get ready now and we'll go have a meal somewhere nice, talk about all this ...mess in a calm adult fashion.'

'Okay,' she smiled. 'That sounds good.'

It sounded anything but to Rebecca and she sincerely wished she had arranged to meet Helen for lunch but the ever present guilt insisted that she at least give Daniel a chance. She was upstairs with her wardrobe doors open trying to decide whether she needed a jacket or something warmer when the door opened and Daniel walked in.

'We're going to have to go back to Darlington Bec, I only came down for a day remember, I can't keep wearing the same clothes much longer.'

He stopped short and stared over Rebecca's shoulder at the wardrobe full of clothes.

Rebecca closed her eyes briefly, waiting for the onslaught.

'Well, well,' he said softly, 'You have been busy, haven't you?'

Rebecca hung her head. After all what could she say? That she had been in Leeds shopping without a care in the world while he had been in Darlington none the wiser.

'I have been shopping,' she admitted meeting his gaze. 'I needed some clothes.' She saw his face darken and sighing she reached out and put a hand on his arm. 'I'm sorry Daniel, I'm so sorry. I know that I went ahead and started all this without you but I truly intended to tell you, it was just never.. I didn't….' her voice trailed away.

Daniel was silent, still staring in the wardrobe.

'Why don't we go into Leeds?' offered Rebecca tentatively. 'Let's start all over again. I…we've won a lot of money and you haven't really felt the benefit of any of it yet. Let's go shopping!'

Several hours later Daniel had finally stopped sulking and Rebecca's guilt was slightly easier as they arrived home. Daniel was still angry but not enough to stop him spending money. He had bought clothes, toiletries, shoes and a new watch the price of which made Rebecca wince. He had quietly seethed as Rebecca paid for all the purchases and had lectured her throughout the day as to how selfish and unfair she was being by keeping the money in her account. It was humiliating, he said, having to ask her to pay for every little thing he wanted. It was unrealistic that he couldn't go to the shop without her coming along with her credit card. He sulked in the coffee shop because he found he didn't have enough change in his pocket and had to ask Rebecca for more. By mid-afternoon Rebecca was beaten. She couldn't argue with him because deep down she knew he was right and she was being unfair. She was so determined to control the money in a way she hadn't been able to control anything for years.

'Okay,' she said quietly half way through one of Daniel's diatribes.

He stopped short. 'What?'

'I said Okay Daniel. You're quite right you need access to money.'

She turned away from the smug look on his face. 'So you're going to move it into our joint account?'

'No, I'll…'

'But you just said that I should have access.'

Rebecca took a deep breath. 'I'm not moving it all Daniel, I've told you. Not just yet. But,' she held up her hand to halt his interruption, 'I will move some over now. So you have access.'

She could see him fighting with his natural need to disagree with her. He wanted control of all the money and she had offered him a tiny taste. But it was better than nothing and he nodded his head stiffly.

'It's a start,' he grunted and then frog marched Rebecca to her bank. He wanted to go in with her but Rebecca refused point blank and made him wait downstairs in the lobby as she went into the inner sanctum.

'So how much do you want to transfer?' asked Richard Dickinson.

'I don't really know, just something so that Dan…so that we can use the main bank account.'

She twiddled her fingers together. 'Daniel is not working at White's at the moment so there will be no salary going in and that means the mortgage payment, the direct debits - things like that need to be met. Plus, Daniel does need to have access to some money,' she said almost challengingly.

Richard smiled reassuringly. 'It's probably a good idea Rebecca. Why don't you put in say - £250,000? It will cover your costs in the meantime, gives Daniel access to ready money and doesn't compromise any of your plans.'

So a transfer was made from Rebecca's account to the joint account and she went downstairs to tell Daniel that he now had access to a quarter of a million pounds.

The initial blaze of triumph on his face lasted approximately 30 seconds.

'Is that all?' he demanded.

Rebecca lifted up her chin. 'For now,' she said quietly.

Daniel glowered, 'Well I suppose it's better than nothing,' he grumbled and they went home.

Despite his displeasure at the amount, Rebecca could see the change in Daniel. He couldn't help the smile on his lips and she knew how he felt. The knowledge that the credit card in your hand could buy whatever you wanted was a heady feeling and she had denied that to him.

'Do you still want to go for something to eat?' she asked, smiling at him as they dumped the bags of shopping on the table.

'Actually,' said Daniel 'I'm starving!'

So they left the unpacking and went to a little pub not very far away. They had been before, many years ago but the prices had been beyond their reach so it had never become a regular haunt.

Daniel drank a whole bottle of very expensive wine to himself plus the glass of champagne he ordered when they arrived. Rebecca stuck to fresh orange after her champagne and watched as Daniel ate everything that was put in front of him and then ordered a brandy and a cigar.

'I'm afraid this is a no smoking establishment sir, I can bring a cigar but you will have to smoke it outside.'

Daniel scowled at the waiter. 'Well that's no bloody good is it. Oh bring it anyway and be quick with the brandy,' he ordered, waving the young man away with a dismissive flick of the hand.

Rebecca smiled apologetically at the waiter as he left. It wasn't the money that had turned Daniel's head, he was always rude to waiting staff and Rebecca usually left anywhere they went with her cheeks flushed with embarrassment.

So Daniel smoked the cigar on the way home, oblivious to Rebecca's indignant glares as she opened the window wide and waved her hand theatrically at the smoke wafting across the car.

But at least the atmosphere had subtly altered. With access to some of the money Daniel was significantly less unpleasant and the evening passed calmly with Daniel soon ensconced on the settee in the snug snoring loudly.

And although Rebecca felt guilty because she hadn't seen Gwen for the last few days she was exhausted from a day spent with Daniel and tiptoeing through the house so as not to wake him up, she decided that Parklands would have to wait until another day and she curled up and spent the evening with a book and a glass of wine.

Chapter 16

'You did what?' Rebecca asked, her hands still immersed in the bowl of soapy water.

'I bought a new car,' said Daniel defensively. 'After all, you bought a car and a house without consulting me. I just bought a car.'

Rebecca took out her hands and wiped them slowly. She supposed he was right. In fact he was right.

She tried to smile. 'Of course it's alright,' she shrugged, 'why shouldn't you? What is it?'

Daniel grinned and threw a pile of glossy brochures onto the kitchen table. 'A Mercedes!' he gloated. 'Top of the range.'

Rebecca really wasn't a car person but she wasn't at all surprised that Daniel had chosen a well-known and expensive car.

'And what's more,' he added, looking even more pleased with himself. 'I told them how you'd bought that silly little car because you didn't know what you were doing and I've arranged to part exchange it. They've got a 4x4 sitting in the courtyard, ex display, immaculate condition. They'll bring it round later in the week and take the Fiat away.'

Rebecca stared at him as he flicked through his brochures.

'My car?' she whispered, 'you've told them to take my car away?'

'Mm.' Daniel had lost interest in Rebecca and was happily reading about the engine performance of his new car.

'But I don't want to change my car.'

‘I wonder if I should have opted for the cabriolet,’ mused Daniel. ‘Thing is the weather is never good enough. You see people driving around in the freezing cold with the top down trying to look as though they’re enjoying themselves.’

‘Daniel, I don’t want to change my car.’

‘I think they just look ridiculous,’ decided Daniel. ‘No, I’ll stick with my choice.’

‘DANIEL!’

Daniel looked up frowning. ‘What’s wrong with you?’

‘You’ve arranged to change my car. **My** car Daniel. The car I told you I was happy with. I don’t want to change it.’

Daniel screwed up his face in irritation. ‘Don’t be ridiculous,’ he said dismissively. ‘It’s not the car you need.’

‘But it is the car I need. And it’s the car I want. You have no right to decide to change it.’

Daniel threw the brochures on the table in exasperation. ‘For God’s sake Bec, what do you know about cars? What do you know about anything really? You bought a totally unsuitable car because you tried to do it on your own. You’ve bought this bloody big house that we don’t need in a place where we don’t want to live because you tried to do it on your own. I think the lesson here Bec is that you shouldn’t do anything on your own. You don’t understand money and cars and houses and businesses. Leave it to me and we’ll be alright,’ and he stalked out of the kitchen with his brochures under his arm to read in peace in the study.

Rebecca stared at his retreating back. At moments like this the guilt faded to almost nothing and she had an overwhelming desire to buy another house far away and make sure that he never found out where she was.

She realised that she was biting her lip so hard that it was bleeding and she tried to relax her stiff body. She folded the tea towel up carefully and put it on the surface before walking to the study and opening the door.

'I'm going to Parklands,' she announced. 'I'll only be a couple of hours and Daniel,' he made a pretence of looking up although he continued to read the brochure. 'Please make sure that the order for the 4X4 is cancelled. I do not want one. I like my car and I will be keeping it,' and with that she smiled pleasantly and walked out, shutting the door quietly behind her.

At Parklands Rebecca couldn't believe the change in the atmosphere. Dotty was still there but she would be leaving in a few weeks and the difference in the old lady was quite shocking. Her lively spirit had vanished, the twinkle in her eyes gone and she sat slumped in her chair by the window oblivious to everyone and everything around her. Two more residents had been told they must leave, one of them sniffled quietly in the corner being consoled by her friends, the other had not come out of her room since the news broke. Mrs Wendover looked beyond exhausted although she still greeted Rebecca with a smile and arranged for a pot of tea to be brought to her and Gwen, who was sitting quietly in one of the large, sunny rooms looking out onto the roses.

'Hi Mum,' Rebecca kissed Gwen on the top of her head and was worried by how much weight Gwen seemed to have lost over the last few days.

Gwen smiled at her daughter but without the usual radiance about her as she patted Rebecca's arm.

'How are you my darling? How is everything?'

Rebecca hadn't seen Gwen since she broke the news about the lottery win and she tried to look happy and carefree.

'Oh it's great! We've moved into the house in Leeds, Daniel is coming to terms with the money and well… everything is ...great.'

But Gwen was a sharp old thing and she could see the dark shadows under Rebecca's eyes and the droop to her shoulders.

'And is Daniel pleased?' she asked.

'Of course he's pleased Mum. We've won millions, why wouldn't he be pleased?'

Gwen smiled and shrugged. 'Money doesn't make everyone happy,' she offered. 'It doesn't seem to be making you very happy at the moment.'

Rebecca hadn't told Gwen the full story, about how she had won but not shared the news with Daniel. About how she had won and kept that glorious feeling to herself for as long as she could, buying houses and cars and leading a totally separate life. But she confessed now. She told Gwen about the lies and the deceit and how Daniel had eventually found out and about the guilt that was now a part of her every waking moment.

Gwen listened to it all silently and when Rebecca finally ground to a halt, there was a long period when neither of them spoke.

'Well, well,' said Gwen finally. 'What a story! And what a sad state of affairs.'

'I know Mum I know!' Rebecca hung her head in shame. 'It was a terrible thing to do and it's not really surprising that Daniel is so angry.'

'Oh I don't mean that my darling,' Gwen shook her head. 'I meant how sad that the only time you were actually happy is when you were living another life that didn't involve Daniel.'

Rebecca stared at her.

'It's something to think about Rebecca. You moved away from Daniel, you lived your own life, albeit for a brief time and you were happy. Happier than I had seen you in such a long time.'

'What do you mean?' whispered Rebecca.

'Oh I think you know what I mean my darling. I know that you've stayed with Daniel for many reasons but none of them the right ones. I know that you're unhappy with him. And you were given a chance not many other people get, a little taste of life without him. And it worked for you Rebecca, it worked and the change in you showed the minute you walked through the door. Now you have to be brave. You have to sit and think, really, really think whether you are prepared to do something about it. Whether that little glimpse of life without Daniel is something that you want to keep.'

Rebecca looked out of the window. Her mother was telling her to leave her husband.

'It's not that straight forward Mum,' she said wearily.

'Isn't it? How much more straight forward do you want it to be? Do you want to stay with him? If the answer is no then you must want to leave him and for the first time in your life you can actually afford to do something about it.'

'But I couldn't leave him now. I mean, how would it look? I win money and walk out!'

'It looks exactly how it is darling. Like you wanted to end your marriage and did so when the timing was right. But that's a decision for you and you alone,' she added briskly. 'It's not my decision or even Daniel's decision Rebecca. Only yours.'

And they drank another pot of tea and the subject changed to Parklands and the unhappy chain of events.

When Rebecca was in the lobby searching in her bag for her keys, Brenda Wendover came out of her little office.

'Oh Rebecca can I have a quick word. Oh don't look so worried, Gwen is fine. She's a bit down at the moment, well most of them are but she's okay. I'm just trying to give everybody as much warning as possible. Parklands is definitely going to be sold. The owner has decided the falling profits are too much to take and he's put it on the market.'

Rebecca's hand flew to her throat in dismay. 'Oh no!'

It may have been something that she had foreseen could happen but faced with the reality it was still a shock. 'When?'

'Oh I don't think it will be a quick sale. These things tend to drag on a little until just the right buyer comes along. I just wanted you to be prepared that's all.'

Rebecca nodded, forced a smile and went out to her car. Parklands as they knew it, gone. Gwen would be devastated. She loved it there. Realistically she could now live with Rebecca, they could make a suite of rooms for her on the ground floor, bring in help. Rebecca would welcome the company but she knew deep in her heart it wouldn't suit Gwen. She liked her independence and at Parklands she felt she had just that. Oh she had a team of people on hand should she need them but she felt as though she was in control of her day. And she loved the company of people like Dotty who she had known for years. Gwen was unsteady on her feet, forgetful and frail but she was surrounded by people who knew how she felt and gave her the respect and dignity that she needed.

But where on earth would Rebecca find another place like Parklands? They were few and far between.

Unless of course she bought it. She could afford to buy Parklands. Gwen would be guaranteed a room for life in her beloved home. The likes of Dotty could be accommodated with some kind of scheme. But it was a lot of money and it wasn't really an investment. It would be just like buying another house, albeit a very large house occupied by lots of other people. But why shouldn't she buy it anyway? She could afford it. Or at least, she could afford it if Daniel forgot this crazy idea to buy White's.

Rebecca's head ached. She didn't know what to think or do next. The guilt she felt over deceiving Daniel was always present. But she could still see the flaw in his idea of buying a company because they wouldn't give him a promotion. And it was so much money. Together with Parklands and the trust fund she had set up for the children it would reduce the balance of her winnings considerably.

Her head aching, she arrived home to the sounds of furious shouting from the study. Dropping her bag in the hall, she tentatively peeped around the door. Daniel's face was almost purple with rage and his voice was choked with anger. As she arrived he ended the call, throwing the phone across the room where it hit the wall, the battery bursting out of the casing and sliding across the floor to stop at Rebecca's feet.

She picked it up waiting for Daniel to speak. He threw himself in the chair, banging his fist on the desk top.

'The bastard. The absolute bastard!'

Rebecca put the battery on the desk and picked up the 2 halves of the phone.

'What is it?' she asked softly.

'Bloody old man White. The fool, the bloody bastard. He won't sell. Said he doesn't feel ready to retire, hadn't thought of it until I mentioned it and he doesn't want to sell.'

The feeling of relief almost made Rebecca gasp out loud. No White's Packaging Corporation. That meant that she could realistically look at buying Parklands. It also meant that there was no reason for Daniel to stay in Darlington. No reason to have more arguments about the money. They could stay in Leeds, give life as the owners of several million a go. Maybe they could repair their failing relationship, get back to how things had been. It was the best news she had heard since confirming her win.

She tried not to look too pleased for Daniel's sake.

'Maybe it's for the best,' she offered, feeling like skipping around the room.

'The best?' Daniel looked at her as though she were speaking a strange language. 'For the best? How can it possibly be for the best! Anyway, I'm not giving up as easily as that. I want White's.'

Rebecca's hands stilled in their job of putting his phone back together.

'What do you mean? If Tom White has said he's not selling…'

Daniel snorted. 'Like I said Bec, what do you know about business? Everyone's got their price and he's no different.'

There was a chill beginning to creep around Rebecca's heart as she waited for him to finish.

'I've told them to put another million on the valuation price. That would be White's pay off. He's not going to say no to that, I guarantee it.'

He smiled. 'He'll say yes, he won't be able to help himself. You just wait. I'll have White's.'

Chapter 17

It was pouring with rain. It bounced off Rebecca's windscreen and blurred the oncoming traffic. She parked as close to the bank as she could but by the time she got there she was soaked to the skin.

A few minutes later she was sitting in Richard Dickinson's office with a cup of coffee in front of her and a towel to dry her hair.

She smiled apologetically at him. 'I'm so sorry Richard. I keep just turning up.'

Richard smiled and shrugged his shoulders. 'You are officially one of our best customers Rebecca. I can hardly complain!'

Rebecca smiled and then drew out two sets of papers, only mildly damp, from the recesses of her handbag.

'These are two - ventures that I'm thinking about at the moment. Would you mind looking at them and just giving me a general opinion?'

Richard leaned back in his chair, took a sip of coffee and started to read.

The night before, after Daniel had gone to bed, Rebecca had gone into the study and gathered together all the papers she could find about White's. The accounts, the valuation, every piece of paper Daniel had received she copied. She checked his emails and copied everything from the broker who had organised the offer, from Tom White himself, anything she could find. Then she had put Daniel's papers back and made a neat pile of the copies. Early that morning she had phoned Mrs Wendover and asked who was selling the nursing home. She had called into the estate agents before going to the bank telling them that she was very interested but wanted more details. They gave her the current accounts for Parklands, the estate agents blurb which put a very positive spin on the whole venture and the glossy brochure which couldn't quite hide the desperate state of repair needed in some areas and was honest enough to suggest that some investment was needed.

It was these two sets of documents that she handed to Richard Dickinson and then sat back, trying to be calm and not fidget as he looked through the papers.

Eventually he looked up at Rebecca sitting patiently in her chair.

'You're thinking of investing in both of these?'

Rebecca shook her head. 'I don't think I should invest in both, it's a lot of money, but both are - options at the moment.'

Richard paused, looking thoughtful. 'Well, strictly speaking you could afford both. It would leave your capital quite low bearing in mind the costs that both of these projects could incur with future investment. It would also mean that you would have to be very careful about spending any more of the actual capital.'

Rebecca nodded.

'But I agree with you, it would be unwise in the extreme to actually go ahead with both.'

He sighed, stretching out his long legs. 'What is it you want me to tell you Rebecca?'

Rebecca shrugged. 'I know I'm not very knowledgeable about these things but one is clearly a good opportunity to buy a recognised and profitable business and the other is - well a project I suppose. No real gain to be made, that sort of thing. Am I right?'

'You are,' agreed Richard. 'White's Packaging Solutions is a profitable business. It's well established and has grown significantly over the last few years. But the recent valuation was at the very top end to begin with. It was a starting point for negotiation downwards. Your husband - I take it this is his project?'

Rebecca nodded.

'Your husband has just added 1 million to the asking price. It's simply not worth it Rebecca.'

Rebecca felt the room spin a little. 'Why?'

'Because you will be paying far over the odds for a business that has just experienced a huge spike in its growth and is unlikely to see another of that size for some years. There is no possibility of improving your initial purchase without significant investment. In layman's terms Rebecca, you are unlikely to get your money back.'

It wasn't the news Rebecca had expected to hear. She sat in silence.

'Parklands on the other hand. Now that's a different story. The business has been starved of funds while its natural assets, the building and grounds have been underutilised. There are 6 rooms on the upper floor which have never been renovated, space for 6 extra guests. The reception rooms are large, very large which means space available for expansion out of just residential care; courses for example, day visits offered via the many organisations in the county that look after the elderly. Parklands have never looked at temporary care, holiday stays for those whose carers need to take a break. Investment is needed but the whole business is ripe for growth and in the right hands is an ideal investment.'

Rebecca stared at him. 'You mean Parklands is a good investment and White's - isn't?'

Richard laughed. 'I suppose that's exactly what I mean Rebecca. Of the two investments I would definitely advise Parklands.'

When Rebecca returned home Daniel was in quite a sunny mood. The level of determination he was showing to buy White's was quite stunning and Rebecca couldn't help but wonder what would happen if they came back and said no to his latest figure.

'Where have you been?' he demanded nursing a whisky as he looked past her into the torrential rain.

'Oh, I just had a few bits and pieces to sort out.'

Daniel grunted. He was not at all happy with this new relationship where Rebecca had things to do that she didn't feel the need to share with him. It had been the other way round for so long.

'By the way, Helen and Emma are coming round for lunch.'

His face darkened. 'What! What on earth for?'

'Because they're my friends and because they would like to see my - our new house and because I invited them,' answered Rebecca calmly.

'For God's sake! Phone them up and cancel. We'll go out for lunch instead. Save you cooking.'

Rebecca watched him stomp off in the direction of the snug and the whisky bottle. Was it her imagination or did Daniel seem quite determined to keep her away from her two old friends.

Putting her dripping brolly in the stand and hanging up her coat, Rebecca wandered into the kitchen, turned on the oven and started to unload bits and pieces from the fridge.

'Have you phoned them?'

Daniel was standing in the doorway.

'No I haven't Daniel. I don't want to cancel, as I said they're my friends and I want them to visit.'

'So you'd rather see your friends than go out to lunch with me!'

Rebecca stared at him for a moment and he had the grace to drop his gaze before adding huffily, 'Well I hope you don't expect me to make myself scarce, not in this weather. I'm staying for lunch as well, this is my house too don't forget.'

Rebecca chose not to point out that it was in fact none of the kind. The house was well and truly hers, but she kept her mouth closed and carried on preparing lunch, taking out three wine glasses just as the doorbell rang.

She was too late to answer it. Daniel was there, welcoming them as though it had been his idea all along. He had been upstairs and changed his shirt which he wore with a cravat that Rebecca had never seen before and stared at in disbelief.

'Helen! Emma! How good to see you both after so long. Come in come in!' and he took their brollies and wet coats and waved them in the direction of the kitchen.

'Bet you couldn't wait to have a peep at our new home eh?'

Rebecca glared at him and stepped forward to kiss her friends.

'Bloody Hell Bec - it's gorgeous!'

'It's a palace - and I thought my house was nice!'

Rebecca grinned. She couldn't lie or pretend. She loved her new house.

She let them admire the hall, ignoring Daniel's attempts to get them into the kitchen. She showed them the snug and the study, the living room, the formal dining room, the vast conservatory and then led them towards the room she loved the most, the huge kitchen with its large table inviting you to sit down, the raspberry settees positioned in front of the French doors giving a view of a rain soaked but enormous garden and the little garden room next door that invited you to curl up beside the fire.

Helen's mouth hung open and even Emma, who was far more accustomed to enjoying the finer things in life, looked shell shocked.

'Okay ladies, a little wine before we eat?' Rebecca glared at Daniel who ignored her, seemingly determined to play the jovial host. 'Rebecca pour your friends some wine. Sit down ladies, sit and admire. Come on Bec, get the wine poured.'

Once the glasses were full Daniel insisted that they raise them in a toast to their good fortune, their wonderful house, the Mercedes that would shortly be arriving on the drive. He poured scorn on Rebecca's little car and her lack of knowledge, told them that he had decided to buy White's because 'they needed someone to take the helm after losing their way' and generally monopolised the conversation while Rebecca silently took the quiche out of the oven, took the salad out of the fridge, cut the ciabatta into slices, laid out olives and relishes and a plate of new potatoes drenched in butter and drank her wine down in one go as she darted increasingly irate glances at the back of her husband's neck.

'So,' interrupted Helen desperately as Daniel paused for breath and Rebecca finally sat down. 'What's it like Becs? Winning all that money, what on earth does it feel like?'

'Oh you know Rebecca,' launched Daniel, 'she hasn't a clue about business and how to control money and the like. She's made some really bad decisions so far.'

He looked smugly around the table. 'You need a business head when you've got lots of money. I think we've decided that I'll be making the decisions from now on.'

The lunch was much shorter than it would otherwise have been. Having eaten, Rebecca took her friends into the toasty warm conservatory where they curled up with a cup of coffee and watched the rain lash against the windows. She suggested that Daniel may have work to do but he shook his head violently and said that's what he paid others to do now and he insisted on joining them, talking nonstop about his plans for White's, his general importance in the business and Rebecca's lack of knowledge about anything remotely resembling business.

In the end, taking pity on her friends anguished faces, Rebecca said that she supposed they had to get back to pick up the children and both Helen and Emma shot out of their seats with a grateful look in her direction and said indeed they had and how lovely it had been before they fled out into the rain.

Rebecca watched them drive away, holding the door open despite the rain hitting her in the face.

'Close the door Bec!' Daniel shouted at her as he walked past. 'I've got some work to do, I'll be in the study,' and minutes later Rebecca could hear the sound of his snores through the firmly shut door.

She spent the rest of the afternoon on one of her raspberry chairs staring outside.

She needed to tell Daniel that White's, even at the original price was a bad idea, that the new price was suicide.

She needed to tell him about Parklands, that not only that she wanted to buy the business but that it was a good investment.

She needed him to understand that she was not changing her car, that she was not leaving Leeds, that she would be giving her friends a donation from her winnings and that she had organised trust funds for the children.

There was so much she needed to tell him but instead she sat there watching the rain fall, her cheeks wet with tears.

Daniel was whistling again. He had done a lot of whistling lately and it was beginning to grate on Rebecca's already shredded nerves. She was used to starting her days with peace and tranquillity around her, not whistling. She glared at the back of his head and poured herself a coffee.

'You do realise that we'll have to go back to Darlington don't you.'

It was said so casually, so friendly, that for a moment Rebecca didn't really take in its full meaning.

'Do you still need some clothes?' she asked sitting at the table.

'No I mean when White's is mine. We'll need to go back, we need to live in Darlington.'

Rebecca almost dropped her cup.

'I mean I really don't know why you bought this house Bec. You must have had a funny turn after getting all that money but we need to be in Darlington, close to White's.'

He opened the paper as though the conversation was already over.

'No,' whispered Rebecca sliding her cup onto the table so it didn't fall from her shaking fingers. 'No.'

'Please let's not go down the 'I want to live back in Leeds' rubbish for God's sake. Get over yourself Bec, we moved to Darlington and that's where we live now. Did you think you could just make a decision to move with no discussion?'

'You did,' answered Rebecca quietly.

Daniel closed his paper throwing it onto the table. 'Oh don't start! We moved to Darlington because we had to. I had to keep my job so you could keep a roof over your head. I had to move to Darlington so that you could carry on living the good life. I had to work my fingers to the bone so that the children had clothes on their back. It's not quite the same as you winning millions and deciding to move to a different town without telling me!'

His face had its unattractive purple flush and he had jumped to his feet to stride around the kitchen in agitation.

'But that's the whole point Daniel, I have won millions and we can live wherever we want and you don't have to work your fingers to the bone and we don't have to live in Darlington.'

Rebecca's voice was rising and until she was almost shouting as she stood to face Daniel's angry eyes.

'Rubbish!' shouted Daniel. 'I'm about to buy a company in Darlington. Of course I need to live there. Are you totally stupid?'

'Don't buy it,' the words were out before Rebecca really had time to think but it was too late to take them back.

'Don't buy White's Daniel. It's too much of a financial strain and…'

'A financial strain! You've just won 15.7 million. Of course it's not a financial strain.'

He leaned in closely, a nasty twist to his mouth. 'Or is it just that you can't bear me to spend any of this money Bec. Is that it?'

'No! No of course not, it's just that…'

'Oh don't start giving me your half-baked explanations about waiting a while and planning and the other crap your bank manager is feeding you.'

'It's not half baked, you're not looking at the bigger picture Daniel.'

He threw back his head and gave a great shout of laughter although it held little amusement.

'The bigger picture? Don't make me laugh! What do you know about finance and planning?'

Rebecca sat back down suddenly exhausted.

'I know enough to understand that buying White's at this inflated price is a bad decision Daniel.'

'You know nothing! You know nothing about White's, you know nothing about business, you know nothing…'

'Which is why I took advice.'

He stopped his pacing.

'Advice? From who…oh don't tell me, the little bank manager? Tell me Bec, what exactly is going on between you and the bank manager? Is he hoping for a little finance of his own?'

His tone was hard, nasty and Rebecca shook her head wearily.

'I had to ask someone Daniel and he was the only one I could think of. I took the papers to him and…'

Daniel's hand shot out and grabbed hold of Rebecca's wrist.

'Papers. What papers?'

Rebecca tried to pull her arm away. 'The ones from the study, I took them to…'

'You've been in my study?'

His grip was tightening and Rebecca was pulling furiously trying to free herself.

'No Daniel,' she spat, 'Actually I went into my study and took papers about a company you want to buy with my money so that I could ask someone who knows what they're talking about whether it was actually a good investment.'

Suddenly her wrist was free but only because Daniel's hand was raised in the air, his fist clenched and his eyes burning with rage.

Rebecca jumped up and faced him square on.

'Do you really think I'm just going to hand over millions so that you can get revenge on someone who didn't give you promotion Daniel. Do you really think I'm that stupid?'

The fist came down but Rebecca was too quick. She stepped backwards knocking her chair over in his path and he stumbled against the table. The pause seemed to bring him back to his senses. He brought his arm down quickly by his side and for a moment Rebecca saw a fleeting look of shame cross his face. But it was only fleeting

'I knew you didn't want me to have any money,' he snarled. 'All these excuses, all these stupid excuses. That's why you didn't tell me in the first place, you were trying to hide it from me.'

The guilt arrived, a great wave of it.

'You're wrong Daniel. Believe me you're wrong,' Rebecca picked up the chair and sat back down. 'I don't begrudge you any of the money. But you're not looking at anything else we might want to do. You're not looking at any other arrangements we might want to make. You're so determined to buy White's you haven't thought about anything else.'

Daniel raised his eyebrows disdainfully.

'What the hell are you talking about. What other arrangements? What else do we need to do?'

'Well there's the children for one thing,' started Rebecca, 'trust funds and tuition fees and ...'

Another shout of disbelieving laughter. 'Trust funds. TRUST FUNDS! Are you barking mad. You won some money Bec, you didn't win a bloody title. What the hell do you want with a trust fund?'

'We need to look after our children, we can take the pressure away from them by paying off the student loans and I don't want them to have to wait until we die to get some money Daniel.'

'Why not? Everybody else has to. Nobody gave me a trust fund when I was their age.'

'That's because your parents didn't have the money,' snapped Rebecca. 'If they'd had 15 million pounds in the bank I'm sure they would have sent some your way!'

Daniel leaned on the table, pushing his face close to Rebecca's own. 'Are you seriously telling me that you're planning on giving the kids a pile of our money? You don't want me to buy White's because you want to give it all to a couple of kids who should be out there earning their own living?'

Rebecca refused to flinch. 'Yes I am.'

'And how much exactly were you planning on putting in this trust fund?'

'£250,00 each when they reach 25 and a further million each when they reach 30.'

For a moment Rebecca truly believed that Daniel was going to have a heart attack. His face changed from puce to grey in a second and he gasped standing upright and stumbling slightly.

'Are you mad?' he whispered, staring at her as though he had never seen her before. Are you completely mad?'

'No. I…'

'ARE YOU FUCKING MENTAL!'

Rebecca did flinch this time.

'You want to give two perfectly healthy children millions of pounds. What for. So they can sit on their arses and never do a stroke of work again? Are you totally stupid?'

Rebecca stared at him, her eyes almost as angry as his own.

'Can you hear yourself?' she asked in disbelief. 'These are your children we're talking about. And you want me to do what? Sit in a huge house while they hold down two jobs each to pay their way through university because you won't help them? Go on exotic holidays while they sit in a grungy bed sit wondering if they can afford to eat? Listen to what you're saying Daniel.'

He took a step back. 'They won't starve,' he grumbled. 'But they need to learn the value of money, they need to work, they need to earn their own money.'

'They will work, that's why I'm not giving it all to them straight away. But I will not sit by and watch my children struggle when I could help them. I simply won't do it Daniel.'

'Well they don't need that much,' he compromised. 'Change it to something less.'

'No.'

Rebecca couldn't remember the last time she had used that word so often in one day.

'I will not.'

His face darkened again. 'They are not having all that money.'

Rebecca stood up and set off towards the door, pausing as she opened it and turning round to meet Daniel's eyes.

'I think there is one thing you really need to remember in this whole debate Daniel. This is my money and I will decide what to do with it. The children get their trust funds,' she turned to leave then paused.

'Oh, and just in case I haven't made myself abundantly clear, I am not selling the house and I am not going back to Darlington,' and she left, closing the door firmly behind her.

Chapter 18

He let her go although not for long and the arguments raged on for most of the day - in the hallway, on the staircase, in every room of the house until almost hoarse with shouting Daniel finally stormed out, slamming the door so hard Rebecca expected it to fly off its hinges.

Sitting in the kitchen she poured herself a glass of wine and with a slightly shaking hand took a long drink. It was so long since she had stood up to Daniel, really stood up to him about anything remotely important that the effort had drained her. The phone rang and with a sigh Rebecca reached over and picked it up.

'Hello?'

'Rebecca it's me. Look, I had to phone and apologise, Emma and I are both so sorry.'

'Helen! Sorry about what exactly?'

'Lunch - leaving so early- not so much leaving as running!'

Rebecca couldn't help the smile. 'It's not a problem Helen, I would have gone with you if I could! I really don't know what got into Daniel, it was like having a stalker.'

She laughed, expecting to hear Helen join in but there was just silence at the other end of the phone. She waited.

'Why do you put up with it Bec? I mean after everything he's done, why on earth do you put up with it? You've got money now, why not leave him?'

It seemed the popular topic of conversation at the moment, whether Rebecca should leave her grumpy husband.

'I can't leave him just because I've suddenly got some money Helen. It just wouldn't be right,' explained Rebecca gently. 'I know he's a pain but it's a shock to the system suddenly having millions in your bank account. He's still getting used to it.'

'I know Bec…. but on top of everything else! It's not just the money, it's.... oh look I know we're not supposed to talk about it but ever since he dragged you off to Darlington I've been waiting for you to phone up and tell me you've left him! Money or no money, you've put up with so much no-one would blame you if you just walked away.'

When Daniel had broken the news that they were moving to Darlington, Rebecca had been so upset she literally couldn't speak about it without crying. In the one kind moment that Daniel had shown during the whole episode, he had asked her friends to let them just get on with it and not discuss all the details with Rebecca. So despite the fact that Helen's eyes were almost as red as Rebecca's own, she had put a brave face on things, never analysing the move, never discussing it in any detail with Rebecca right up until the day the removal truck pulled out of the village and Rebecca stood shaking at the passenger door of Daniel's car. Helen had thrown her arms around her friend's neck and pressed her lips to her ear. 'I'm here for you Bec, if you want to come back I'm here for you,' she had whispered and then Rebecca had climbed in the car waving goodbye numbly to Helen and Emma.

She had hated Darlington with a passion but it wasn't a reason why you left your husband.

She sighed. 'Helen, he's my husband and I can't just abandon him because I've had some good luck. He deserves more than that.'

Helen snorted. 'You're too good for him Rebecca, always were!'

Rebecca paused for a moment. 'You see Helen, I didn't tell him.'

'What?' Helen's puzzled voice echoed down the line. 'Didn't tell him what?'

'I didn't tell him I'd won. I won weeks ago. I came to Leeds and collected the money but I just - didn't tell him. I bought the house and I didn't tell him. I bought a car and I didn't tell him.'

She paused, waiting for Helen to comment but there was nothing but a stunned silence on the other end of the line.

'He finally found out because he - well he thought I was having an affair because I was spending so much time in Leeds. He followed me and found me at the house so I had to tell him everything.'

Still nothing from Helen.

'Helen, are you still there?'

'He thought you were having an affair?' whispered Helen. 'He followed you to Leeds because he thought you were having an affair? Oh my God!'

Rebecca sighed. 'Well it's the only conclusion he could come up with because I was spending so much time in Leeds. But the point is that he had to follow me here before I actually told him the news.'

'Why didn't you tell him?'

Such a simple question, if only there was a simple answer.

'Oh Helen, I don't know.' Rebecca passed a hand wearily over her face. She had been trying to answer this for so long. 'I really don't know. It was just so much fun, being in charge, deciding things for myself. It all got out of hand and then

Daniel had trouble at work, well he didn't think it was trouble he thought it was good news and he needed it - the good news I mean. I suppose I thought it might help him, change him back somehow into the Daniel he used to be but it didn't and it actually made things worse and then I still couldn't tell him….'

She realised that she was rambling and stopped with a sigh. 'I don't know why I didn't tell him Helen but the fact is that I didn't. He had to find out and of course now there will always be that unspoken question, was I ever going to tell him? He will always wonder.'

'It's a bit hard to keep 15 million pounds a secret Bec. Especially from your husband!'

Rebecca laughed half-heartedly. 'I know, and I truly was going to break the news but I didn't and now he doesn't really trust me. I feel so guilty Helen. It was an unforgivable thing to do.'

Helen's voice was quiet, serious. 'Are you staying with him out of guilt Bec? Because that really isn't a good basis for a marriage you know.'

Rebecca took her time answering. Was she staying purely out of guilt? It was undeniable that the happiest she had been in the last 5 years were the weeks she had spent in Leeds without Daniel.

'I don't know,' she whispered, 'I really don't know Helen.'

And in an echo of the words whispered in her ear 5 years earlier Helen whispered back. 'I'm here for you Bec, if you want to come back, I'm here for you.'

The conversation continued in a somewhat strained way for a few more minutes and eventually Helen said goodbye and Rebecca replaced the phone softly in its cradle.

She was disturbed and restless. Winning money shouldn't be so stressful she thought, she should be happy, full of plans and dreams. She had been exactly that until Daniel had become part of the experience. How quickly it had all turned so sour.

She had no idea where Daniel was. She didn't actually care. She was exhausted from the constant battles and she was determined that for once she would get a say in the path their futures followed. But it was such hard work. Maybe she would be better just giving him half of the money. Let him make his own decisions. But with what she had already spent on the house, what she planned to give the children and friends, the money she wanted to put to one side for Gwen, if she divided what was left it wouldn't be enough for Daniel. It had been her decision to buy the house, maybe she should sell it and insist that the children were taken care of and then they split the rest. But what about Parklands, what about saving the home Gwen had lived in for so many years?

Rebecca groaned and put her head in her hands. Why did it have to be so complicated she thought? Why did she have to win the money in the first place.

The next morning Daniel stayed out of her way. Rebecca was tense and on edge, waiting for the argument to begin to rage once more. But Daniel stayed in the study, she even thought that she could hear him whistling again. She felt certain he was expecting her to submit. She had for the last 5 years. Daniel would decide and Rebecca would accept. But this time it was different. Rebecca had the upper hand and she needed to hang onto it as hard as she could. No submission this time.

By lunch time she was in desperate need of some fresh air and without saying anything to Daniel, she slipped out and into her car, heading aimlessly in the direction of Leeds. She didn't need to shop, she had done enough shopping for a lifetime over the last few weeks. Sarah had lectures, and although she briefly considered visiting Gwen she really didn't want to go to Parklands. It would remind her of the difficulties it faced, of the difficulties Rebecca faced. She could help the residents of Parklands, she could help Gwen. She just needed to make a decision.

Aimlessly she parked the car and wandered around the shops. She was in the home ware department of Debenhams, looking with listless eyes at the new summer stock spread across the shelves. It would soon be warm enough to sit in the garden. The little courtyard just outside the kitchen doors would be a perfect place to sit with a coffee in the afternoon or a croissant in the morning. She needed to organise the gardener, get the trees and shrubs tidied up. She had meant to phone the telephone number the previous owners had left her and ask their old gardener to come back. She had meant to look for some lovely wooden garden furniture and perhaps a great big gas BBQ like you the ones you saw on American TV, the sort that could cater for the masses. She had meant to do lots of things really but it was amazing how time consuming her daily battles with Daniel were and how totally exhausted they left her.

She was admiring some fresh picnic ware that would look lovely on the table in the courtyard when she looked up to find a young woman staring at her.

It took a moment to place her but then the frown on Rebecca's face cleared and she smiled.

'Holly! I'm sorry, I didn't recognise you for a minute.'

She stepped away from the display table and walked towards the young woman who was holding the hand of a small girl with masses of blonde curly hair whilst pushing a buggy containing a sleeping baby.

Rebecca stopped uncertainly, if she hadn't known better she would say that Holly was staring at her with nothing less than hatred in her eyes. They had only met a few times. She was the pretty young wife of Joshua who worked at White's and had been given the job Daniel thought of as his own. They had sat next to each other at the last Christmas party and had spent the evening having a wonderful conversation about children, as Holly stroked the huge bump where her second child still lay.

'I heard that you'd had a little boy.' Rebecca leaned forward to peer into the buggy and Holly drew back as though she had been stung.

Rebecca stared at her in confusion. 'I'm sorry,' she offered, 'I was just looking… he's beautiful.'

Holly nodded tightly and turned the buggy around and set off in the direction of the door.

Rebecca watched her with her mouth hanging open. What on earth had happened? She watched Holly walk stiffly around the displays and then just as she reached the door, Rebecca couldn't take any more.

'Holly!' she shouted and sprinted after her. Holly didn't stop and Rebecca had to move quickly to reach her before she disappeared into the crowds. 'Holly!' She grabbed at the young woman's arm only to let go immediately as Holly turned swung around, undiluted hatred filling her face.

'Oh my God Holly, what on earth has happened?'

'Happened?' spat Holly. 'You can really stand there and ask what's happened?'

Rebecca looked around. Holly's voice was far from quiet and their exchange was bringing a few interested glances. But she didn't care.

'Holly,' she pressed gently, 'please tell me what's wrong.'

Holly took a step back, her eyes flicking over Rebecca with a look of such contempt that Rebecca couldn't help but blush.

'You look well Rebecca. Winning millions obviously suits you.'

Rebecca frowned shaking her head. 'You're angry because I've won some money?' she asked disbelievingly.

'No!' ground out Holly. 'I couldn't care less what you do or how much you've won. But what right do you have to ruin other people's lives with your money? What gives you the right to destroy my life just because you've had some luck?'

Rebecca's confusion was written all over her face and for a moment Holly's features softened a little.

'You don't know do you?'

'Know what?'

'You have no idea what Daniel has done.'

At the mention of her husband's name Rebecca's heart dropped like a stone. She had no idea what Holly was about to say but she had a feeling that she was not going to like it.

'Please tell me,' she demanded.

Holly closed her eyes for a brief moment and sighed as she opened them to meet Rebecca's anxious gaze.

'He's been into White's. He went in to tell them all that he was buying the place.'

Rebecca nodded. It wasn't a secret and although she would have waited until the deal had completed, she could see that wasn't Daniel's style. He would have wanted them all to know what he was planning.

'He went around the room,' continued Holly, her face hardening again. 'He gave each person a slip of paper. They all had one word written on them. Going. Staying.'

Rebecca's heart was hammering, her face was flushed and her breath ragged.

'Then he laughed and told them that when he was in charge that's what would be happening to them. Josh's paper said going. Daniel told him that he was the person he would enjoy sacking the most.'

Rebecca felt sick, she clutched her throat as she felt the bile rise.

'Josh had to come home and tell me that he was losing his job because Daniel Miles had won the lottery. Daniel was so angry with Josh for being promoted that he was going to buy the business just so he could sack Josh.'

Rebecca was shaking. She truly wondered if her legs would carry on supporting her. She was shaking with shame and humiliation.

'Is that fair?' demanded Holly. 'Is it fair that you winning can leave us with nothing?'

Rebecca couldn't speak. There were tears rolling down her face as she shook her head.

'I'm so sorry,' she whispered, her lips hardly able to form the words. 'I'm so, so sorry,' and turning her back she fled.

She ran through the people, knocking them out of her way, uncaring of the shouts and the swearing. She pushed her way up the stairs towards the car park hardly able to breathe for the sobs that racked her body and when she finally made it to her car, she sat inside for almost an hour crying as though her heart would break.

How could he do such a wicked thing she wondered. The Daniel she knew would never be so outrageously callous, so cruel. What on earth had happened to him over the last few years to make him so hard, so uncaring? Was it her? Had she made the monster he was now?

Eventually the tears stopped and she calmed down enough to think about driving the car. Her hands still trembled, but only slightly and the tears had left her eyes enough for her to see ahead.

She thought about driving home and realised that she didn't want to go back to her beautiful house. She had been so happy there for those few short weeks before Daniel joined her. But now it was just another battle ground. The joy of her home had disappeared within hours of Daniel arriving.

Briefly she considered booking into Quebecs. But that was more avoidance and that was exactly what had brought her to this situation in the first place. If she had been honest with Daniel right from the beginning, maybe things would never have come to this.

Sighing she left the car park and turned the little Fiat in the direction of home. The relief she felt when she drove up the long drive to find it empty was immense. She didn't know where Daniel was but at least he wasn't here. She parked the car and walked into the lovely, light filled hallway, her eyes falling on the curt note left on the hall table.

GOLF, it said. BACK TOMORROW.

Her heart lifted. A whole night without him, a night in her beautiful home without another argument. She hung up her coat and turned on the coffee machine as her mobile started to ring.

'Rebecca?'

It was Richard Dickinson from the bank.

Rebecca smiled. 'Hello Richard.'

'Er, I just thought that you should know Rebecca. Not that there's anything to worry about, we obviously don't take any instruction from anyone but you, but you should know…'

Rebecca frowned, it was unlike Richard not to come straight to the point.

'What is it Richard?' she asked gently.

'Daniel,' he said bluntly.

Rebecca's heart sank. 'What has he done?'

'He came to the bank today, insisted on seeing me and demanded that the trust funds for the children be stopped. He said that you'd had second thoughts and wanted to allocate much lower amounts. He wanted a new fund drawing up.'

There was a long silence.

'Rebecca, I just thought that you should know. If that's what you want then of course it's no problem but you know that I won't take any instruction about this account from anyone but yourself.'

Another long silence.

'Rebecca?'

'Sorry, yes I'm here.'

Rebecca was numb with shock, struggling to speak.

'Thank you for letting me know Richard. The trust…'

'Is exactly as we agreed the last time you were in the office. In fact, the paper work is now ready to sign...whenever you're ready.'

Rebecca nodded then realised he couldn't see her.

'Thank you. I'll speak to you soon,' and she hung up, placing the phone carefully on the kitchen table. Sitting down with a bump she stared at her hands. They hadn't stopped shaking fully since her meeting with Holly earlier and now they trembled again as she wound her fingers together and rested them on the table.

How could Daniel do that to his own children? How could he put White's and his need for revenge above everybody and everything else? To be so cruel to White's employees, people he had worked alongside for years. To try and stop his children benefiting from their good fortune.

Rebecca shook her head, the tears falling silently down her cheeks. It was time to stop this. It was time to take control.

Chapter 19

Rebecca slept fitfully. She had spent the evening on the settee in the living room. The weather was much warmer but Rebecca found herself shivering as she curled up, pulling the red throw over her for comfort as much as anything else. She hadn't had the heart to choose a DVD or read a book. The TV stayed off and she spent the evening simply staring out of the window at the ever darkening garden until it was pitch black, both outside and in. Eventually she went upstairs to bed and lay there staring at the ceiling, her heart so heavy that it was a pain deep in her chest.

Morning came and a subdued Rebecca showered and dressed, going through all the motions mechanically, her mind whirling with the previous day's knowledge. She ate her breakfast without tasting anything and cleared away before getting into her car and setting off to Parklands.

The difference in the atmosphere was unbelievable. There was an overwhelming air of despair that hit Rebecca as soon as she entered the lobby. The soft sound of sobs echoed down the hall with muted voices coming from the TV lounge.

Rebecca walked through, looking around for Gwen. She was sitting near the French window, clutching Dotty's hand in her own as they both gazed out of the window in silence.

'Hi Mum.'

Leaning down Rebecca kissed her mother's paper thin cheek and noticed again that Gwen had definitely lost some badly needed weight.

'Dotty,' she said gently stroking the back of the elderly woman's hand. There was no response. There had been little response from Dotty since she'd been told she had to leave Parklands.

Rebecca sat down next to the two women, smiling reassuringly at them.

'Don't worry Mum,' she said with a grin. 'It's all going to be alright.'

Gwen for once had no bright smile to give back.

'I don't think so Rebecca my darling, I really don't think so,'

Rebecca patted the back of her hand. 'I've told you, don't worry. Now, where is Mrs Wendover?'

She looked around, the TV lounge was quite full, many of the residents gathering together in their grief. Ruby was sitting next to one weeping woman, patting her gently on her back and talking to her in a soothing voice. Then Rebecca noticed Mrs Wendover, crossing the lobby and heading into her office.

'I'll be back in a minute Mum,' she whispered and shot off.

'Sorry Brenda. Can I have a minute?'

Brenda Wendover looked nothing short of exhausted. And desperate.

'Oh Rebecca. I'm really busy, will it wait my dear?'

Rebecca smiled as she took Mrs Wendover's arm. 'I'm afraid it won't Brenda,' she said firmly. 'It won't wait a minute longer.'

Moving decisively, she steered the slightly shocked woman into her office and settled her behind her desk.

'What on earth…'

'Mrs Wendover, Brenda, do you have any brandy?'

Brenda's eyes came out on stalks. 'Brandy?'

'Yes. Brandy.'

The two women stared at each other for a few minutes until shaking her head in confusion Brenda waved in the direction of the filing cabinet.

'Top drawer. Often need it when I'm breaking bad news. Good for shock.'

Rebecca grinned. 'I know,' she said as she rescued the bottle and two glasses from the shelf above. She poured two generous measures and put one of the glasses in front of Brenda.

'Rebecca I…'

'Brenda, I have some very good news for you,' she smiled at the wary woman.

'You have? Oh, have you found somewhere for Gwen already?'

'I certainly have,' Rebecca couldn't help the grin that split her face. 'An absolutely fantastic place, a lovely setting, great location, beautiful old building, wonderful staff.'

Was it her imagination or did Brenda look a teeny bit put out. 'Well that's wonderful Rebecca, I'm so pleased for Gwen.'

'Don't you want to know where it is?' teased Rebecca.

'Well I'm sure wherever it is, such a wonderful place will be good for Gwen and …'

Rebecca reached over and touched Brenda's arm gently.

'Brenda, it's here. This is the fantastic place with the wonderful caring staff where I want Gwen to stay.'

Brenda stared at her as though she had lost her mind and then glanced down at the brandy sitting untouched in front of them both.

'Rebecca,' she started gently,' I thought that you understood…'

'You remember that I won the lottery?'

'What? Well yes but I…'

'Brenda, I am going to buy Parklands. I'm going to buy the house and the business. I want you to stay on as manager, I won't be getting involved. Well that's not quite true. My bank manager has suggested all sorts of ways that we could improve the business and….' she stopped.

That could all wait. Brenda was staring at her in disbelief.

'I'm buying Parklands Brenda. Lock stock and barrel. Nobody needs to leave. Dotty and the others, we'll do them a special deal, set up some sort of sponsorship scheme. They can all stay Brenda. As can you. Will you stay? Will you stay and run Parklands for me?'

She could see the tears start to gather in the corners of Brenda Wendover's eyes.

'Are you serious Rebecca? Are you really going to buy Parklands?'

Rebecca nodded. She grinned from ear to ear and nodded.

'Oh!' Brenda's hand flew to her chest and for a moment Rebecca thought that it had all been too much for her. 'Oh, I can't believe it. That's just too perfect. I can't…'

Rebecca pushed the brandy in her direction.

'It's going to happen Brenda. Parklands is saved and we are going to keep it just as it always has been - with a few improvements of course.'

With a shaking hand Brenda picked up the brandy glass and raised it in Rebecca's direction. Rebecca picked up her own and gently they clinked glasses.

'I don't know what to say Rebecca…I don't...' She put the glass back down on the desk and clasped her hands together to stop the shaking.

'Thank you, Rebecca. Thank you from the bottom of my heart.'

Through the tears she was smiling and Rebecca smiled back.

'I can't say how much this means to me…'

Rebecca stopped her. 'It means a lot to both of us Brenda,' and they raised their glasses and drank.

The following few hours were like every Christmas and birthday rolled into one. At first no-one could quite grasp the news. The staff repeatedly asked if it was true, the elderly residents looked on in confusion. Then slowly the reality hit them all and one by one they started cheering and whooping and laughing and crying. Many residents phoned relatives to let them know the good news and many of the relatives wanted to speak to Rebecca or Brenda to make sure that there was no mistake. Some residents wanted to say thank you. Several just sat quietly in their favourite chair, smiling happily as they let the relief wash over them. Bottles of champagne left over from Christmas were found and glasses were filled and passed around. Giggles filled the air and the atmosphere was so profoundly different from earlier that day that it felt to Rebecca as though she had walked into a different place. Gwen sat quietly in her chair, a look of such pride and happiness on her face that Rebecca felt the tears start again. Something of a celebrity, Gwen was getting praise from all sides for having raised such a wonderful daughter and albeit indirectly, being the answer to their prayers. She smiled and let the thanks wash over her as she sat and watched her daughter. Eventually they had a quiet few minutes together.

'That was a very good thing you did my darling,' whispered Gwen.

Rebecca took her mother's hand in her own. 'I just needed to know you would be okay, you would be happy.'

'You did all this, spent all this money for me?'

Rebecca thought for a moment. 'Not just for you,' she said truthfully, 'some of it was for me as well,' and they smiled at each other as they sat holding hands and watching the celebrations unfold.

Hours later, with a slight headache from the glass of champagne and the sheer emotion of the morning, Rebecca made her excuses and left. She'd had another conversation with Brenda Wendover, assuring her that there was no mistake, Rebecca was indeed buying Parklands. She outlined the possibilities suggested by Richard, the expansion of the very top floor, the idea of using the large grand reception rooms to hold courses for the elderly, escape days for those generally housebound, Parklands as a weekend or weekly retreat - all manner of improvements and diversions that would make Parklands into a profitable retirement home once more. There was so much to discuss and once Brenda was convinced this was going to happen she joined in with huge enthusiasm, mentioning several ideas she had thought of herself until eventually, giggling like school girls, they arranged a formal meeting for a few days' time when they would sit down and decide the future of Parklands.

Rebecca drove away, smiling and waving cheerfully from the window of her car. But as she pulled out of the driveway the smile disappeared from her face altogether and her heart began to hammer with dread. She drove a little way down the road, pulling in at a layby where she turned off the engine and sat very still, staring out at the countryside to one side of her and the fast moving traffic to the other.

It had to be done. She had come to that conclusion in the early hours of the morning as she tossed and turned and fought her natural inclination to run for the hills and leave all these decisions behind her. It had to be done.

She took out her mobile phone and searched for the number she had entered before she left the house that morning.

'Hello?'

Rebecca paused. She really did not want to do this.

'H-hello. Is that Mr White. Tom White?'

'Yes. Who is this?'

Another long pause. It wasn't too late. She could put the phone down and go home, lock the door and pretend none of this had ever happened.

'Hello Mr White. It's Rebecca. Rebecca Miles.'

Tom White was surprised, Rebecca could hear it in his voice. He was also a gentleman, a kind, elderly man who had never been anything but courteous to her whenever their paths had crossed.

'Rebecca! Well this is a surprise my dear, I haven't spoken to you in a long, long time. What can I do for you today?'

Rebecca's hand was shaking and the phone was banging against her cheek. She gripped it more tightly, trying to steady her nerves.

'I needed to speak to you Mr White…'

'Oh please Rebecca, call me Tom.'

Always so polite, always so nice.

'I needed to speak to you Tom. It's about White's and the offer Daniel has made.'

There was silence.

'You see, I don't know whether you realise this but I won the lottery and Daniel is using the money to buy White's.'

There was a small chuckle from Tom White.

'Daniel has offered to buy White's Rebecca. He hasn't bought it yet.'

'Oh I know, I'm sorry, I didn't mean…'

This was so hard. Rebecca closed her eyes. She could hear the drone of the traffic on the road and the soft sound of Tom's breath on the phone. What did she mean?

'I understand that he increased the offer a few days ago, offered you one million pounds personally if you would agree to sell the business?'

'Yes. He did.'

'What I needed to say Mr Wh… Tom, is that Daniel is unable to stand by the offer he made to buy White's. You see, the money he was planning on using is actually mine and I have decided not to … support him in the take-over.'

Tom White said nothing.

Rebecca gripped the phone tightly again. She had to do this. It was hard but she had to do this.

'The thing is Mr White I don't think it would be a good idea if Daniel took over White's. I don't think it would be good for White's or the people who work there. I think Daniel is - confused at the moment and he has made a decision based on…'

Hatred, revenge, spitefulness.

'…based on the wrong reasons. The money is mine and I will not let him have what he needs to buy White's. I understand that he has offered you a substantial amount of money if you say yes and accept his offer but I'm phoning to ask you to say no to this deal. And if you do, I will still pay you the million he promised you.'

Chapter 20

Rebecca stayed in the lay-by for almost an hour after the conversation with Tom White. She could, of course, just tell Daniel that he couldn't have the money. That she wouldn't let him have the millions he wanted. That she had bought Parklands and his dream of owning White's was over. But her guilt at the way she had handled the whole business of winning made her want to at least try to save Daniel's feelings. If he just thought Tom White had said no then it ended the matter. Even Daniel would understand that he couldn't just keep offering more and more money. He had tried to buy White's and his offer had been turned down. It was time to forget about White's and move on. Whether they could move on together, Rebecca was beginning to seriously doubt but at least he wouldn't have the humiliation of knowing that Rebecca was behind the refusal. He wouldn't ever know that she was so disturbed by his mean spirited nature, his need for revenge and the humiliation of others, that she had bribed Tom White to say no to Daniel's latest offer.

Eventually, her head aching with thinking, she pulled out onto the road and headed for home. She wondered if Daniel would be back yet and offered a silent prayer that he was still busy on the golf course. The thought of doing battle with him again left her drained and exhausted. Pulling into the drive, her heart sank as she caught sight of another vehicle parked a little way into the entrance, only to realise that it wasn't Daniel's car. Passing by and pulling her own car up to the front door, Rebecca climbed out and walked back down the drive.

'Can I help you?' she asked pleasantly as a young man who had been examining a clipboard jumped out and approached her.

'Hello, you must be Mrs Miles?'

'Yes, and you are...?'

'I'm from Homefront Mrs Miles, I'm just here to put up the sign. I won't be two minutes then I'll be out of your hair.'

He smiled, turned away from Rebecca and walked to the back of the estate car.

'Homefront?' said Rebecca frowning. 'I'm sorry, I don't recognise the name.'

'Homefront,' echoed the young man opening the boot and letting it swing upwards. 'The company who are selling your house Mrs Miles.'

He laughed as though it wasn't at all unusual to come across home owners who had forgotten the name of their estate agents and reaching into the back of the car, he pulled out a large sign that had emblazoned across the centre FOR SALE.

For a moment Rebecca thought she might actually pass out. The ground suddenly rushed upwards to meet her and the young man's voice drifted off into the distance. She put a steadying hand onto the bonnet of his car and watched as he pulled out a pole.

'Mr Miles has instructed that the sign needs to go right at the end of the drive, where people will see it clearly.'

He grabbed a hammer.

'Lovely house,' he sighed looking enviously down the drive. 'A lot of people who have this kind of house, you know - an exclusive kind of a house - they don't always bother with a sign but Mr Miles explained that you were after a quick sale and wanted a sign up pronto.'

He hitched the sign and the pole under one arm and swung the hammer in his other hand. 'Won't take long Mrs Miles,' he said cheerfully. 'I just need to...'

'Put it back.'

Rebecca's voice was so calm, so reasonable, so low that the young man paused and looked at her questioningly. 'Sorry, didn't quite catch that...'

'I said,' this time Rebecca's voice was like a roll of thunder rushing across the fields to break over their heads, 'PUT IT BACK!'

The young man stiffened. The hammer stopped swinging and he stood very still, staring at the woman before him who suddenly seemed to have grown several inches.

'Er, you mean you've changed your mind about the sign?'

Rebecca was walking towards him and instinctively he took a step back. She looked wild, her head held high and her eyes blazing.

'I have not changed my mind about anything. This house is not for sale. This is my house and I do not wish to sell it. Mr Miles has nothing to do with this house, he doesn't decide whether it will be sold, whether it will have a board, he has no say in this house.'

Rebecca was now nose to nose with the young man who took another hasty step backwards.

'This is MY house. MY HOUSE. MINE. Do I make myself clear?'

The young mad nodded. Rebecca stared at the sign still in his hand and he threw it hastily back into the car.

'Now will you please take this sign back and tell Homeland or Homefront or whatever it was called, that this house belongs to Rebecca Miles and is not for sale.'

'Yes ... yes I'll do that right now.'

He threw the pole and the hammer in the boot, wincing as he heard the hammer hit one of the signs.

'You tell them not to come here again with a sign, a pole or anything to do with the sale of my house.'

'I'll go now and...'

'Tell them this is MY HOUSE.'

'I will, I'll tell them Mrs Miles, I'll tell them right now,' and with a nervous backwards glance he leaped back into the car under the watchful eye of Rebecca and reversed down the driveway to screech out onto the road and disappear.

Rebecca stood motionless, watching the car until it disappeared from view and long after, just in case the young man decided to sneak back and put the sign up anyway. Eventually she turned in the direction of the house, her house, and walked up the drive to the front door. She put her hand on the shiny brass handle and then her legs gave way and a huge sob ripped through her body as she sank onto the stone step and sobbed and sobbed. She just couldn't stop, almost howling as she gave vent to all the frustrations of the last few days. The sobs kept coming, shaking her body as she sat on the cold stone. In the distance she could hear a phone ringing and wondered if she should go inside and answer it but it stopped. It rang again, much nearer and for a moment Rebecca looked around in confusion until she realised that it was the mobile ringing in her bag. Reaching in blindly she pulled it out and pressed the answer button, still unable to stop the sobs that were now erupting involuntarily.

'Rebecca - is that you? Bec? What's the matter? Oh my God, Rebecca what's happened?'

Rebecca tried to answer Helen but she was beyond speech and shaking her head frantically, all she could manage were a few garbled words mixed with yet more huge body wrenching sobs.

'I'm on my way over Bec. I'm only a few minutes away. I'll be there soon...'

And the phone went dead.

Numbly Rebecca stayed on the step. Her bottom was cold, her back ached, her head throbbed and her face was soaked with tears. She took a couple of deep breaths and managed to control her crying. A couple more and the sobs subsided. A couple more and she felt some control coming back. Just a few more she thought, just a few more breaths and it would be okay. She wiped her face with an old tissue she found in the depths of her pocket and sighed deeply.

A car screeched into the driveway and raced in Rebecca's direction to skid to a halt. Helen flung open the door and almost fell out in her haste.

'Rebecca! Oh Rebecca what's happened. Are you all right?'

She was crouched by her friend scanning her body, looking for signs of injury, trauma.

'What happened?'

Rebecca took another deep breath. 'There was a man here,' she started.

'What!' Helen jumped upright. 'Did he hurt you? Oh my God shall we call the police, has he gone?'

Rebecca put out a calming hand, although it was shaking badly.

'No! I don't mean that. He had come from Home something.'

Another sob shuddered through her body and Helen sank back down onto the step to put a comforting arm around her shoulders.

'He had come to sell the house, well he wasn't selling it, Home something was. He had the sign.' Rebecca shook her head. 'Daniel had gone to an estate agent and told them to sell the house, my house. Someone was here to put up a sign when I got back.'

Helen grimaced. 'Well let's face it Rebecca, it's not the first time he's sold a house from under you and made you move.'

Rebecca gave a snort. She hadn't thought of it like that. 'I suppose you're right. It's just this time he did tell me he thought we should sell and I said no. He just ignored me and decided to go ahead anyway.'

'Again, typical Daniel behaviour Bec!'

Rebecca stopped talking. Her head was thumping and her chaotic thoughts were whirling through her brain.

'I know,' she eventually whispered. 'I just thought this time....'

Helen hugged her friend. 'Come on, let's get you inside,' and she pulled Rebecca to her feet, helped her find her keys and steered her in the direction of the kitchen.

As Rebecca sank onto the raspberry settee Helen looked doubtfully at the coffee machine then put the kettle on and dug out a jar of instant coffee from the back of the cupboard, leaving Rebecca with her thoughts as she busied herself making them both a drink.

Rebecca stared down the garden. The courtyard was full of herbs now, little pots set by the kitchen door where she could reach out and pick what she needed. She had wandered around the garden and found the perfect spot for a small vegetable patch, she even had a collection of seed packets in one of the kitchen drawers ready to get planting. She loved this house and she was staying put.

'Bec?'

She turned to find her friend holding out a steaming cup and she took it gratefully, warming her hands on it. She was shivering even though the kitchen was warm.

'You know,' began Helen carefully as she sank next to Rebecca on the settee and put her own cup down on the floor. 'You do know that it's time to call it a day Rebecca?'

Rebecca looked at her questioningly.

'With Daniel. It's time to stop this farce and just admit that it's over.'

For once Rebecca didn't jump to his defence. The guilt that usually washed over her had finally disappeared.

'This can't go on sweetheart. He's taken advantage of you, treated you dreadfully and you've gone along with it all. I have to admit, I've spent the last five years waiting for the phone to ring and you to tell me you'd finally seen the light and left.'

Still Rebecca didn't join in. She knew that Helen was right. Oh not about moving to Darlington, she could actually appreciate that Daniel had been trying to do the right thing. He had handled it badly but he had been trying to improve things for his family and she hadn't supported him at all. They were both to blame for the dull, unhappy lives they had led in Darlington. But the Daniel he had become was not the Daniel she had married and his actions over the last few weeks had left her despising him.

'I should have told him about the money,' she said wearily.

'Oh come on Rebecca. This isn't about the money! This is about everything that happened before the money.'

Helen sighed in exasperation. 'Look, I know we're not supposed to talk about this Bec but it's been five years, let's face some home truths. Most men I know, every man I know who's had an affair, he…. well he's expected to pay! He's expected to be sorry, show some remorse, offer his soul if only he can be forgiven. If his wife wants him to change his job, he does. If his wife wants him to move to Outer Mongolia, then he does. If he wants to save the marriage he pulls out all the stops and does whatever she says.'

Rebecca stared at her.

'Daniel is the only man I know who had an affair and then dictated the terms for the reconciliation. He behaved appallingly, selling the house and dragging you up to Darlington. To take you away from all your friends at the time you needed them most! And quite why you agreed to it all I'll never know,' she grumbled taking a sip of her coffee. 'But then to let him walk all over you for the last five years! Bec, come on, where's your fight, where's your anger?'

She took her friends hand, not noticing the glazed expression on her face.

'We are aware that he tries to stop you keeping in contact with us you know. You wouldn't believe the number of phone calls we make to be told you're out with your friends, you don't have time to see us. He did actually come out with it shortly after you'd left – he suggested it would be better for you if we didn't contact you at all, ever again. Let you forget it all and move on.'

She snorted, shaking her head in anger. 'As if we'd fall for that one! No, we just kept phoning until we spoke to you. We were convinced one day you'd wake up and walk out. We've gone along with this charade for five years now Bec but enough is enough. Leave him!'

Rebecca carefully pulled her hand away from Helen's grip and stared at her friend's flushed face.

'What on earth are you talking about?'

Helen stared back.

'What?'

'What are you talking about?' Rebecca's voice was louder, a frown digging into her forehead. 'What are you trying to say! What affair, who had an affair?'

Helen looked completely confused.

'I don't understand Bec....'

'What affair are you talking about,' Rebecca's voice was still rising, tremulous. 'Daniel didn't have an affair!'

They stared at each other for a second, Rebecca bewildered, confused as she watched the panic that chased across Helen's face, the doubt, the horror.

'Bec - you knew. Daniel said you knew...'

She broke off her hand flying to her mouth.

'Knew what? What on earth are you saying! We moved to Darlington because Daniel was worried about his job. We moved because, God help him, however badly he handled it all he was trying to keep us all safe. There was no affair.'

Rebecca stood up, putting her cup shakily down on the table.

'There was no affair! Who on earth told you that there was?'

Helen shook her head. Tears were sliding down her cheek. 'Oh God Bec, I'm so sorry, I'm so, so sorry.' She bit her lip, her face crumpling as she reached out to take her friend's hand again. 'Bec please believe me we thought you knew, he said you knew. He told us we mustn't mention it, that you didn't want to talk about it.'

Images were flashing before Rebecca's eyes. Daniel standing before her telling her gruffly that he had broken the news of the move to Helen and Emma, that he had told them how very upset Rebecca was feeling, that she didn't want to talk about it. Images of her two friends wrapping their arms around her whispering to her that when she was ready to talk they would be there, ready to listen. She remembered the last day, Helen whispering in her ear 'I'm here for you Bec, if you want to come back I'm here for you.'

Rebecca looked down at her fingers held in Helen's grip. Bewildered she looked up at her friend.

'He had an affair?'

Helen was crying now. In a daze Rebecca grabbed a tissue and passed it to Helen before sinking back down onto the settee.

'Daniel had an affair?'

Helen nodded. 'Bec, I'm sorry, I really thought you knew, I thought you didn't want to talk about it, I thought ...'

Rebecca waved her apologies away with a shaking hand.

'But I didn't know, I never did so perhaps it's time we did talk about it.'

And she turned to her friend to find out the real reason why the Miles family had left Leeds five years earlier.

Half an hour later Rebecca stood up and retrieved a bottle of wine from the fridge. She looked at it and then put it back and took out a bottle of brandy from the cupboard, pouring two large tumblers.

Daniel had been having an affair and he had been caught red handed. He should have been playing golf. Rebecca actually remembered the weekend quite well. Daniel had returned from his short break in a foul mood. He had stormed around the house complaining about everything from the children's shoes in the hallway to the basket of laundry on the kitchen table.

Rebecca had teased him a little about giving up golf if it made him this unhappy but for once he wouldn't be coaxed out of his temper and in the end she had shrugged and ignored him. He had gone to work in the same mood and for the rest of the week it was like walking on eggshells whenever he came home. Even the children had pulled faces behind his back and asked Mum what was wrong with their grump of a Dad. Rebecca tried to talk to him but he didn't want to discuss anything, he seemed unbelievably angry and almost frightened. By the end of the week Rebecca had started to feel quite worried. There was a desperation in his face that she had never seen before and although he hardly spoke a civil word to her all week she was starting to feel quite anxious that there was something seriously wrong with him. The following weekend Daniel had dropped his bombshell. He needed to move to keep his job. He had put the house on the market, no board that time. They had already had an offer and they were moving to Darlington. A huge part of Rebecca's acquiescence following the move had been because of the struggle she had seen in Daniel during that week. She had seen how frightened he had been, how desperate, and deep down she accepted that what he had done, he had done for his family however much it had hurt him. So she had moved to Darlington despite her urge to say no. She had co-existed with Daniel over the last five years, hating every minute of it and allowed her life to deteriorate partly because she had believed that Daniel too had made a sacrifice and that his changed personality was his way of coping with the disappointment of the whole move.

It was funny mused Rebecca, how an unspoken belief could dictate a person's life. She believed she had known how Daniel was feeling. She believed that she understood his emotions, his despair, his reasons. They had never discussed anything, Daniel wouldn't discuss anything. But Rebecca had justified his actions and lived her life for the last five years holding onto that belief. And now it turned out that she had been wrong, very, very wrong.

Daniel hadn't played golf that weekend. He had actually been conducting an affair with Christine Myland who lived in the same village but several streets away. Friends of a sort, Rebecca and Christine regularly encountered each other as they carried on with village life. They would smile and chat if they bumped into one another. They would often meet at parties. If an event was organised they were more than likely both there, albeit sitting at opposite sides of the room.

But Daniel, it would seem, had developed a much closer relationship with Christine over a period of a few months and many of his golf weekends had actually been cancelled in favour of a night away with Christine, who had supposedly started a pottery course which involved weekend seminars and courses attended all over the country. But their little romance had been unexpectedly outed one Saturday. The country house hotel they had chosen for their weekend away had also been chosen by Sheila and David Goodfellow who also lived in the village and who were celebrating 40 years of married bliss. They had come across Daniel and Christine in a pose that left nothing to the imagination and Daniel had known that it was only a matter of time before the affair was posted on the village notice board.

It had actually taken several days. Mr and Mrs Goodfellow were not the gossipy, malicious sort and they did not run back to the village and burst into the local pub to broadcast their news. But feeling uncomfortable with the discovery, Sheila Goodfellow had asked one of her friends if she felt that the news should be made available to Rebecca. The friend, again not the gossipy, malicious type, hadn't really been sure if it was their place to enlighten Rebecca and as a result the two of them had consulted another friend, slightly more gossipy, although fortunately for Daniel still not malicious. It was the second friend's opinion that if the roles were reversed and it was her husband spending weekends at a hotel with another woman, she would most certainly want to know about it and the decision was made that somehow Rebecca should be told.

Meanwhile Daniel, desperate to avoid the fallout if at all possible, had put the house on the market the very next day after the unfortunate meeting with the Goodfellows, had received an early if not exciting offer and agreed to sell. By the time the news of the affair had reached the shocked ears of Helen and Emma, who had been selected by Sheila Goodfellow as the ones who should break the news to Rebecca, Daniel had news of his own. Yes, he admitted to them in an unexpected visit to Helen's house one evening, he had been having an affair. Rebecca was absolutely distraught, as could be imagined and they had decided that the best course of action would be if they moved away. Quickly. Rebecca really didn't want to discuss the nasty business with anyone, she was far too upset and he hoped that they would support their friend by doing what she wanted, refraining from discussing the sordid details of exactly why they were moving. And when Rebecca emerged from her house with red rimmed eyes the next day, it confirmed everyone's belief that Daniel's affair had become public and poor Rebecca Miles was too upset to discuss it with anyone including her two best friends. So the village patted her on the hand and murmured condolences and she smiled through teary eyes and thought how nice everyone was being and how much she would miss this lovely little village and finally they left Leeds for Darlington with Rebecca none the wiser about her husband's indiscretion and with her friends firmly convinced that sooner or later she would come to her senses and turn against Daniel and the new life he was offering her in payment for his affair.

Rebecca sighed and looked into her friend's anxious face.

'We just thought you knew Bec. You were so upset the morning after Daniel told us about it all, we believed that you knew. And you just kept saying you didn't want to talk about it so we thought he was right and once you'd moved and you were far away from Christine and the village you would feel better about life.'

They sat in silence, sipping their brandies, Helen still looking distraught but Rebecca was strangely calm.

'What happened to her?' she asked in an offhand way.

'Who? Oh Christine?'

Rebecca nodded.

'Moved away. Not long after actually. She was the talk of the village, everyone was quite angry with her. Not that she seemed particularly bothered. Sheila had a show down with her in the post office one day and Christine just shrugged and said it took two and he'd been quite willing.... oh,' Helen stopped. 'Sorry. That's sounds....'

Rebecca shrugged. 'Don't worry Helen, it really can't get any worse.'

Helen continued. 'Anyway, a few months later it came out that she had run off with her pottery teacher! Yes, she was actually having lessons. Her husband sold up and moved in with the women he used to do a car share with and last I heard they were expecting a baby and Christine was living in York with the pottery teacher and his mother.'

'I wonder if they ever saw each other again,' mused Rebecca.

Helen shrugged. 'I don't really know. I got the impression that Daniel couldn't wait to leave the village and her behind. I really don't think he would carry on seeing her,' Helen paused, twisting her fingers together. 'I do think that he regretted it Bec. He was so eager to get you out of the village and away from everyone, I really think he didn't want you to know and was - protecting you.'

It was the nicest thing that Helen had said about Daniel in five years and Rebecca squeezed her hand.

'Thank you Helen, but I think we both know that Daniel was probably just protecting himself.'

Chapter 21

It was getting dark outside and wherever he was, Daniel would no doubt be home soon.

'Do you want me to stay?' offered Helen. 'Shall I phone Emma and get her round as well? We can throw him out for you if you want.'

Rebecca smiled and hugged her friend. 'No. I'll be all right, truly. I need to talk to Daniel alone.'

'Okay,' said Helen doubtfully. 'But if there's any suggestion of trouble give me a ring and I'll get...'

Rebecca laughed. 'There won't be any trouble Helen. Really, I'm okay.'

So Helen left, driving away much more slowly than she had driven in and Rebecca waved her off then closed the front door, turned the heating up and the outside garden lights on and waited for Daniel to come home.

The door slamming made Rebecca jump. She had drifted off, still curled up on the raspberry settee. Sitting upright she waited.

The door opened and in came Daniel. There was defiance written all over his face. He would know by now that Rebecca had been told of his visit to the bank. He would know by the absence of the board that she knew all about his plans to sell the house.

'Hello Daniel.'

He looked around the kitchen, his eyes resting on the brandy bottle and two empty glasses.

'Helen came round,' offered Rebecca.

'So I see,' he sneered.

Rebecca stayed on the settee and watched him look at the bottle again before grabbing a clean glass and pouring himself a hefty measure. He'd obviously been drinking already, Rebecca could smell the beer from where she was sitting.

'How was your golf?' she asked politely.

He stared at her suspiciously. 'Okay.'

'You were gone a long time.'

'I didn't think I had to account for every minute I spent away from the house. I had some time to myself, much like you've been doing recently,' Daniel snapped, draining the glass and pouring another.

Rebecca didn't answer. And neither did she experience the wave of guilt that usually came over her when Daniel mentioned her less than perfect behaviour over the last few months.

'The bank phoned me.'

He stiffened, turning his back towards her and staring at the rapidly emptying brandy bottle.

'They told me about your visit.'

He shrugged. 'I told you it was too much money to give them Bec. I made it quite clear that we were going to have to scale down this 'trust' of yours.'

'And I had a visit from Homeland ...'

'Homefront.' he interrupted.

'I had a visit from someone with a for sale sign that they wanted to put on my drive.'

'For God's sake Bec! Don't you listen to anything I say? I made it quite clear that the house would need to be sold. The trust was too much and the house was too much. We need to be in Darlington. We need to move back there. You shouldn't have bought this house and I told you that we were going to sell it and I told you...'

'Shut up.'

'And I told you...what?'

'I said shut up Daniel.'

He glared at her, his face turning dark and his mouth opening to respond.

'You need to shut up and listen Daniel. Because I made it quite clear to you that the trust fund would go ahead and I would not be selling this house. No!' she added as Daniel started to splutter in anger. 'Like I said Daniel, you really need to shut up and listen for a change. I have decided that I will give a substantial amount of the money I won to my children. I bought this house because I wanted it. And neither of those things are going to change Daniel. Neither of them.'

'Who the bloody hell do you think you are to start telling me what we will and won't do!' his voice erupted with rage. 'I will decide where we live, I will decide what we'll spend the money on! We've already established that you know nothing about business and finance. You know nothing Rebecca. Nothing!' he spat. 'You've made a complete mess of everything you've tried to do since you won that money and it's time you let me take over. When I buy...'

'No.'

So calm, so quiet and yet the single word filled the kitchen.

'No Daniel. You do not decide what we are doing with this money. This is my money and I will decide.'

'Yours! Oh now we're getting to the truth. That was the problem all along wasn't it Bec? All that rubbish about not being able to find the right time and place to tell me. You weren't worried about timing. You didn't want me to know. Well, let me tell you,' he walked towards her, his face contorted with anger. 'What's yours is mine and that money is as much mine as yours. I have an absolute right to it and tomorrow we stop messing about and you will move it all over into our joint account. Tomorrow Bec, no more excuses, no more pathetic excuses, tomorrow it goes into our account.'

'No.'

Again. Quiet, controlled, steady. Five years of 'no's coming to the fore.

'No Daniel,' she was beginning to enjoy the sound of that word on her tongue. 'No that is not what is going to happen. You're mistaken you see. The money is totally mine. You have no right or say over it what so ever.'

She watched him gape at her in disbelief, whether at the news or her defiance she didn't know but she could see him gearing up for another onslaught.

'Don't you want to know why Helen came round?'

He stopped. 'What?'

'You always ask what we've talked about whenever I see Helen or Emma. You always want to know what we've discussed, where we went, what we did. You want every detail of every conversation we have. So don't you want to know what we talked about this time Daniel?'

She saw the fear flash across his face, the sudden uncertainty in his gaze.

He shrugged his shoulders. 'I imagine it was nothing but idle, malicious gossip. That's all those two are any good for. Spreading trouble.'

Rebecca smiled.

'Fortunately for you Daniel both of them are far from that.'

He was standing, quite rigid, by the kitchen work surface, his hands fiddling with the glass he still held, his gaze anywhere but on Rebecca.

She let the silence linger, spreading over the kitchen and the two people standing there.

'She told me about your affair Daniel.'

His head shot up, he met her eyes as he threw the glass onto the black surface.

'Affair! What the hell are you talking about? Affair! I told you that woman is poison. She ...'

'She told me about the affair Daniel. She told me about Christine and the hotel. About explaining to Helen and Emma that I didn't want to talk about it. About pretending that we were going to Darlington because I wanted to escape the village.'

Daniel stared at her, his mouth opening but nothing coming out.

'She told me the whole sordid story Daniel. Every last detail. And I told her my story. The story of how I left the house I loved in a place where I was happy, uprooted my children from their school and their friends and moved to Darlington because I actually admired the fact that you would make such a sacrifice for the family. I told her how I had spent five miserable years up there, hating myself for hating my life. Hating you for making me live that life but never prepared to walk away because you had made the same sacrifice, you had been prepared to do whatever you needed to support your family.'

The fight suddenly disappeared from him. Before Rebecca's eyes he shrank. All the bluff and bluster went. The anger, the hate. It all went and in a matter of seconds he looked almost identical to the Daniel she had loved for so many years. He had put on weight, his face was a little jowly, his hair slightly thinning. But the posture he had adopted for the last five years, the thorny nature, it all disappeared before her eyes. His eyes were full of sorrow, His face full of regret and he shook his head as he half held out his hand before letting it drop to his side.

'I'm sorry Rebecca,' he said simply. 'I'm so sorry.'

The phone rang. It echoed around the house but neither of them moved.

'You'd better answer it. It may be important,' instructed Rebecca and sank back down on her settee.

Daniel didn't move for a moment then slowly, sluggishly he reached out for the phone.

'Hello? Oh hello Tom.'

Rebecca could hear the muted voice of Tom White speaking on the phone. She watched Daniel's face as he nodded silently, his eyes closed.

'Okay, I see. Yes, that's fine. Thanks,' and he hung up the phone.

Neither spoke for a moment as Daniel pulled out one of the kitchen chairs and sat down heavily.

'That was Tom White,' he said unnecessarily. 'He's not taking my offer. Doesn't want to sell.'

When Rebecca had pleaded with Tom White to say no, offered him a million pounds to say no, she had it in mind that she could still save her marriage.

'I asked him to turn the offer down.'

Daniel frowned. 'What?'

'I asked him to say no. Actually I didn't ask him, I told him to say no because I wouldn't fund the sale.'

Rebecca didn't mention the bribe she was prepared to offer. There could be too much honesty.

It was a sign of the change in Daniel that he just smiled ruefully. 'I see.'

'And in case you're wondering, I spoke to him before I found out about your affair.'

Daniel nodded.

‘I saw Holly in Leeds. She told me about your visit and your threats to the staff. I couldn't stand by and let you do that Daniel. It wasn't right.’

His face was flushed with shame and he squeezed his eyes shut.

‘I think it was probably the right decision Bec.’

Rebecca nodded. She watched him slide back in the chair, looking up at the ceiling. She remembered him sitting like that in the house in Leeds. He would stare at the ceiling for inspiration then wink at her and admit he hadn't got a clue.

‘Why did you do it Daniel?’

He winced. ‘For all the wrong reasons Bec darling.’

He used to call her darling all the time. He would come home and wrap his arms round her and kiss her and tell her about his day. It was always long and tedious and grumbly but Rebecca had never minded. She would carry on cooking, making all the right noises in all the right places and when he finished he would kiss her again and tell her that it was a good job he had his best friend to come home to at the end of the day.

‘How could you destroy everything that we had?’ she whispered. ‘How could you Daniel?’

Daniel's face was full of sadness. ‘I was worried about work, I just didn't seem to be making the same connection with people. Business was down, my sales were down.’

‘So you slept with Christine Myland?’ Rebecca asked caustically.

‘Yes.’

Rebecca's eyebrows shot up. ‘You had an affair because you were worried about work?’

‘I know it sounds too simple Bec, but that's exactly why I slept with her. I just couldn't bring myself to tell you that things weren't going so well. I didn't want to see the disappointment in your face….’

'Don't you dare blame me Daniel!'

'No,' he added hastily, 'it wasn't your fault Rebecca. It was never your fault. She was there one evening at a party. I can't even remember whose it was. And she was flirting with me and just for a few hours I could forget about everything, forget about the mortgage and the job and the problems.'

He saw Rebecca's face darken. 'I know Bec! I know. I was a married man with responsibilities I wasn't supposed to forget about them. I'm not trying to defend myself, I'm just telling you what happened.'

Rebecca nodded stiffly. 'Go on.'

'Well she suggested that we meet for a drink and even as I said yes I knew where it would lead. I almost phoned her half a dozen times to cancel but ... well I turned up.'

'And that's when you started the affair.'

It was a statement not a question.

Daniel nodded.

'For a few hours every week it was like I was someone else. And I started to need it.'

Rebecca heard her heart make a little cracking noise.

'You needed her more than you needed me?'

Daniel paused.

'More than you needed me Daniel?'

He nodded. 'I had always needed you Bec. Always. But I suppose I had started to feel that maybe you didn't need me. It was stupid and foolish and I have regretted it every day since but I started to need those hours of being someone different. Of being someone who had no problems, who only had to turn up to make her smile, whose only responsibility was to keep going to the bar and keep laughing and smiling.'

Rebecca stood up and walked to the brandy bottle, pouring herself a glass. 'And when you were found out?'

Daniel groaned. 'It's the classic case of realising when you're about to lose something or someone, just how much they mean to you. I couldn't let you find out Bec. I just couldn't take the risk that you would know what I had done. I couldn't bear to see the hurt on your face, I couldn't live with the thought that I could have risked our marriage like that.'

'So you lied.'

Again not a question but a statement.

Daniel hung his head. 'I thought it might work. I truly thought if I could get you away fast enough it might work.'

'You didn't think anyone would tell me?'

He laughed, a wry laugh. 'It worked for five years Bec.'

Rebecca stood in the dark kitchen and stared at the man she had loved.

'But why did you change so much Daniel. If you loved me and wanted to save our marriage, why did you stop being the man I loved?'

Daniel stood up, his shadow looming over Rebecca. 'I hated myself Bec,' he said simply. 'I think I became everything that I despised because I truly hated myself. In my head I was a monster and I started behaving like one.'

Rebecca shook her head. It wasn't enough. He had loved her. He had made the move to protect her. He had wanted to save their marriage. And yet he had become the very opposite of everything she had loved.

'I don't think I understand Daniel. I really don't think I understand.'

And as she turned and walked out of the door she heard him say softly behind her, 'I don't understand either my darling.'

Fifteen minutes later Tom White rang on Rebecca's mobile phone.

'Rebecca my dear, I'm sure that by now you will know I have said no to Daniel's offer.'

'Yes, I do. Thank you Tom. About the money I'll….'

'Oh no, no, no. I didn't do it for the money Rebecca. I admit I considered selling the business. It would be a lot of money to put into the family coffers. But I would never have gone through with it. Like you Rebecca, I knew that White's needed protecting from Daniel. I don't want your money. The matter is now closed.'

And saying goodbye he hung up.

A few minutes later Helen's soft tones came on the line.

'Are you okay sweetheart?'

Rebecca nodded and then remembered to speak. 'I'm okay Helen. I'm okay.'

'Remember, if you need me...'

Rebecca wasn't quite sure what she needed at the moment. She was angry, sad, angry again. She felt a huge bitterness at essentially losing five years of her life and also for the effect it had had on her children. She relived the years in Darlington over and over again in her head to see if she had missed the signs. Should she have realised she wondered? Was he trying to tell her all that time? She thought about the Daniel she had known before and the Daniel he had become and wondered if she had helped create the monster. And most of all Rebecca couldn't help wondering what would have happened if she hadn't won 15.7 million pounds on the lottery. She would still be in Darlington living a lie, hating her life and having no idea what to do about it.

She looked around her beautiful home and smiled a sad little smile. It wasn't just a house the money had bought her. Maybe, just maybe it was a chance to get her life back.

Chapter 22

Summer had most definitely arrived. The sun was shining, the birds were singing and the air was full of the smell of freshly cut grass and barbecues. Rebecca smiled as she drove towards Parklands. It had been a long, cold and miserable winter in more ways than one and she relished the feel of the warm air on her face through the open window. She swung the 4X4 into the driveway and parked outside the front door. On the surface Parklands looked exactly the same as it always had. The gardens had always been well maintained, in part due to the residents who loved to spend the odd afternoon pruning and weeding. But inside the improvements were many and continuing.

The decorators had been called in and room by room they were working their magic. Scaffolding had to be used due to the high ceilings and rooms had been closed to residents for a while but gradually all the old cornices had been repaired and restored, the ceiling roses had been returned to their former glory, the chandeliers rescued and cleaned and the walls were now free of peeling paint and damp spots. The downstairs was almost complete and the rooms were returned to their former glory, fresh, welcoming and gracious.

Grabbing a couple of boxes from the back of her car, Rebecca peeped into what had been the events room. Tired and shabby with old magazines covering aged coffee tables and walls in desperate need of a good coat of paint, it had still been a lovely large room with French windows opening onto the rose garden outside and had been the setting for the occasional game of bingo and a sing song. It was hardly recognisable now. Cleaned, decorated and restored, it was now full of comfy armchairs and fresh flowers. It also held a couple of huge pine tables where various demonstrators would come along and give lessons or talks. At the moment the room was full and Rebecca could see Gwen amongst the crowd, engrossed as she painted roses on a porcelain cup. Several of the residents were taking the class but the majority of the group were day visitors who now came in steady and welcoming numbers to partake in the activities Parkland offered and helped greatly in the balancing of the books at the end of each month.

Nodding in satisfaction Rebecca headed to Mrs Wendover's office where the manager of Parklands was sipping a coffee as she looked through a magazine.

'Rebecca!' Brenda threw down the magazine and reached out to take one of the boxes. 'I wasn't expecting you today.'

Rebecca glanced down at the magazine, interiors for larger homes. and smiled. On the desk was a small stack of similar titles and by the side of the desk stood another stack of paper samples and scraps of fabric.

The top floor was still undergoing renovation and the lift needed to be extended to reach the new rooms but eventually they would have at least 6 large suites all with their own bathrooms. The bathrooms would be new and shiny and the rooms themselves decorated in keeping with the proportion and style of Parklands. They had decided that it was only fair to carry out similar redecoration on the existing bedrooms and as word had gotten out many of the residents had approached Brenda to give her little pieces of fabric or pictures of how they would like their room to look.

'I have something for you,' said Rebecca putting one of the boxes on the table and opening up the top, 'and I thought there was no time like the present!'

Brenda gave a little gasp and what Rebecca decided almost counted as a squeal as she looked at the mass of fabric swatches, paint charts and wallpaper samples inside.

'Rebecca, where on earth...?'

Rebecca laughed. 'I mentioned our renovation project to Annie and she of course has a contact for everything and everyone and the next thing I knew I had this provided by a local interior firm. Anything that we like in here they can provide and if they want us to do the design as well - they will.'

Rebecca saw the slight shadow cross Brenda's face and she continued gently.

'But of course I told them we were doing the design and planning ourselves.'

After the initial shock of having Rebecca come to the rescue, Brenda had thrown herself into the saving of Parklands with an energy and enthusiasm that took even Rebecca by surprise. She was spilling over with ideas and a determination to make them work and she was thoroughly enjoying being able to finally spend a little money on the ancient décor.

'Oh look at this!' She pulled out a soft apple green check with a tiny pink rose. 'This would look absolutely beautiful on the chairs in the reading room and this...' out came a yellow and blue regency stripe, 'this is exactly what Dotty was saying she would love in her room. Oh Rebecca, thank you!'

Dotty had been told she could stay at Parklands indefinitely due to a fund now set up to help some of the original residents. The old lady had cried and cried much to the concern of everyone until they realised they were tears of happiness and relief and since then she had been unable to stop laughing. Gwen was so proud of her daughter that she beamed from ear to ear and the already happy atmosphere at Parklands had improved even more.

There hadn't been a moment since she had signed the paper work that Rebecca had regretted her decision and both she and Brenda were working long and hard to make their dreams for the lovely old house a reality.

Rebecca left Brenda exploring the contents of the boxes, said her goodbyes and returned to the 4X4. Daniel had been right, it was a good car to have. She still had the little Fiat and if she was heading into town she would leave the Range Rover on the driveway. But with Parklands now a part of her everyday life it was exactly the car she needed.

She turned in the direction of home, winding down the window again to take advantage of the summer air. The weather had been glorious for the last month and Rebecca had finally managed to live out her fantasy of taking her morning coffee and croissant in the courtyard with the smell of her herb garden filling the air.

It had been an eventful and fulfilling few weeks. The children had both finally visited. Sarah had come first. Rebecca had collected her in the Fiat and taken her on a tour of the house. And although Rebecca had described her beautiful new home to her daughter in detail, Sarah's mouth had hung open in wonder as Rebecca took her from one room to another finishing in the kitchen where Daniel was opening a bottle of champagne.

'I can't believe it,' she had whispered, taking a glass from her father and sinking onto the raspberry settee, 'I just can't believe it!'

Rebecca had laughed. 'It's true my darling, quite true.'

They had wandered around the garden, Sarah squealing in delight at the tennis court hidden behind the trees and making plans for a tennis party in the summer. Finally, they came to rest in the courtyard with the sun dappling through the trees. Daniel had fired up the huge BBQ and they spent the rest of the afternoon chatting and planning for a future that included millions in the bank.

Daniel had wanted to confess all to the children, had wanted to get Toby and Sarah together and tell them the whole story. But Rebecca had refused. She felt so bitter and angry, not at Daniel having the affair, she had recovered remarkably quickly from that news, but from the frustration of losing five years of her life. No confession could bring that back and no amount of 'sorry' could alter the fact that Daniel's lies had taken those years away from her. She didn't want the children to feel the same and she told Daniel firmly that he would have to live with his guilt. He wasn't going to make himself feel better at their expense. So Daniel had kept quiet and if Sarah had wondered at the change in her father she said nothing.

Eventually Toby had visited as well, He had taken the move to Darlington hardest of all and his relationship with his father had never really recovered. He had never been back to Darlington for more than a couple of days since he had left for Bristol but the lure of Leeds was different and he finally agreed to join Sarah and his parents for a weekend.

Knowing about a lottery win was one thing, seeing a lottery win was a step further and like Sarah he had wandered round the house in shock, examined the cars on the driveway in a daze and shook his head in disbelief as he took in all the new signs of wealth. He had been as cool as ever towards his father and Daniel kept to his word and said nothing. No excuses about why he had taken them away from the life they had loved, no reason as to why he had been such an overbearing unpleasant man for the last five years. Rebecca had caught the regret in his eyes more than once but she stood firm. Daniel would have to rebuild the relationship with his children without revealing that the cracks could have been avoided.

They had spent the weekend as a family for the first time in years, chatting late into the evening and enjoying a family meal around the kitchen table. Daniel had been subdued but pleasant and Rebecca could feel the curiosity burning in both her children but she smiled her way through their visit and hugged them both tightly to her, relishing the feel of having her family restored.

Rebecca had told the children she would take them into Leeds on Sunday evening, drop Sarah at her flat and take Toby to the train station. As they gathered in the kitchen before leaving she had sat them down at the table and discussed finances. She'd already told them that their student loans would be paid in full. She had already started paying a monthly allowance into their accounts for which they had both declared their undying thanks and gratefully resigned the jobs they had been holding down to pay their way through the term.

But now she placed a set of papers in front of each of her children and gently explained about the trusts she had set up, the money that they would receive on their birthdays.

Daniel had said nothing and Rebecca thought that she could still detect the disapproval in his eyes but he had smiled and nodded while in tears, both of his children flung their arms around their mother and thanked her over and over again. And if anyone had noticed that Daniel wasn't part of the conversation they had said nothing. And if Daniel had felt isolated as they all wept and hugged, he had said nothing.

Eventually Toby had leapt to his feet and said that he was going to miss his train if they didn't get moving at which Rebecca had smiled and taken them both by the hand to the large garage where she had opened the door and showed them the two cars that were waiting for them. More tears followed, more laughter, more hugging and this time Daniel was slightly more animated as he joined them in exploring the interior and lifting the bonnet so he and Toby could examine the engine.

Eventually Toby and Sarah had left. Toby had decided it was too late to set off to Bristol and he was going to spend the night with Sarah in Leeds and leave the next morning. Laughing at their good fortune and grinning at the prospect of a night in the Student Union Bar with their new found wealth, Toby and Sarah had waved goodbye and set off down the long driveway. Rebecca had stayed in the doorway for a while, shivering slightly at the slight wind that had picked up and staring into the distance, still able to feel the excitement of her children.

She had smiled, this was what she had expected from winning the lottery and she had finally had the moment, albeit several months late.

And the moment had continued when the following week she had invited Helen, Emma and their families to Sunday lunch. She had asked Annie to join them too and the afternoon had come straight from her daydreams as her friends sat at the huge wooden table, drinking wine, laughing, chatting and putting the world to rights with the smell of roast beef drifting through the air and a feeling of happiness and goodwill filling every corner of the room.

Daniel hadn't joined them. He had suggested that he might play golf that day and Rebecca had agreed. Meeting her old friends with her new knowledge was something that she could handle better without Daniel being present and Daniel had no desire to be the object of everyone's contempt for the afternoon. When the afternoon had finished and everyone had finally gone, shouting their goodbyes as they drove away, Rebecca had flung open the kitchen doors and wandered into the courtyard with a glass of wine. She trailed her fingers through the mint and the basil and inhaled their aromas before lifting her face to examine the full moon rising in the sky. This was perfection.

Rebecca arrived back from Parklands, parking the 4X4 next to the Fiat and sat in the car for a moment before taking a deep breath and climbing out. Daniel was in the kitchen. He was staring out of the window, his hands thrust deeply into his pocket.

'Hello.'

He turned in her direction.

'I was waiting for you.'

Rebecca nodded. 'Sorry, I just had so much to do, I had...'

She trailed off. For a long moment they just stared at each other, Daniel eventually breaking the silence.

'Right, well. Okay then.'

He walked slowly into the hallway, Rebecca following him.

It had been after the Sunday lunch with Helen and Emma that she had asked him to leave. He had started to argue and then stopped. He started to plead and then stopped. In the end he had simply nodded. His shoulders had drooped and his face suddenly aged.

Maybe she had known all along that they couldn't survive the events of the last few months. But part of her, the part that still felt guilt when she thought of how badly she had behaved, decided that she ought to at least allow some time to pass. Give her battered emotions some time to recover. But it had made no difference.

'I need to start again Daniel - you have to understand I can't forgive and I can't forget but I can start again and it has to be without you.'

He had given in without a fight.

Rebecca offered to sell the house and split what money was left but Daniel had refused. She offered to set him up in business somewhere and he refused. He wanted to walk away empty handed and she refused and it took several hours of talking before Daniel agreed to take one million pounds and the sale of their Darlington house. He had decided not to return to Darlington, which annoyed Rebecca intensely although she couldn't quite say why. She didn't ask where he planned on going, she found that she has very little interest. It was over.

His cases were packed and standing neatly by the front door and in silence he carried them out to the Mercedes and stacked them in the boot and on the back seat.

Putting in the last one he closed the door and turned in Rebecca's direction.

Rebecca bit her lip.

'Daniel...'

He took a step towards her, a minute, hopeful step.

'Thank you, Daniel.'

He stopped, nodded and turned back towards the car.

For a moment he stood staring at the driver's door, fiddling with the key in his hand and then turning he strode towards Rebecca, reaching out to wrap his arms around her and press his face into her hair.

'I'm so sorry my darling, so very sorry.'

And then he was gone, the sound of his car wheels making their way down the driveway all that was left.

The air was still warm, pleasant, silent and Rebecca smiled. She decided that it was time for a coffee in the courtyard and turning around with a serene smile on her face she walked into her house and closed the door.

Google Your Husband Back
By Julie Butterfield

Kate has the perfect marriage, a handsome husband and a beautiful new baby - so she is more than a little surprised when one Monday morning Alex announces that he's leaving. Shocked and distressed at both his absence and his silence, Kate turns to Google for some answers. Why has her husband left and more to the point what can she do to make him come home? Together with her faithful friend Fiona they come up with a strategy to persuade her errant husband to see the light and return to his loving wife. Unfortunately for Kate, even Google doesn't have all the answers.

Did I Mention I was getting Married? By Julie Butterfield

Two years ago Rebecca Miles won the lottery and ended her marriage to her overbearing and unpleasant husband Daniel. She had every intention of putting the past behind her and starting again, but it turned out to be so much more difficult than she had imagined. Then Daniel announces he is getting married again and as Rebecca broods over how he has found it so easy to move on her daughter phones with good news - she's getting married too! Determined not to be left behind Rebecca finally throws caution to the wind and meets someone who can give her the new start she so desperately wants. Now her ex-husband is back in her life, the future Mrs Miles wants to be her best friend, she has her daughter's wedding to plan and a ramshackle old wedding venue to renovate to its former perfection in just a few months, if only she can find a builder who will take on the job. There are challenges, surprises, love and heartbreak ahead but at the end of a long, hot summer, will there be any weddings?

10533528R00143

Printed in Great Britain
by Amazon